The
Lady's Code

Samantha Saxon

BERKLEY SENSATION, NEW YORK

For all the smart women in my life: Charlotte Wood, Cynthia Wood,
and Melanie Sharpless. I love you all very much.

THE BERKLEY PUBLISHING GROUP
Published by the Penguin Group
Penguin Group (USA) Inc.
375 Hudson Street, New York, New York 10014, USA
Penguin Group (Canada), 90 Eglinton Avenue East, Suite 700, Toronto, Ontario M4P 2Y3, Canada
(a division of Pearson Penguin Canada Inc.)
Penguin Books Ltd., 80 Strand, London WC2R 0RL, England
Penguin Group Ireland, 25 St. Stephen's Green, Dublin 2, Ireland (a division of Penguin Books Ltd.)
Penguin Group (Australia), 250 Camberwell Road, Camberwell, Victoria 3124, Australia
(a division of Pearson Australia Group Pty. Ltd.)
Penguin Books India Pvt. Ltd., 11 Community Centre, Panchsheel Park, New Delhi—110 017, India
Penguin Group (NZ), Cnr. Airborne and Rosedale Roads, Albany, Auckland 1310, New Zealand
(a division of Pearson New Zealand Ltd.)
Penguin Books (South Africa) (Pty.) Ltd., 24 Sturdee Avenue, Rosebank, Johannesburg 2196, South
Africa

Penguin Books Ltd., Registered Offices: 80 Strand, London WC2R 0RL, England

THE LADY'S CODE

A Berkley Sensation Book / published by arrangement with the author

PRINTING HISTORY
Berkley Sensation mass-market edition / August 2006

ISBN: 0-425-21107-X

BERKLEY SENSATION®
Berkley Sensation Books are published by The Berkley Publishing Group,
a division of Penguin Group (USA) Inc., 375 Hudson Street, New York, New York 10014.
BERKLEY SENSATION is a registered trademark of Penguin Group (USA) Inc.
The "B" design is a trademark belonging to Penguin Group (USA) Inc.

PRINTED IN THE UNITED STATES OF AMERICA

10 9 8 7 6 5 4 3 2 1

One

"*Who* are you?"

Lady Juliet Pervill glanced about her cousin's library, scanning the room for a means of escape while keeping an eye on the gentleman so determined to keep her there.

"That is of no importance, Lady Juliet." The older man slurred his words as he rounded the settee, inching ever closer toward her while he, too, kept an eye on the library door. "What is of paramount significance, however, is why I am here."

"Why?"

"Your father." The gentleman paused, his brown eyes flickering with hatred. "Lord Pervill has taken rather a large sum of money from me and I want something in return."

Juliet swallowed, seeing for the first time the level of danger this man posed. " 'A pound of flesh.' "

The gentleman grinned, creating small wrinkles at the corners of his eyes, which betrayed his age if not his malice. "Something like that, yes."

"It won't matter." Juliet's backside collided with Lord Appleton's mahogany desk and she sucked in a breath. "You have met my father. He won't care what you do to me."

"But you see, my dear, I care." The man stripped his gloves from his fleshy hands and Juliet could feel the panic rising in her chest. "I care very much."

"I'll scream."

"I wouldn't if I were you." The gentleman held her eyes, his threat clear. "Furthermore, no one will hear you this distance from the ballroom. It was rather unwise of you to venture this far into Lady Felicity's home unescorted."

"I . . ." Juliet clutched the note from Lord Robert Barksdale in her right hand and the man laughed.

"I see you received my message."

"You wrote the note?" Juliet asked, knowing that he had and feeling a fool.

She had been given the note from a footman and thought perhaps Robert Barksdale was finally going to make her an offer.

"Yes, cruel of me, I know, but your Lord Barksdale does need a bit of prodding, don't you agree."

"No," she whispered, and the corners of the man's mouth lifted.

"He said that you weren't very pretty, but I disagree."

Juliet needed no clarification as to who "he" was, her bastard of a father.

"Yes, well, that is quite comforting in my present situation, knowing that my assailant finds me attractive."

The gentleman's laughter lacked the sneering contempt of his early amusement.

"Attractive and amusing." He sighed. "Pity."

The man reached for her and Juliet bolted for the door. But her slight frame was no match for him, and he had no difficulty catching her about the waist and throwing her down on the velvet chaise.

"I'm going to enjoy this."

"Please, don't." Juliet refused to cry. She could see pleasure shining in his dark eyes as he used his stout body to trap her against the vermilion cushions.

"Don't fear, my lady," the man whispered as he bent his head to kiss her neck, spirits wafting off him. "I've no intension of hurting you." He chuckled. "Not really."

The vengeful man kissed her collarbone and Juliet turned her head, her skin crawling. She felt his hand on the sleeve of her gown and Juliet froze. He tugged at the soft silk and then kissed the swells of her breasts, now very nearly exposed to his reprehensible view.

Juliet closed her eyes, not knowing if she would survive, when she heard a rather substantial gasp coming from the direction of the library door.

Her attacker sat up, running his thick fingers through his graying hair. Juliet turned with reluctance, her eyes growing wide when she saw Lord and Lady Winslow, the *ton*'s most infamous gossips. However, the thing that tore her heart in two was the expression on the face of the young gentleman standing behind them.

Lord Robert Barksdale.

Juliet met his wounded eyes and shook her head, saying, "You don't understand, Rober—"

Lord Barksdale was staring at the carpet in disbelief and then turned, his crisp footsteps echoing down the wooden corridor.

Lord and Lady Winslow exchanged a significant glance and then followed, no doubt already formulating the manner in which they would spread the news of Juliet's wanton ruination to the more interested members of the *ton*.

"Well," her assailant said, staggering to his feet. "Good

evening, Lady Juliet." The man grinned. "Tell your father that Lord Harrington sends his regards."

The gentleman walked toward the library door and Juliet sat up, furious. "This is your revenge on my father!" she shouted after him. "To ruin me?"

"Yes." The gentleman grinned. "As he has ruined me."

Two

At two o'clock the following afternoon, Juliet was still seething, in bed, with her cat and a tray full of cakes. Well, half a tray of cakes.

"Juliet?" The melodious voice of her beautiful cousin Lady Felicity Appleton rang out shrilly from the door.

"What do you want, Felicity?" Juliet barked, pounding on the pillows at her back before leaning against them.

"You've received two letters, dearest."

Felicity opened the door and held out the letters, which had been sent to the Appletons' home, the entire *ton* being aware that Lady Juliet Pervill resided with her cousin when visiting town.

"Read them."

"Perhaps you would like some privacy while—"

"Read them, Felicity."

"Oh, very well."

Her beautiful blond cousin sat on Juliet's bed as she did

everything else, gracefully. She broke the seal of the first communiqué and read aloud.

" 'Lady Spencer regrets to inform you that the invitation to the Spencer ball extended to you last week has now been . . . withdrawn.' " Felicity looked up, her fawn-colored eyes clouding to an intimidating chocolate. "Well, I don't think I like Lady Spencer any longer and I shall write her and decline my invitation as well."

"Felicity," Juliet sighed. "You cannot refuse every event from which I have been excluded."

"Yes, I can."

"No, you can't, darling." Juliet grabbed her cousin's hand. "Or you shall become an old spinster like me and we will be forced to live together with nothing better to do with our time than raise . . ." Juliet lifted her tabby, and the feline protested with a low meow. "Cats. Oh, God, that is depressing. Read the other one."

Felicity glanced at the seal and smiled. "It's from your mother."

Juliet covered her face with her hands, groaning, "She knows already? Do you think she has received my letter explaining about Father and Lord Harrington?"

"I don't see how she can have received it. We've only sent it two hours ago."

"Oh, just read her letter." Juliet grabbed a cake and shoved it into her mouth.

" 'My darling, Juliet.' " Felicity smiled, her fondness for her aunt clear. " 'I was told this morning of the unfortunate events which occurred at your uncle's home last night and I wanted you to know that you are welcome at the estate whenever you wish to visit . . . or perhaps to talk. Shall we say, this weekend? All my love, Mother.' "

Juliet chuckled as she shook her head. Her mother had never been one for subtlety. A result, she guessed, of marrying Juliet's bastard of a father.

"In the meantime . . ." Felicity rose and walked to the

window, throwing back the cobalt velvet curtains. "I thought we could take a stroll in the park."

Juliet looked at the mountain of moist handkerchiefs littering her bed and knew that her eyes must be as puffy as the Prince Regent.

"Are you mad, Felicity? I am not going out today. We both know what is waiting for me out there." Juliet pointed toward the exceedingly bright window, squinting. "I will be turned away from every reputable house in London."

Felicity put her hands on her hips and in an unusual show of temper said, "Then what are you going to do, Juliet? You cannot just let the man succeed. Just sit here and let your reputation be ruined all because your father is a selfish so-and-so."

"Bastard," Juliet agreed with a nod.

"Yes, that's it exactly. A selfish bastard!"

Juliet laughed, never having heard her cousin curse or speak ill of others, for that matter.

"All right," she said. "Just give me a few days, Felicity. It's not every day that a girl is ruined."

Felicity's anger turned to sympathy and she sat on the edge of the bed, brushing hair from Juliet's bloodshot eyes. "I know, dearest. I am sorry." Felicity embraced her and Juliet sighed, wallowing in self-pity. "That is why I am giving you two days to formulate your plan."

Juliet lifted her head and raised a sardonic brow. "Two whole days? You are generous, cousin."

"Yes, I thought I was quite generous, and besides"— Felicity patted her on the knee as she rose—"we both know you are only weeping because you think you ought."

"Wouldn't you cry if you had been ruined?"

"Oh, yes." Felicity nodded. "I would."

"What does that mean? *I* would."

"It means, Juliet, that I would weep for the loss of my reputation whereas you do not give two figs about yours."

But her cousin was wrong. Well, in part. It was true that

she did not care about the *ton*'s opinion of her. However, she did care about the repercussions of ruination.

She cared very deeply.

Felicity walked to the door and looked back over her right shoulder, saying in all seriousness, "You know that you are welcome here for as long as you wish to stay."

Juliet nodded, unable to speak, and then the door closed, leaving her alone with her withered dreams of a life she would never have.

Mister Seamus McCurren sat reading the *Gazette* as his valet meticulously cut his dark sideburns to echo the sharp line of his square jaw.

He turned the page of the newspaper, the subtle scrapping away of whiskers hissing in his ear, when he came across a singular capital E, which appeared to be a printing error in the second paragraph of the news narrative. The only difficulty being that his office had noted three other such "errors" appearing in various publications in the past two months.

"Damn!" His valet struggled to pull the straight razor from his face before Seamus was nicked by the blade. He looked at his startled servant, saying in a subtle brogue, "Finish up and then call for my horse. I need to get to the Foreign Office as quickly as possible."

"Yes, sir."

A half hour later, Seamus was standing over his enormous desk staring down at all four newspaper articles. The arithmetical odds against multiple publishers printing the same error were monumental and therefore must be assumed by his clandestine office to be intentional. Yet, he could find no other patterns in the articles in which the errors occurred, simply one bloody E.

Seamus stared with frustration at the character that should not have been there. His studies at Oxford had given him a unique perceptive of words and of their origins, their usage. But it was his subsequent research of ancient texts that had given Seamus a true understanding of the development and repetitive patterns of the written word.

It was this understanding that had enabled him to decipher two French codes in the short amount of time that he had been working at the Foreign Office. But this code . . . eluded him.

He called to his assistant, James Habernathy, and with great reluctance said, "Inform his lordship that we have intercepted another message."

"Yes, Mister McCurren." The shorter man bowed, leaving his office. Seamus stared at the article, knowing that another attack on British military instillations was eminent.

Shortly after his discovering the previous three articles, the French had attacked British positions they should not have known existed.

Yet, they did.

"I'm told you have found another message." Seamus looked up to meet the inquisitive eyes of his esteemed employer.

"Aye." Seamus nodded to himself as he tossed his pencil on the desk in disgust of his own stupidity. "But the words, they fight me."

"There is no set pattern in any of the articles which have been identified thus far?" Falcon asked.

"None that I can see," it pained Seamus to admit. "I have studied all four articles for similarities in length, structure, letter placement, word choice, repetitive patterns, and sequencing and have found nothing other than one anomalous letter E with which to connect them."

"And you are sure the attacks are related to this E anomaly?"

"Aye." Seamus crossed his arms over his chest and leaned back in his leather chair. "The attacks on three classified military locations within a two-week period of this irregularity appearing in a London publication are too much of a coincidence to be anything but related."

"I agree." The old man nodded, sighing as he looked down at Seamus. "Continue working on decrypting their code. British lives hang in the balance."

Seamus stared at the E in the *Gazette*, knowing that there was nothing to be done but wait for the next attack to occur. Nothing to be done but wait for more British troops to die.

"Aye," Seamus said, frustrated beyond belief. "I know."

Three

"*Juliet*, this is not what I had in mind by way of a plan." Lady Felicity Appleton sat in her landau, twisting her pretty lace handkerchief to ribbons. "The entire *ton* will be at the Earl of Spencer's ball."

"Exactly!" Juliet smiled, pinching her cheeks and adjusting her pale blue ball gown. "That is precisely why it will work."

"No, dearest." Felicity met her eye, shaking her head lightly. "All your plan will do is further shame you in the eyes of polite society."

Juliet swallowed the lump in her throat, refusing to feel sorry for herself as she turned and looked at her concerned cousin.

"Felicity, I am the gossip of the season and not welcome in any reputable home in London. What could I possibly do tonight to make my situation any more shameful?"

Her beautiful cousin took a moment, trying and failing

to think of something more devastating than a lady's loss of her reputation.

"Nothing, I suppose," Felicity said regretfully.

"Now." Juliet held out her gloved hand. "Give me your invitation."

"I don't want to watch you do this, Juliet." Lady Felicity shook her head, the blond curls dangling down her cheeks swinging attractively. "I'll just wait in the carriage until the entire scene is finished."

"Please, come inside." Tears moistened her eyes, and Juliet struggled to steady her quivering chin. "I don't think I can do it without you, Felicity. When I leave that ballroom, I shall need one person whom I can look to that will not hold censure in their eyes. Please, come with me," she begged, holding her breath as she waited for an answer.

"Oh, Juliet, I had not thought of it in such a way. Of course I will accompany you, but are you sure that I cannot talk you out of doing this?"

"No, if I am going to be unjustly ruined, then I am damn sure going to take my blackguard of a father with me."

Felicity grasped Juliet's hands and searched her eyes. "Your father already has a horrible reputation, Juliet. Why are you really doing this?"

Juliet tried to look away, tried to manufacture a lie that Felicity wouldn't recognize instantly as a falsehood.

"It is so unfair, Felicity," she whispered and her cousin wrapped her gentle arms around her. They silently held each other as they had been clinging to one another their entire lives.

"I know, dearest," Felicity whispered. "And if I could take your place, I would willingly do so."

Juliet lifted her head and met her cousin's kind eyes and knew that Felicity meant every word.

"Right." Juliet sniffled, wiping her cheeks of wasted tears. "No more or I shall look as if I have been crying, which quite frankly would be more humiliating than the spectacle I am about to make of myself."

Felicity laughed. "You look stunning, Juliet. Oh, I almost forgot." She opened her reticule and pulled out an enormous sapphire necklace and matching bracelet. "If you are going to exit polite society, do it with a bit of flash."

"I thought my plan had a great deal of flash."

"Oh it does," Felicity said, fastening the necklace around Juliet's neck. "I just thought your attire should be equally as ostentatious."

"Well, my lady." Juliet yanked at her gloves as they rolled to a stop. "Shall we enter the den of hungry lions?"

"After you, dearest." Felicity bowed her elegant head as Juliet laughed at her cousin's subtle humor.

Then, with a deep breath, she stepped from the carriage, knowing that the *ton* was waiting to feed on its latest victim.

The Spencer ball was a bloody bore and Seamus could not wait to leave. However, he was here at his brother's request and knew that the viscount would arrive at any moment with his beautiful bride, Lady Nicole Dunloch.

Daniel had married the lass a little over a month ago and recruited the entire McCurren clan to ease her path into polite society. Not that the stunning woman needed much assistance, but Seamus had promised his brother nonetheless. So, here he stood, bored to tears and counting the minutes until he could leave the ball without enduring too much grief.

He positioned himself by a potted shrub, grateful that he was merely the second son of the Earl of DunDonell but not willing to take any chances of being seen by the more desperate of this year's debutantes.

Seamus pulled his pocket watch from his gold brocade waistcoat and sighed, staring at the front entrance of Lord Spencer's tawdry town home.

A group of guests sitting some ten feet in front of him burst into robust laughter, drawing his attention away from the door. Seamus turned to stare at the gentleman holding court over his attentive hangers-on and tried not to visibly roll his eyes.

The man was well into his forties but was still dressing as though he were a young buck just swaggering into society. God in heaven, but there was something to be said for subtlety. Seamus glanced at the exquisite sleeves of his own black superfine, thankful that at six-and-twenty he knew the difference between garishness and sophistication.

He had never needed, as this man obviously did, the approval of his peers. Seamus had always done what he pleased, caring only that he retain the respect of his parents and his six brothers.

But this man . . .

Seamus sipped his champagne, knowing he would never understand gentlemen such as these, men who lived purely for their own pleasure. The *ton* was littered with them, which was no doubt why Seamus felt so out of place in the drawing rooms of London society, choosing instead to do something with his time and his mind.

"Oh, my lord!" one of the gentleman's court said, her eyes growing wide as she stared at the front entrance of the Spencer town home.

Seamus turned, curious as to what this worldly woman could possibly find surprising, and saw nothing more than two young ladies. A tiny brunette and a stunning blonde who was dressed in a spectacular white gown embroidered with silver thread. His eyes flickered over her slender frame, thinking this beautiful lady knew a thing or two about sophistication.

Conversation at the Spencer ball died as the women walked down the stairs and Seamus could see why, noting the lady's sheer grace, her elegance. Heads of guests drew together as if tethered and the hiss of whispers became deafening.

Seamus waited to be enlightened, knowing that he was missing some crucial bit of information about the alluring woman and making him want to know all the more.

The corner of his mouth lifted as the ladies made their way toward him, affording Seamus a much better view. He watched the fair lady grow more beautiful the closer she came, soft brown eyes that were kind and trained . . . He turned back toward the group before him. The lady's eyes were trained on the pompous fop holding court not ten feet in front of him.

The dandy smirked, looking up at the duo as he said, "Well, I'm surprised to see you show your face in public."

The blonde's eyes widened, her beautiful mouth falling open in shock, and Seamus wished that he paid more attention to the politics of polite society. But before he had a chance to speculate, the little brunette hauled back and slapped the dandy so hard that the gentleman's champagne glass went flying across the floor while her bracelet came hurtling toward Seamus's head.

He caught it in midair and smiled as others gasped. Turning away from the blonde, Seamus looked at the little brunette for the first time.

The girl had no idea that the clasp of her bracelet had broken because the whole of her attention was focused on the gentleman she had just walloped.

"How dare you speak to me in such a manner when my situation is entirely your fault!"

Situation?

The fop grinned caustically as he rubbed his wounded cheek. "Well, darling," he chuckled. "It is hardly my fault that you were caught entertaining your lover at Lady Felicity's soiree."

The blackguard indicated the beautiful blonde, who had

gone completely white as her eyes darted to the smaller woman. The fair lady took an instinctive step backward, and as Seamus watched the narrowing of the brunette's striking blue eyes, he could see why.

"I was assaulted at Lord Appleton's home by a man that sought to take revenge on you, because as the *ton* well knows, you are a lying, cheating, gaming, philandering bastard who cares nothing for anyone bar himself!

"Unfortunately, for me, this Lord Harrington appears to be the only member of polite society that did not realize your daughter was included in that category!"

Seamus laughed aloud and the woman's sharpened eyes trained on him, prompting him to raise his champagne glass in encouragement.

"Don't mind me, lass."

Her lightly freckled cheeks went a subtle shade of pink and she lifted her chin and said for the benefit of the aghast guests, "Do not ever contact me again, Lord Pervill, because as of this instant, I renounce you as my father."

The brunette spun about and made for the door, leaving her companion to add, "Yes, and I am afraid that you are no longer welcome in my home, Uncle."

"Thank you for telling me," Lord Pervill said, amused.

And being the epitome of a lady, the man's elegant niece nodded, saying, "You're quite welcome," before turning to join her cousin, who was speeding toward the front door.

Glancing down at the costly bracelet, Seamus hastened to intercept them. He grasped the brunette's upper arm, which proved to be a dangerous miscalculation.

Startled, and more than a tad angry, the lass spun round, throwing a rather sharp elbow, which would have connected with his right ribs had he not leaned dramatically to his left. He was stunned to see her features lined with disappointment when the lady realized that he was not her intended target.

"I take it you were expecting your father."

"Oh," she gasped, her large eyes growing larger with surprise. "Oh, I'm so . . ."

Words failed her so Seamus provided them.

"You seemed to have lost your bracelet the moment you lost your temper," he said, holding up the diamond and sapphire band by the tip of his index finger.

"I thank you for returning it." The lass reached up and yanked the jewels from his finger. "But I'll not apologize for my temper."

Seamus met her bright blue eyes. "I would never dream of asking, Lady Juliet," he said, grinning as he bowed while the cousins continued along their determined path.

As Seamus watched the entertaining pair leave, their names kept rolling around in his mind. *Lady Felicity Appleton and Lady Juliet Pervill?* He had heard the names before and was racking his brain when his brother strolled up alongside him, having finally arrived at the ball.

"Evening, Mister McCurren."

Seamus looked in his brother's direction. "And where is your lovely bride?"

"Lackland has just taken her out for the first set." Seamus glanced across the ballroom floor and easily located his younger brother dancing with the ebony-haired lady.

"Your wife looks beautiful."

"Aye." Daniel grinned like an idiot and Seamus smiled, pleased to see his brother so contented. "She always does. Have you been here long?"

"Long enough," Seamus moaned, and his elder brother chuckled, knowing how much Seamus abhorred society events.

"You can dance the next set with my wife and then be dismissed to join your mistress with my heartfelt gratitude." Daniel placed an enormous hand over his insincere heart.

"I no longer have a paramour." Seamus sighed without any real regret.

"You jest?" Daniel's turquoise eyes widened in proportion to his surprise. "When did this occur?"

"Last month." Seamus shrugged, not wanting to discuss the matter of his former lover's cold ambitions to inherit his brother's title. So he changed the subject. "Who are Felicity Appleton and Juliet Pervill? I know the names, but I don't recall where I have heard them mentioned."

"From me, no doubt," Daniel said, adding by way of explanation, "Do you recall the Earl of Wessex and his younger sister Sarah Duhearst, now the Duchess of Glenbroke?"

"Aye, Daniel. I've met the duchess once or twice at your house, remember?" Seamus could not keep the sarcasm from his voice.

"How the bloody hell am I supposed to remember who you've met at my house. Right, so you know the duchess." His brother took a moment to remember what he had been saying. "Well, Lady Felicity and Lady Juliet are cousins who met the duchess years ago when they were still in the schoolroom, been thick as thieves ever since."

"What happened to the lass, the brunette?"

Daniel looked to see if anyone was standing near them and then moved closer, just to add to his precaution.

"A week ago, Lady Felicity Appleton hosted her annual New Year's ball. Her cousin was naturally invited as were half the people you see here tonight. Unfortunately . . ." Daniel hesitated, disliking gossip particularly as it pertained to a friend. "Shortly after midnight, Lady Juliet was found in a rather compromising position with a gentleman."

"Lord Harrington." Seamus nodded.

"How did you know?" Daniel's auburn brows furrowed.

Seamus shrugged, "I heard someone mention the gentleman's name. It's not important, go on with the tale."

"There is no more to tell. They were seen by Lord and Lady Winslow and the lady's most ardent admirer, Lord Robert Barksdale. Lady Juliet has been in seclusion at her cousin's town home ever since the regrettable incident."

"Hmm." Seamus sipped his champagne, his mind turning from the curious cousins to his duty for the evening. "So, may I dance the next set with your wife and then flee to my own home?"

"Aye." Daniel smiled, adding, "Unless you want to stay and select your next paramour."

"Not bloody likely," Seamus said, resolute. "I've decided it is far cheaper for me to hire a harlot than to woo another lady."

"I give that declaration all of a week. You've always enjoyed quality, Seamus." Daniel met his eye, grinning.

"Well, I see your wife is finished with our little brother. So, I'll just go have a spin while you circle the seventh ring of hell, which is surely where you're headed." Seamus slapped his brother on the back so hard that he was sure his hand would hurt the entire time he danced with the black-guard's wife. But it was damn well worth the pain. "Good evening, Daniel."

Four

Falcon paced his office, walking a wooden plank as if it were a rope strung fifty feet off the floor. And at times his work did seem a tightrope, an intricate show of balance. Knowing which steps would propel Britain toward victory and which of his decisions would prove fatal to the country and the war.

He had agents carefully dispersed throughout Europe gathering information, and it was his job merely to interpret their findings. The problem for him came when the puzzle was incomplete, when he knew there was a vital piece of information missing, which rendered any speculation or recommendations he might provide Wellesley . . . useless.

This was the case with the most recent of French codes.

For the most part, the French were careless and their codes elementary in nature. It had taken his cryptographers no time at all to intercept and decode their messages, thus allowing him to provide Wellesley with valuable information in a timely manner. Yet, while each code had its own style and flavor, this new anomaly was proving elusive.

The writer of the E code, Falcon feared, was not your typical French cryptographer. This code, he was sure, was concealing a level of complexity that his men had yet to crack. But how did one crack an anomaly?

By deviating from the normal patterns of cryptography.

A knock at his office door interrupted Falcon's tortuous deliberations, and he returned to the dignity of his desk before looking up and saying, "Yes."

His secretary entered the room with a deferential bow.

"Lady Juliet Pervill wishes an audience, my lord."

"Send her in," Falcon said, remembering clearly the intriguing young woman.

The lady had proved exceedingly helpful some months ago in identifying a French assassin working in London. He had been struck then by her composure as she described in detail the horrific scene she had stumbled upon.

The girl had instantly understood the significance of what she had seen, had known instinctively that the murders were not the work of footpads, and had come to the only person to whom her information would be useful.

Him.

The lady walked into his office, interrupting his recollection, her pale yellow morning gown and elfin stature giving her the appearance of a schoolgirl.

Just as he remembered her.

Falcon rose to his feet, saying with a polite bow that would not aggravate his back, "Good afternoon, Lady Juliet."

"Good afternoon." The girl smiled nervously, which immediately piqued his already honed interest.

He indicated a sturdy wooden chair facing his well-worn oak desk and then asked, "Would you care for a cup of tea?"

"No, thank you." The lady sat, her blue satin slippers scarcely touching the floor as Falcon nodded for his assistant to leave them in privacy.

The door clicked closed and he seated himself in his leather chair, taking a moment to reassess the woman. Light brown hair, shimmering with health and an intelligent face dusted with faded freckles across the bridge of her nose. Her eyes were an unusually vibrant blue and she had an overwhelming air of competence that seemed to come as naturally to her as breathing.

"How might I be of assistance?" Falcon asked, sure that her visit had in some way to do with the unfortunate episode surrounding the girl one week ago.

Lady Juliet fidgeted in her chair, obviously attempting to decide which path to take as they proceeded down the road of conversation.

"Were you aware, my lord, that I have received honorary recognition from Oxford University?"

Falcon shook his head. "I was not aware that women were bestowed recognition, honorary or otherwise," he said, impressed and wondering how this was pertinent to their conversation.

"They're not," she confirmed. "The assumption was made that J. Pervill was male and—"

"And . . . you did nothing to clarify that assumption." The girl inclined her head, neither confirming nor denying his assertion. He continued, asking, "For what was your honorary recognition bestowed?"

"Mathematics. Well, more specifically, I won recognition for my theses in differential calculus."

"Theses?"

"Yes, I've written three," she explained. "Although the suppositions of these papers were, to some degree, interrelated."

"I see." Falcon stared at the small woman, who looked as though she should be shopping, not formulating mathematical theory.

"I . . ." She bent her head to search her reticule and then

lifted it, holding out a letter. "I've brought a letter of recommendation from mathematics professor Quinby of Oxford."

Falcon read the astounding two-page letter and glanced at the brilliant woman seated before him. "This is a marriage proposal."

Embarrassed, the girl cleared her throat and stroked the back of her upswept hair.

"Well, yes. Professor Quinby came to my home to meet J. Pervill and saw that I was . . . not—"

"Male?" Falcon chuckled.

"Quite. However, if you read further, you will see that the reason for Professor Quinby's proposal was his . . ." The girl turned her head so that she could read the letter to recall the correct phrasing. "'Undying admiration of my immense mathematical mind.' See it is right there." The lady's delicate gloved finger darted out to point toward the bottom of the correspondence.

"Yes." Falcon nodded, to keep from laughing. "I might be old but I can read, my lady."

"Of course you can read, my lord," she said, blushing. "You would not have risen to the position that you hold at the Foreign Office otherwise."

"Ah." Falcon leaned forward, intrigued. "And what position is that?"

"Well, I am not sure precisely, but from our previous conversation, you appear responsible for dealing with any number of serious matters."

"Yet, you have not come to me this afternoon to discuss my position within the Foreign Office."

"No, indeed not, my lord." She looked at her lap. "You no doubt have heard of my . . . situation. Perhaps more accurately described as my ruination?"

Falcon nodded regretfully. "I have, yes."

He had also heard why the girl claimed to have been accosted, and from what information he had obtained about her wastrel of a father, Falcon had no doubt that Lady Juliet's assertions were true.

Unfortunately, the *ton* was not so reasonable.

"Well." The girl lifted her chin. "If I am to be condemned to a life of isolation, I thought I should rather do something with my time than spend the remaining years of my life wasting away in the countryside writing mathematical theory for Professor Quinby."

"That is far more useful a life than the pursuits of polite society."

The lady looked him directly in the eye.

"I want my skills to mean something, to be used for something other than having my ideas procured by men to further their intellectual ambitions. I want to work for you, my lord, for Britain."

Falcon sat back, the implications of her offer sending him slightly off balance. "Ladies of polite society do not work for the Foreign Office."

"Well, that is rather the point, is it not? I am no longer recognized as a lady of polite society. I am an outcast whose behavior is beneath the notice of the *ton*. And," the young woman stressed, "you do not strike me as the sort of gentleman with whom social stricture holds an ounce of weight."

"And what does hold weight for a man such as myself?" Falcon raised a brow, curious to hear her reasoning.

"Getting results." She held his eye. "Choosing the person best capable of accomplishing the assigned task. Whether that person be noble or common. Male or . . . female."

"And how do I know you are more capable than the men I already have working for me, Lady Juliet?"

"You don't," The woman shook her head and shrugged. "But as I shall work without compensation and with utmost discretion . . . you have very little to lose."

They stared at one another, eye to eye, and Falcon could not help admiring the mettle of a girl who was ruined last week and today sat before him, offering her service to the Crown.

"Very well." Falcon sat up, his mind mulling over the possibilities. His eyes sparkled, the full extent of the lady's potential coming to him in one brilliant flash. "You shall report to me at ten o'clock tomorrow morning."

The girl broke into a bright smile, her freckled nose crinkling as she tried to contain her excitement.

"I'll not let you down, my lord, I swear it."

"Let us hope that you do not," Falcon said, thinking that the lady was correct.

He had little to lose by commissioning Lady Juliet Pervill, but much for Britain to gain.

Five

Seamus McCurren dragged himself into the Foreign Office at ten o'clock, having never gone to bed.

He had spent the entire evening gaming at *Dante's Inferno* and in the end he had still come out losing. Not much blunt, but it was vexing nonetheless. He had wandered home at sunup to be shaved and change his attire, but his external appearance was merely a palatable façade of fatigue.

"Morning, James," he mumbled to his assistant.

"Good morning, Mister McCurren." The man eyed him suspiciously, prompting Seamus to inquire, "What?"

"Are you feeling well?"

"Just get me some coffee, will you?" Seamus's brogue was extracted by his irritation. But the man's brows were drawn together in concern and Seamus thought to ease his anxiety. "I'm just tired, James. I had a very late night last night."

The married father of five smiled.

"I see." What his assistant saw, he had no notion, but the

man must have thought Seamus needed reviving because he dashed out the door, saying, "I shall just go and retrieve a strong cup of coffee for you." His secretary was halfway out the door when he stopped. "Oh, you've just received a report and I've left it on your desk."

Seamus nodded, too tired to respond, and then opened the door to his large office and settled in his comfortable desk chair. He sighed heavily as he sank into the rich leather then reached for the report, leaning his chair back and propping his feet on the corner of his desk as he read.

The report was from the Naval Office, giving a detailed account of the sinking of a British supply frigate just west of Bordeaux. However, it was not the loss of the ship that landed this report on his desk, but the manor in which the ship had been sunk.

The frigate had been ambushed, by all accounts, by three French vessels that appeared to have been lying in wait at the port city of La Rochelle. And while this information could easily be disputed as a coincidental encounter, its occurrence within two weeks of the E anomaly appearing in the *Gazette* made the attack suspect.

"Damn."

Seamus was reading the report for a second time when James knocked on the inner-office door.

"Yes," Seamus said, continuing to read.

However, no coffee was produced and he looked up to find Falcon standing in the doorway.

"Good morning."

Seamus dropped the front two legs of his chair to the floor as he sat up to meet the astute eyes of his powerful employer.

"Morning," he greeted politely, but upon seeing a woman at the old man's side, Seamus dragged his boots off the abused desk and rose to his feet. "Good morning, madame," he said and bowed with as much elegance as he had remaining before focusing his attention on the lady's face.

"May I introduce you to Lady Juliet Pervill," Falcon offered.

"That is not necessary, my lord." The girl's astonishingly blue eyes met his as she held out her hand in his direction, adding, "Mister McCurren introduced himself three nights ago at the Spencer ball."

Seamus kissed the back of her hand, taking her bait. "Aye, but I'm astonished that you remember, Lady Juliet, as I recall you were rather occupied at the time."

"Oh, no, speaking with my father never requires more than half of my mind," the lady said.

Seamus hid his amusement behind a polite smile and offered to his unexpected guests, "Please, do have a seat."

The lady sat in Seamus's chair while the old man found a wooden bench tucked in the corner of the spacious office.

Falcon looked up at Seamus, who remained standing. "Lady Juliet will be assisting the Foreign Office with our inquiries and I have determined that the best use of her skills would be in this department."

The thought of a woman running underfoot stiffened his smile, and Seamus stared at Falcon and then glanced at Lady Juliet. A knock at the door broke the awkward moment, and when James Habernathy entered the room with his coffee, Seamus could have embraced the man.

"That is a very generous offer, my lady. However, I already have a secretary. Thank you, James," Seamus said, overly appreciative as he took his warm cup of coffee from the man's dutiful hands.

Seamus took a long sip to prove his assistant's usefulness. Lady Juliet raised a brow and then turned, irritated, toward Falcon.

The old man rose, saying, "You may go, Mister Habernathy." When the door had closed, Falcon's brandy-colored eyes met his. "I'm afraid you are misunderstanding the situation entirely, Mister McCurren. Lady Juliet will not be your subordinate. She will be your colleague."

Seamus waited for the end of the jest, and when none came, he laughed. "Pardon me?"

"I will be moving a second desk into this office and you will be working hand in hand to decipher French communiqués intercepted in Britain."

Seamus glanced at the woman glaring back at him and then turned to Falcon. "Perhaps, my lord, it might be more appropriate if we discuss this matter at another time."

"This matter is not up for discussion, Mister McCurren. You have done excellent work thus far, but you need help and Lady Juliet is eminently qualified to provide you that much-needed assistance."

"Or guidance." The lady smiled caustically, eliciting a turn of the head from the old man as he looked directly at her.

"Or guidance"—Falcon nodded—"in untangling this latest code. Lady Juliet has been briefed and her clearance is of equal status to your own."

It was an intellectual slap in the face and Seamus was set back on his heels. The petite woman made a great show of evaluating him from the tips of his boots to the top of his less than academically adequate head.

"Well," she said to Falcon as if Seamus were not standing in the middle of the bloody room. "It appears as though it will take a day or two for the man to adjust. I can certainly see why his intransigence of thinking might prove ineffectual in decoding French communications."

"Thankfully, we were fortunate enough to acquire your services, Lady Juliet," Falcon said with a nod of respect. "I shall have your desk ready by tomorrow morning and all pertinent papers will be awaiting you."

"Thank you, my lord." Lady Juliet rose and the two small people walked around Seamus as if he were a lamppost. "I look forward to working with you."

Falcon opened the door and the woman left without once glancing in Seamus's direction. No sooner had the door closed than he voiced his protest.

"My lord, you cannot be serious?"

"Oh, but I am, my boy. Lady Juliet will be working with you as of tomorrow."

"The lady is unqualified, not to mention impolite."

"The woman is brilliant and you deserved every barb she gave you." Falcon's tone brooked no opposition. "My decision is final."

"Then put the lady in her own office."

"It is more beneficial for the Foreign Office if two scholarly heads are put together." Falcon opened the door and smiled. "Besides, I don't have another office to put the lady in. Good day, Mister McCurren."

Juliet was still fuming from her encounter with Mister McCurren by the time she returned to her uncle's town home.

She stripped her reticule from her wrist and was mumbling to herself when Felicity glided into the entryway.

"Juliet, you have a visitor." Her cousin's eyes were wide with excitement, which immediately caused Juliet to narrow hers.

"Who is it? If it is Father, you can tell—"

"It's Robert Barksdale," Felicity said, watching her cousin's face carefully. "He has been here for over an hour, and from the dark shadows beneath his eyes, I'd say he has not slept overly much this past week."

"That makes two of us," Juliet mumbled with an accompanying stab of pain. "Where is Lord Barksdale?" she asked, suddenly tired.

"We were having tea in the small drawing room."

"Thank you, Felicity." Juliet gave her cousin's hand a squeeze as she met her gentle eyes.

"I will be in my sitting room if you would like to talk."

Juliet let go of her cousin and took a deep breath before walking to the drawing room and the gentleman she had hoped to marry. She tried to vanquish the memory of shock and hurt that had been on Robert Barksdale's face the last time she had seen him.

She had not written him after the unseemly incident, had not known what to say. However, if she were being truthful, Juliet had been hurt that Robert could believe her capable of such a thing. She had wanted him to come to her and ask for an explanation of what had happened that night in the library.

But he had not, until now.

"Good morning, Lord Barksdale," Juliet said as the footman closed the door behind her, leaving them alone.

Robert was staring out over the park, his brown jacket cut to display his fit shoulders and elegantly ridged back. He turned at the sound of her voice and Juliet all but gasped when she saw his face. He was pale, which only emphasized the dark lines under his midnight blue eyes.

"Look that bad, do I?" Robert smiled.

"Yes, you look horrible," Juliet said, truly concerned, and he laughed.

"My dear Juliet, your honesty is one of your best and worst attributes."

"Let us sit down, Robert." Juliet walked forward and he met her in the middle of the room, where they stood three feet apart and simply stared at one another.

"You look beautiful."

"I have the benefit of face powder." Juliet plopped on the settee and Robert joined her.

They sat in painful silence until Juliet could stand it no longer.

"It's not true, Robert." Tears spread across her eyes but she refused to let them fall.

Robert smiled miserably, his hand caressing the side of her cheek.

"I know," he whispered and Juliet leaned her head against his shoulder, relief lifting her burden.

"I was so frightened, Robert." He rubbed her back, allowing Juliet to talk as he held her in the safety of his arms. "I thought he was going to . . ." She closed her eyes, unable to form the words.

"Why didn't you run, Juliet?"

"I did!" she said, irritated. "But you saw the man."

"Yes." Robert stiffened and Juliet pulled her head back and stared at him.

"You believe me, don't you?"

"Yes." Lord Barksdale pulled her against his chest and Juliet closed her eyes, comforted by his strength. They sat for a long while before Robert whispered in her ear, "I want to marry you, Juliet. I've wanted to marry you for quite some time."

Juliet planted her left hand in the middle of his chest and pushed herself upright.

"Robert," she snorted, looking at him in disbelief. "I hardly think this the time for a wedding. It would be far more prudent to wait until the gossip dies down before we marry." His troubled eyes darkened, and if he were not a man, Juliet would have sworn he had tears in them.

"Robert?" she asked, alarmed.

He stood up and turned away from her, rubbing his forehead with his right hand.

"My father . . ." Robert turned around, staring down at her as she sat waiting in utter confusion on the settee. "The earl will not permit it."

Juliet laughed once and then again. "What . . . what do you mean, he will not—"

"My father will not permit me to marry you, Juliet."

His declaration caused her to sit back against the plush cushions of the settee; her left hand covering her abdomen and her right covering her gapping mouth.

"Father has threatened to disinherit me if I marry a woman of questionable reputation. He even went so far as to have legal papers drawn."

"How efficient of the earl."

"That is not entirely fair, Juliet. Father has a valid point. I mean, you were seen half dressed with a gentleman who is not your husband." She was stunned by the underlying bitterness in Robert's voice. "Any children we would produce would be tainted and therefore tarnish the title."

"Soiled goods?" Her face was setting as quickly as her heart.

Robert ran his fingers through his brown curls, throwing his hands toward the floor.

"Do you think I want this, Juliet?"

"I don't know what you want, Robert." She rose, hurt and angry.

Juliet took one step in the direction of the door before Robert stopped her by gently grasping her upper arm.

"Please, wait," he asked, knowing better than to demand.

He guided her to the settee and then bent to one knee as he held her right hand. Juliet's heart thumped in her chest as they stared eye to eye. She searched his face, thinking this could not be happening; it had taken a horrible scandal to bring the man to one knee.

"I am in love with you, Juliet Pervill. I have been absolutely mad about you for two years." Juliet grinned, her heart melting as she stared into his vulnerable eyes. "I am on my knees." He grasped both of her hands. "Asking, no begging you." Juliet started to cry, elated. "To become my mistress."

Juliet blinked, staring at the mouth that had formed the wrong word.

"What?" she breathed.

"Father has agreed to buy us a house in town so that we can—" His proposal was cut off when Juliet slapped him.

"How dare you, Robert Barksdale." She was shaking, cut to the core.

"Juliet, be reasonable." Lord Barksdale stared at her. "No one will marry you, and you are far too passionate a woman to live your life alone." Robert swallowed truly distressed. "The thought of you with another man . . . What choice do I have, Juliet?" He rose to his feet. "Marry you and become a pauper or take you as my mistress so that I can take care of you the way that I have always wanted?"

She could see in his eyes that he was still hoping she would change her mind.

"The choice you have, Robert." Juliet was lifted to her feet by her fury. "Is when to become a man." She wanted to hurt him as much as he had wounded her. "I never want to see you again, Lord Barksdale. Please, leave this house immediately."

Robert stared at her in disbelief, the reality of her words taking a moment to sink in. Then he walked toward the door. However, he stopped when they were shoulder to shoulder, facing opposite directions.

His left hand grasped hers and he whispered to the walls, "I do love you, Juliet," before letting her hand go and walking through the drawing room doors and out of her shattered life.

Six

ornamental flourish

"*Tell* me everything you know about Lady Juliet Pervill."

"Good God, not you, too, McCurren." Christian St. John, Seamus's lifelong friend and second son to the Duke of St. John, slurped his brandy angrily as they sat in an isolated corner of White's gentlemen's club. "Just because I am of close acquaintance with the cousins does not mean that I will spread gossip about—"

"I know all the gossip." Seamus rolled his eyes. "What I want is the truth."

"Oh." Christian's stormy Nordic blue eyes cleared. "No way on earth Juliet Pervill would have an assignation, particularly in Felicity Appleton's own home. She is far too sensible."

Sensible? He did not think the lady's laboring for the Foreign Office a very sensible course to take.

"I want to know about the lady's character."

"Why?" His companion's fair brow rose with speculation.

"Interested? Might need to wait until the gossip dies down a bit before—"

"Christian." Seamus sighed, keeping the man on point.

"Very well." Christian rolled his eyes as if supremely disappointed that he was not playing along. "Lady Juliet Pervill is the only child of Lord and Lady Pervill. Lady Jane was a wealthy debutante swept off her feet by the handsome, if somewhat narcissistic, Lord Neville Pervill. The moment the ink was dry on their marriage license, Lord Pervill began gaming and whoring until he discovered that Lady Jane's father had placed his daughter's inheritance in trust so that her philandering husband would be unable to touch the majority."

Seamus thought back to the Spencer ball and the man who would have been so transparent to anyone but a very young and uncommonly innocent girl.

"By then it was too late," Christian continued. "Lord Pervill had lost the affections of his young bride. Lady Jane gave him a monthly allowance on the condition that he leave their country estate so that she might raise their infant daughter alone. He moved to their house in town, which is why Juliet Pervill stays with her cousin Lady Felicity Appleton whenever she visits London."

"While that is all very fascinating"—Seamus nodded—"my question was of Lady Juliet Pervill's nature."

"Oh, Juliet is great fun. Although she is very blunt at times," Christian said. Seamus thought that a considerable underestimation. "But I would say her overriding characteristic is her wit.

"Juliet Pervill is by far the cleverest woman that I have ever met. Felicity once told me that she studied something . . ." Christian stared at the paneled wooden walls as if they held the key to his memory. "Somewhere? Oxford, I think. Or perhaps it was Cambridge?"

"It's of no significance." Seamus waved away the inquiry, thinking it truly did not matter. Lady Juliet Pervill was going to be ensconced in his office tomorrow morning whether he liked it or not.

"The whole scandal has been very distressing for both the cousins." St. John sipped his brandy. "I even considered asking Juliet for her hand in marriage."

"Really?" Seamus sat up, shocked.

"Yes."

"Why didn't you?"

Christian shrugged, looking down at the carpet in an infrequent moment of contemplation, which was quickly replaced by an infectious grin. "Juliet wouldn't have me."

"How do you know if you haven't asked?"

"As I've said . . ." Christian held up his near empty snifter. "Juliet is a very clever girl."

"A lady does not have to be particularly clever to refuse you, St. John. She need only look at your string of women to see that fidelity is not your strongest suit."

"Mean-spirited of you, Seamus, but unfortunately true." Christian nodded, not at all remorseful. "Although I must tell you that my current mistress is absolutely spectacular. Have I told you about the baroness?"

"No." Seamus shook his head, always entertained by Christian's outlandish exploits.

"It must be the snow, because every Russian lover I have ever had truly understands how to warm a man's bed." Christian St. John grinned.

"You realize that one of these days you are going to get yourself shot?" Seamus warned.

"That is what my brother and father repeatedly tell me and I don't need to hear it from you, Mister McCurren. And . . ." Christian lifted his brown Hessians to the leather ottoman between them, adding, "I don't see you rushing to the chapel anytime soon. In fact, Daniel told me that you had just broken it off with your paramour. How long were you with the lady?"

"None of your bloody business," Seamus said, annoyed with his indiscreet older brother.

"That's right, nine long months." He was going to kill Daniel. "Nine months with the same woman and in the end we arrive at the same damn place. However, I had a far more entertaining journey."

"That is debatable, St. John," Seamus smiled mischievously. "You forget, I've meet your paramours." Christian made an obscene gesture in his direction, and Seamus could not stop himself from adding, "Did you learn that from one of your so called 'ladies'?"

"Sod off, McCurren."

Seamus chuckled, thoroughly enjoying himself for the first time all day.

Juliet had no idea how long she had been sitting in the drawing room when Felicity suddenly appeared at her side.

"Dearest, it is time to dress for dinner."

Juliet wiped her eyes of any lingering tears and then stood up to face her concerned cousin. "Would you mind having my dinner sent to my room, Felicity. It has been a trying day."

Felicity nodded with understanding, and Juliet left the drawing room with the intention of going to her bedchamber. Yet, Juliet knew if she were alone in her room, she would cry, so she walked instead to the quiet of the conservatory.

The room was dark, lit only by the moon, and she preferred it that way. Juliet made sure to sit on a bench not visible from the conservatory doors. This room had always soothed her and she regretted not having learned more about the plants flourishing in the lovely openness of the glass-lined room.

Juliet raised both brows, thinking she would have plenty of time to study botany now that she was ruined.

She did not mind the rebuff of polite society, never really having cared for the constant balls and events. She enjoyed the music and dancing well enough, but much preferred smaller gatherings with close friends.

No, there was only one thing about being a ruined woman that Juliet suspected she would never truly get over.

She wanted children.

Not as many as Felicity wanted, mind you. Juliet did not think her temperament was particularly suited to a large brood, but she desperately wanted some children. A boy and a girl would have been ideal.

But Juliet knew she would never have children.

She herself had been the legitimate child of a scandalous father and that was difficult enough to overcome. She would never subject a child to the burden of being the illegitimate offspring of a scandalous mother.

Unfortunately, this also meant that she would have to swear off men. And Juliet rather liked men. She was mad about them, in fact, their lovely arms and muscled chests, even their masculine smell.

And she liked the way they thought, direct and to the point.

Juliet had always felt much more comfortable speaking to men. The inane chitchat that women seemed to have mastered drove her completely mad.

Juliet had to admit she was looking forward to working in the Foreign Office. Although she would have to be careful with the men with whom she worked. While Felicity attracted men and offers in mass quantity, Juliet was not without charm to certain gentlemen. Usually, lecherous older gentlemen, but as the years of her miserable ruined life droned on, they might at some point come to look quite appealing to a thirty-year-old virgin.

However, the war with France would be decided before then, one way or the other. Juliet's services would no longer be needed and she would no longer be thrown together with attractive gentlemen like Seamus McCurren.

Juliet's brows furrowed, surprised by her own carnal thoughts.

To be fair, the man was stunningly handsome. She had

always been attracted to tall men, perhaps because she herself was just this side of short. When they had entered his office today and those long legs were outstretched with buckskins hugging his muscular thighs, Juliet had taken a moment to enjoy the sight.

But the thing she found most attractive about Seamus McCurren had been his eyes. His eyes were a complex blend of colors that in some way reflected the complexity of the man. She had looked into his golden eyes both at the Spencer ball and today but was unable to divine what the man was thinking and that rarely ever happened to her.

Juliet did not particularly like the sensation.

Nor did she like the fact that the man seemed able to see straight into her mind. *Oh, God!* She wondered if the arrogant Mister McCurren knew that she found him attractive? That would be the final blow to her pride.

Thank the lord the Scot was such an ass.

Come to think of it, the more time she spent in his office, the less attractive Seamus McCurren had become. No, Juliet would go to the Foreign Office, analyze documents, and go home, making sure to avoid any gentlemen she did find appealing.

She was looking forward to the work. It sounded extremely interesting, particularly this new code that had been found by one of Falcon's men, but not yet deciphered. Her mind would then be occupied with this puzzle and not the painful encounter with Robert Barksdale.

Robert.

His picture formed in her mind and tightened her chest painfully. Robert was the first man to truly take an interest in her, and she did not know if that would ever happen again. Robert enjoyed her humor and her company and had even begged kisses from Juliet on more than one occasion, his attraction to her clear.

But his asking her to become his mistress had betrayed every moment of their friendship, making Juliet wonder if he had ever truly understood her as she thought he had, as she hoped that he had. Robert Barksdale had said that he wanted to marry her and she had wanted to marry him.

Until today.

"Juliet?" Felicity called from the conservatory door. "Are you in here, dearest?"

"Yes." Juliet sighed, rising.

"Your dinner is being taken to your sitting room," Felicity informed her, knowing the location of her favorite spot in the conservatory. "You are going to eat?"

"Of course I am, Felicity." Juliet smiled halfheartedly. "I have to be well nourished if I am to be of any use to the Foreign Office tomorrow morning."

Felicity nodded. "They are fortunate to have you."

And she, Juliet lamented, was very fortunate to have them.

Seven

The proprietor of Dante's Inferno walked into room number four and stared down at the side of the nude man tied to the corners of the four-poster bed. The man turned his rust-colored head, grinning with anticipation until he saw that it was not the whore he had paid to ride him.

"Who the hell are you then?" the man growled. "I bloody well did not pay to be watched."

"I've no intension of watching you rut, Major Campbell." Enigma walked to a wooden chair next to the well-used bed. "And to answer your question, I am the owner of this establishment."

The man's eyes narrowed. "I've paid my fee, and if you're wanting to rob—"

Enigma chuckled. "I don't want your money, you simpleton."

"What do you want then?" the man asked, lifting his head off the bed.

"Information." The man stilled and Enigma smiled at the

understanding in the major's bloodshot eyes before proceeding with the interrogation. "You told my whore that you are enjoying your last night of freedom prior to being transported to the Peninsula. What is your regiment's destination?"

"Our destination?" Rage contorted the major's lean face and he yanked against the ropes securing his wrists. "You're a bloody collaborator!"

"More of an opportunist," Enigma said, reaching for a lamp and carefully allowing three drops of oil to drip on the man's chest before setting a candle to the shiny liquid.

Major Campbell screamed, the distinct stench of burning hair filling the small room. Enigma waited a moment longer then snuffed out the small fire consuming the man's flesh, looking him in the eye.

"You will tell me what I wish to know, one way or the other, and then I will kill you. However, I will give you this choice, Major Campbell." Enigma lifted the full lamp, the thick oil sloshing beneath the glass. "We can spend hours in one another's company before I ultimately set you alight. Or you can tell me the information I wish to know now."

The major was trembling with pain as he glanced at the melted flesh on his chest and hesitated for only a moment before saying, "What do you want to know?"

"Everything."

Enigma left the room some ten minutes later and turned toward a large guard waiting in the brothel corridor.

"Send Chloe into room four, and when they have finished fornicating, kill Major Campbell. Use opium and then dump the major's body near one of the dens."

"Why not just kill him now?"

"Really, Mister Collin, we're not a pack of thieves." Enigma laughed, dumfounded. "The major did pay for a ride."

"My apologies." The guard lowered his dark head in submission, the scar on his cheek a gleaming contrast to the rest of his face.

"I shall send for Chloe straight away."

"Excellent, and then come to my office," Enigma ordered, already calculating the next move. "I have another article to submit to the *Herald*."

Seamus McCurren arrived in his office at precisely half past eight the following morning.

He had come at such an ungodly hour to ensure that the location of the desk provided the inconvenient Lady Juliet was placed where he wished it to be.

Well, that was not entirely accurate, for he wished it to be located in the corridor. But if he was to be shackled with the harpy, then he would damn well position her desk as far away from him as was possible.

"Good morning, James." His secretary glanced up from his desk, stunned to see Seamus arriving so early. He staunchly ignored the man's surprise, opening the inner office door and asking, "A cup of coffee, if you ple—"

The words dispersed in his mouth at the sight of Juliet Pervill sitting behind a small desk that had been placed in front of the office window. Her chestnut hair was twisted in a severe chignon at the back of her neck and she wore a gray gown that made her skin appear as drab as the dress.

The lass glanced up and nodded politely toward Seamus while speaking to James Habernathy. "Have you located the documents I requested?"

"Uh." Mister Habernathy looked toward Seamus for assistance. "No, ma'am, I was just on my way to prepare Mister McCurren's morning coffee."

Seamus raised a triumphant brow and acknowledged the woman's unwanted presence. "Good morning, Lady Juliet." Then making clear that James was *his* secretary, he said, "Black would be fine."

The lady's light blue eyes flashed and she set her gaze on Seamus. "Surely, this late in the day Mister McCurren is in no need of refreshing?" Then her eyes pierced his discomfited secretary. "And do you not think it more urgent, Mister Habernathy, that our office deals with the security of this country before the comforts of its occupants?"

James paled and Seamus took pity on the poor man. "You may retrieve my coffee when you have finished gathering the documents so"—he turned his head and met the woman's unflinching gaze—"*urgently* needed by Lady Juliet."

"Yes, sir," James said, leaving before the lady had an opportunity to take a second bite.

Annoyed, Seamus sat down and turned to face the bothersome creature.

"Would you be so kind as to tell me, *Mister* McCurren," she began, having caught his slight, "the details of the discovery of the E code?"

Hackles raised, Seamus lifted his head and spoke over his right shoulder. "As his lordship has no doubt told you, the anomaly appeared four times in three publications, which—"

"Means the mathematical probability of a consistent printing error is highly unlikely," she finished, as if reading his mind. "Yes, I agree."

"I am so pleased our conclusions meet with your approval," he said, picking up a new report in need of analysis.

Seamus had not even read half the page when he saw the tiny woman standing beside his tidy desk. "And you have found no pattern in these articles?"

He sighed and looked up at the lass, her dusting of freckles more visible as she stared down at him.

"No."

"And you have found four anomalies printed in three publications over the past two months?"

"Yes."

"May I see them?" the lady asked, failing to take the hint.

Unaccustomed to having his findings questioned, Seamus met her clear eyes, holding them. "There is no pattern in those articles, Lady Juliet."

"Nevertheless." The girl smiled. "I would like to read them."

Seamus handed her the clippings, knowing that she would find nothing in them.

"Do let me know your conclusions," he said, smiling before returning to the document on his desk and completely ignoring her.

The woman mercifully wandered off and he heard not a peep from the opposite side of the room until James Habernathy returned to the office with a stack of newspapers and a laden luncheon tray, both of which he set atop the lady's small desk.

"Lady Felicity sends luncheon with regards."

"Oh, how thoughtful of her," Lady Juliet remarked as though she had just been invited to tea. "Thank you so much for bringing it to me, Mister Habernathy."

"Not at all," James said with considerable pleasure, adding an overly reverent inclination of his head.

Annoyed at his secretary's lack of loyalty, Seamus continued to read while ignoring the subtle clanking of bone china ringing in his ears. However, what he could not ignore were the delicious aromas wafting in his direction from the opposite side of the all-too-small room.

"Well." He rose, his stomach suddenly very empty. "I'll just leave you to dine."

As Seamus walked from the room, he could feel Lady Juliet's hostile gaze ushering him out of his own bloody office.

He closed the door, thinking that summarized the problem with the entire arrangement. How was he to concentrate with the woman glancing over his shoulder at every turn?

The lass had not been there half a day and she was already distracting him from the critical work that needed to be done.

Seamus ate his midday meal alone at his club; all the while trying to decide how long he should wait before informing Falcon that this forced partnership was unacceptable.

A week? Yes, that would be enough time for him to assert that he had truly made an effort to work with Lady Juliet.

A week! God in heaven.

Seamus rolled his eyes as he wandered back to his office, his steps increasingly languid. He eventually opened the outer-office door but James was nowhere to be found. Seamus placed his hand on the knob of the inner-office door and took a deep breath, opening it.

He was startled to find Lady Juliet not at her desk as he had left her, but on her hands and knees with multiple newspapers spread across the dingy wooden floor.

The woman looked up excitedly and opened her mouth to speak. But upon seeing Seamus, she closed it and looked down at the papers again. He watched her glance from one page to another, her large blue eyes growing wider as she read.

Then he heard the office door open and the old man stepped past Seamus with James Habernathy at his heels.

"Well?" Falcon asked the girl.

Lady Juliet jumped up and smiled like a child bursting with a newly discovered secret. "I've found something."

Seamus stiffened and he remembered to close his mouth.

"Show me," Falcon ordered, wasting no time.

"This morning I had requested that Mister Habernathy obtain copies of the newspapers in which the four anomalies first appeared."

"Yes," Falcon nodded, following.

"As I waited for the papers, Mister McCurren was kind enough to give me his clippings of the articles and informed me that there had been no pattern evident in any of them."

Seamus cringed at her kind assessment of the exchange.

"Having read Mister McCurren's essays on the repetitive sequencing of languages . . ." Shocked, Seamus glanced at the tiny woman. "I knew that he was most assuredly correct. So, I began to examine the newspapers as a whole."

"Do get on with it, Lady Juliet," the old man demanded, impatient.

"These two anomalies"—she pointed with her feminine finger—"here and here, appear in the same publication. While these anomalies"—she pointed toward the two remaining newspapers—"appear in different publications."

Seamus found himself walking toward the newspapers, his heart racing with anticipation as he stared down.

"But if you will note the dates on which the anomalies appear in the same publication . . ." How could he have been so stupid? "They both appear in the first week of the month," she concluded.

"It is not a coded message at all," Seamus said, turning to look at the astute woman. "It's a—"

"A marker." She nodded, encouraging his comprehension.

"Forgive me, but I do not understand," Falcon said, and the lady explained.

"Both of these E anomalies occur in the same publication during the first week of the month. This one"—she pointed—"was printed in a different publication in the second week and that one was printed in the fourth week.

"All the French need do is read this publication the first week, this one the second"—the girl twirled her hand—"so on and so forth.

"If the E anomaly appears in any of these three publications, then the French agent knows he has information ready for retrieval. Markers have been used as far back as the Mesopotamians when they—"

"Are you saying, Lady Juliet, that we must now identify their retrieval site?" Falcon asked, decidedly discouraged.

"I'm afraid so." The lady nodded in apology of being the barrier of bad tidings. "But, of course, it could be a physical location rather than a separate publication. We simply do not have enough information to draw those conclusions."

"Lady Juliet is correct," Seamus was pained to admit. "We must first begin by identifying the last marker published in the third week of the month. We can eliminate these three publications." Seamus looked at the floor. "And as all of these are daily newspapers, I would recommend we begin with a search of the remaining daily publications in town."

"Exactly," Juliet Pervill agreed with a vigorous nod.

"I shall have James compile a list of all daily newspapers," Seamus said, thinking aloud. "And then I will do an analysis of the most likely candidates for the third marker."

"We," Lady Juliet chimed in.

Seamus glanced down at her, confused. "Pardon?"

"We . . . 'will analyze the most likely candidates for the third marker.' " She held his eyes.

"Yes, of course," Seamus conceded, his stomach tightening. " 'We' will analyze the information."

"Very well, keep me apprised of your progress," Falcon said to them both and then turned to the lady, asking, "How did we ever manage without you, my dear?" The old man nodded in approval. "Well done, very well done indeed."

Seamus tried not to feel the blow to his pride, but he should have identified the markers himself.

"Thank you, my lord."

Falcon left the office and Lady Juliet glanced at Seamus, embarrassed.

"Well, back to work then," she said, walking toward her messy little desk.

Seamus followed, not letting her off that easily. He sat on the edge of her oak desktop with his arms crossed over his chest, reassessing the increasingly interesting woman.

"You've read my work?" Seamus asked, staring down at her.

"Yes." Lady Juliet nodded, failing to look up as she gathered papers and placed them in the appropriate files. "I thought it best that I know something of the gentleman I was to work with. Well." She shrugged. "More than I already knew."

"Ah." Seamus's dark brows rose at her presumption. "And what is it that you 'knew' of me prior to reading my academic articles?"

"I've known your brother, the viscount," she clarified as he had six brothers, "for several years. I have also met you on two previous occasions."

Seamus wrinkled his forehead, remembering the unsightly scene at the Spencer ball, but for the life of him, he could think of no other.

"Two occasions? What was the second?" he asked, neither of them needing to revisit the infamous meeting with her father.

"It was the first, actually," the lady corrected, blushing prettily and bringing some color to her cheeks despite the unfortunate gown. "Several months ago, I observed you coming out of the Duchess of Glenbroke's home as Lady Felicity and I were heading in."

Seamus stared at her, looking closely at her freckled face, those bright blue eyes.

A memory flashed through his mind and he said, "You ran into the lamppost."

Seamus smiled, flattered as he remembered that Lady Juliet had run headlong into a lamppost because she had been gawking at him.

Well, gawking at his backside.

Realizing that he had recalled correctly every detail of the encounter, the lass hastened to explain, "You . . . you looked so familiar and I could not understand why as your coloring is so different from that of your brother's."

"I'm a bit darker." Seamus stated the obvious.

"Yes." She jumped on his observation with relief. "But your features are . . ." The lady motioned to her own face.

"Similar?"

"Yes." She nodded as if he had hit the nail on the head and Seamus let the silence lengthen, enjoying her discomfort as they stared at one another.

"Similarities tend to occur with siblings, but then you have no siblings, do you, Lady Juliet?" The lass blinked and Seamus continued to surprise her. "But you did manage to occupy yourself, receiving honorary recognition from Cambridge?"

"Oxford," the lass corrected, visibly surprised. "How did you—"

"I thought it best to 'learn a bit about the woman I would be working with,' " Seamus lied and she blushed.

"What was it you study? I can't quite remember," he lied again.

"Differential calculus."

Bloody hell!

"Aye, that's it." He snapped his fingers and pointed at the lass in a great show of recollection. "Differential calculus. Unfortunately, I was unable to obtain *your* articles. What was the supposition of these papers?"

"Well . . ." The lady looked at the desktop, no doubt searching for the right words of simplification. "The articles are somewhat interrelated and deal with the arc differential in proportion to the earth's curvature."

Lady Juliet met his eye as she continued to describe her theories, clearly checking to see if his feeble mind was following her train of thought.

"You see, the curvature of the earth will eventually affect the accuracy of the calculation, thus causing inaccuracies in navigation, for example, which will increase exponentially in direct proportion to the distance."

The only problem was that he was not following . . . not really.

Seamus watched her lips, his heart pounding as he listened but understood only bits and pieces of what the lass was saying. Her pretty little mouth continued to teach and her moist, red lips were calling to him to listen.

Seamus's nods of agreement were pulling him forward and he was intent on kissing her when the lass suddenly stood.

"Then I shall see you tomorrow," the lady was saying, "and we can put our heads together to find a solution to the problem of the last marker?"

He just stared at her, caught somewhere in the world between his mind and his flesh, choosing the path of proprietary over the inexplicable road that beckoned to his body.

"Right." Seamus blinked as he watched the woman walk out his office door, and the moment it closed, he shook his head in confusion as his heart continued to race. "What the hell just happened?"

"How was your first day at the Foreign Office?" Felicity asked, Juliet's excitement obvious from the moment she entered the drawing room.

"My day was quite enthralling." Juliet plopped in her chair and tried to capture the feeling in words. "I had not been there half the day before I was able to be of assistance. I can't tell you the details, of course, but I felt so . . ."

"Useful?"

"Yes, that is it exactly." Juliet snapped her fingers and then leaned back against the comfortable leather chair, wondering how her cousin knew. "I was useful today."

"And did any of the gentlemen at the Foreign Office make advances toward you as we had feared?"

"Not a blessed soul." Juliet grinned. "Of course, this

means we shall have to commission the modiste to fashion more hideous gowns."

Felicity laughed, observing, "You do look like death warmed over, Juliet. I myself can hardly bear to look at you."

"Thank you, darling. Would you prefer that I dress for dinner so that you might stomach your food?"

"Please," Felicity begged and then in all seriousness asked, "So, this is something that you will continue to do? Assist the Foreign Office?"

"Yes. I don't know how to explain precisely." Juliet's forehead knitted as she tried to find the proper words to spare Felicity injury. "I have a colleague who understood what I was saying today, followed every blessed word, and so often people are not really—"

"Capable of keeping up with your intellectual pace?" Felicity grinned.

"Yes, I'm sorry."

"It's all right, dearest," Felicity eased her guilt. "It is not as though I'm lacking in intellectual capabilities, it is merely that compared to your intellectual prowess I, along with most mere mortals, pale in comparison."

"As do I when I stand next to you."

"Oh, I do wish you would not say such things, Juliet," Felicity pleaded with a touch of ladylike irritation. "You know how much I dislike being pretty."

"Yes, and I shall never in my life understand why."

Felicity looked at Juliet with a sadness that was increasing in its frequency. "It is very tiresome."

Juliet nodded in confused sympathy. "Then you shall have to accompany me to the modiste so that Madame Maria might have you resemble a corpse as well." Felicity laughed and Juliet mused, "I should think an orange gown—"

"Oh, dear." Felicity's perfect nose wrinkled in distaste.

"Would make you sufficiently sallow, and perhaps if

you were to slump over"—Juliet rolled her shoulders forward as her cousin continued to laugh—"men would not be quite so aware of your exquisite figure."

"I could grow exceedingly fat."

"Even better." Juliet smiled, wondering why her cousin would choose the life of a fat spinster over the many gentlemen who had offered for her hand.

Eight

Falcon's weekly chess match with the Duke of Glenbroke was, for him, a time of reflection, of reassessing the decisions made and the steps yet to be taken by his secretive office.

The fact that the duke reported the activities within the Foreign Office directly to the Prince Regent meant nothing to Falcon. It was Glenbroke's unerring quest to do what was best for Britain and not the individuals perilously laboring under Falcon's command that made them the perfect complement to one another.

The duke requested information and Falcon provided it with little or no explanation as to how the information had been obtained.

The Duke of Glenbroke preferred it this way, as did he, allowing Falcon to concern himself with the safety of his agents and the task at hand, while the duke concentrated on the information with little knowledge of the individual sent to retrieve it.

With the exception of today.

"I've just commissioned a new agent."

"Oh?" Glenbroke stared at the chessboard, his silver eyes fixed. "Your funds are already stretched rather thin. Are you sure you can afford him?" the duke asked, sliding his rook into position.

Falcon permitted the implications of the duke's move to sink in before allowing himself to answer. "This particular agent won't cost my office one farthing."

"I'm intrigued," the duke said, watching the chess pieces lest one disappear. "How did you manage that? Recruit another volunteer?"

"Quite." Falcon moved his queen and then leaned back from the intellectual effort.

"Good man, Seamus McCurren," the duke mumbled, distracted by their game. "I still can't believe you gathered him into your fold. Am I acquainted with your latest acquisition?"

Falcon stared at the duke, knowing what the man's reaction would be, yet wanting to witness it nonetheless. "Yes."

The duke's steely eyes sharpened into seriousness. "Please, tell me you have not commissioned Christian St. John?"

"Good Lord, no!" Falcon chuckled. "Not even if the boy volunteered. Entirely unpredictable, that one. No, no, no."

"Who then?"

"Lady Juliet Pervill."

"Lady J—" The duke choked on a gush of air. "Lady Juliet?"

"The lady volunteered after having been ruined." Falcon grinned to himself. "Interesting girl, Lady Juliet."

"Juliet Pervill is more than just interesting." The duke was irritated as Falcon knew he would be. "She is my wife's dearest friend."

"That's as it may be, but the lady also harbors a skill I find myself in desperate need of at the moment. Once she has assisted me in this matter, the duchess is welcome to continue with her elaborate plans to reconcile the girl with polite society."

The duke grinned. "I see you've received your invitation to our ball?"

"Yes, thank you, Your Grace, but I believe I shall be sitting this one out."

Glenbroke chuckled and then his brows furrowed when he remembered, "What skill does Lady Juliet possess that you need so badly?"

"Did you know the lady was affiliated with Oxford?" The duke shook his head and Falcon clarified, "She was given an honorary degree in mathematics."

"Ah, your precious codes," Glenbroke nodded with understanding and more than a little amusement. "I thought Seamus McCurren was seeing to the decrypting."

"Oh, he has been. Done a wonderful job thus far, but this latest code is dangerous." Falcon stared at the walls, the heavy weight of certainty pulling at his chest.

"Dangerous? Aren't all French codes dangerous?"

"Yes, but this one . . ." Falcon shook his head, thinking aloud. "I sense that this one . . . is a great threat to the security of our country."

"Why this one more than any of the others?"

"I don't know." And he did not, but Falcon had learned never to ignore his instincts and he was not about to now. "You see, the difficulty in decoding the majority of these French codes is in the detection.

"Once the code has been detected, men such as Seamus McCurren make short work of deciphering them. Not so with this code." Falcon sighed with frustration. "We have known of this code for two months and are no closer to decoding it than we were the day it was first detected."

"And you believe Juliet Pervill can help you break this code?" the duke asked.

"She already has! Lady Juliet identified the code as a mere marker for a much more complex system of cryptography. A system, I fear, that is at the core of the French espionage effort here in London."

"I suppose it will keep that brilliant mind of Juliet's occupied while my wife labors on her behalf." The duke glanced up, now deadly serious. "Juliet Pervill is under your protection?"

"Yes." Falcon nodded and continued to reassure the man. "The lady has been placed in Seamus McCurren's own office and I am just down the hall."

"Excellent." The duke moved a pawn. "I should never hear the end of it if my wife believed I had knowingly placed Juliet in harm's way."

"You may assure the duchess, Your Grace," Falcon said with confidence, "that Lady Juliet's position within the Foreign Office is nothing more than a glorified librarian and equally as dangerous."

On Friday morning, Juliet walked into her office at eight forty-five with seven books of various sizes and colors weighing her down. She dropped them on the table with a resounding thud and then removed her coat before seating herself at her functional, but at the same time charming, desk.

She stared as rain crashed against the window, leaving streams of water that joined to form rivers. Juliet traced the lines with her forefinger, wondering what force was being exerted to pull the water in diagonal lines rather than directly down the windowpane.

Was the irregularity of the glass a factor in the path the water took? There appeared to be too many streams to rely upon this variance to explain the water's movements. Therefore, the water must hold some attraction to itself, enough of an attraction to pull it sideways. But how much of an attraction, and was the pull a constant—

Juliet's musings were interrupted when she heard the outer door open. She quickly reached for a book and opened it, bending her head as if she were engrossed by hours upon hours of riveting reading.

The inner-office door opened and the silence made her grin. She had noted Mister McCurren's irritation yesterday when he had arrived to find her already there. So, Juliet had risen at eight this morning to ensure that she arrived in the office before him.

Childish, she knew, but satisfying nonetheless.

"Morning." The crisp baritone greeting sounded as though it had been pushed past clenched teeth.

Juliet made a great show of reluctantly pulling her eyes from the fascinating book she had yet to read so that she might welcome her tardy colleague.

"Good morning," she beamed, glancing toward the door with the intention of returning to her book.

However, when she saw Seamus McCurren framed in the doorway, his green jacket complementing his chestnut hair, his unusual golden eyes circled by dark lashes, his full masculine lips . . . Juliet simply stared, appreciating the view.

Uncomfortable, the gentleman broke eye contact with a respectful inclination of his head and then walked toward his larger desk. She enjoyed that, too, his muscular thighs flexing beneath his buff buckskins as he sank into the leather chair. Juliet cocked her head, having one last look, before reluctantly returning to her far less appealing book.

She sighed.

Men where so lovely to look at, and Juliet wondered if she would be able to control her lecherous side, if she would be able to content herself with just looking at the multitude of handsome young men working at the Foreign Office.

Her eyes wandered from the pages of her book, drawn by the ugly brown gown that she had forced herself to wear. Her nose wrinkled with distaste, but she knew it was for her own good.

She was a weak woman when it came to men, always had been.

She had adored kissing Robert Barksdale and he was not even her masculine ideal. If she had been born as beautiful as Felicity, she would have ruined herself years ago.

Juliet gave a snort of laughter, certain that God had made her plain for that very reason.

"Did you say something?"

She could feel her cheeks burning when Juliet realized that she had laughed aloud.

"Uh, no." She shook her head. "My apologies, this book is rather amusing and I'm unaccustomed to reading in the company of others."

"Mmm." The deep tone contained doubt and a note of superiority that irritated Juliet to no end, but Seamus McCurren did not stop there. "Does this novel you're reading lend insight into the breaking of French codes?"

Her jaw dropped at the insinuation that she was frittering away her time on some frivolous novel.

"None at all," Juliet sang, turning to face the arrogant Scot. "However, as the last marker will not appear until sometime next week, assuming of course that the French have a message to convey at all, I thought to amuse myself with a bit of research."

Seamus McCurren stood to his impressive height, and with each elegant step he took toward Juliet, her heart leapt out of her chest.

"And you find researching differential calculus . . . amusing?" he drawled, looking down at her with a raised brow of intellectual condescension.

"Somewhat." He was standing over her now and Juliet licked her lips to ease the words from her mouth. "The conclusions that ancient mathematicians have drawn are somewhat amusing in their simplicity."

"Such as?" The Scot held her eyes, the glistening of brown and gold in his rendering her speechless.

She shrugged and Mister McCurren reached out to gently pry the thin book from her unsteady hands. His long, rough fingers brushed hers and her stomach flipped as Juliet watched him draw the book toward his spectacularly sculpted features.

His head tilted downward as he read and Juliet suppressed the urge to stroke his perfect sideburns, which he no doubt knew emphasized the line of his even more perfect jaw.

"This is written in ancient Greek?" Seamus McCurren's beautiful eyes were once again on her, demanding an explanation.

"Well, yes. I find that many of the subtleties of mathematical theory are lost in the translation from one language to—"

"This is a Persian text." Seamus McCurren had lifted another of her books.

"Yes, the Persians were by far the most accomplished mathema—"

"Is this Mandarin?" he inquired, his brows draw together in astonishment.

Feeling the need to defend her diverse collection of texts . . . and herself, Juliet jumped up and reached for the tiny red tome.

"Please, be careful with that book, Mister McCurren. It is very old and I have not yet learned enough Mandarin to interpret the theories fully. I have recently acquired the services of a tutor to assist me in translating the—"

Juliet sucked in a breath, shocked when her words were smothered by Seamus McCurren's sumptuous lips.

The fingers of his right hand speared her severe chignon as he drew her head closer with persuasive pressure at the nape of her neck. However, it was the large hand cradling her jaw that very nearly burned her as much as his demanding lips.

Juliet closed her eyes, astounded by how different this kiss felt compared to Robert Barksdale's.

This man was assured, confident, and skilled in his movements. Very skilled at enticing a woman to want that little bit more, that one last touch. Juliet was becoming lightheaded the more that they kissed . . . and she was most definitely confused.

Why would a man of Seamus McCurren's obvious experience kiss her?

And then the answer was clear.

"Stop!"

The slight Lady Juliet shoved him in the chest so hard that Seamus had to take a step backward to steady himself. He stared down at the lass in utter shock of what he had just done, his chest and lips on fire where they had touched her.

The lass lifted her chin, her jaw setting as she stared up at him, saying, "I realize that you do not wish to work with me, Mister McCurren, but I would have thought this tactic quite beneath you."

"No," Seamus protested, appalled that the lady would think such a thing but unable to explain his actions . . . even to himself. "You miscompre—"

"Well, I can assure you that the Foreign Office will not be so easily rid of me," the lady railed on, not listening. "You see, Mister McCurren, my mother's marriage to my bastard of a father taught me one very valuable lesson. Perseverance. And whether you wish it or not, sir, I shall continue to work in this office come hell or high water."

With that declaration, the lass swept her dingy brown skirts to one side and resumed her seat behind her cluttered little desk. Seamus glanced about the office, so stunned by his own actions that he could scarcely move.

Not only did Seamus not know what to say, but he now had no choice but to sit in the room with the very woman he had just taken liberties with while trying to pretend that he had not.

And as to why he had taken those liberties in the first place, he had not a bloody clue.

"As you wish," Seamus mumbled, not knowing what else to say.

Sitting in his chair, he discreetly put the back of his hand against his forehead and was disheartened to detect no fever. Seamus glanced at Juliet Pervill from the corner of his eye, baffled as to what had possessed him to kiss her.

Her unsightly gown and ashen face had drawn his attention to the bright blue of her eyes and cherry red of her lips. And as those feminine lips continued to move, he had wanted . . . No, more than that, he had been *compelled* to kiss the woman.

Surely, he was ill?

"If I had my wish, Mister McCurren, we would not be working together at all." What was she saying? He turned to listen. "I have been here all of two days and you have been nothing but a liability in my efforts to decrypt this French code."

"A what?" he scoffed, offended.

Lady Juliet stopped writing and swiveled round in her wooden chair so that she might look at him. "A liability, a deficit, a hindrance. Surely, as an expert in the written word, you have come across that one."

Seamus's previous humiliation dissolved with the lady's continued insults. "I know the meaning of the word, Lady Juliet."

"Hmm," she mused, expressing doubt.

"Furthermore"—he was attempting to be reasonable— "if we are to continue working together, I suggest that we discuss the manner in which we—"

"Let's not."

"Pardon?"

"Let us not 'work together.' Go our separate ways, so to speak." She lifted her shoulders as if she were the most reasonable woman in the world. "I have all of the information compiled by the Foreign Office pertaining to this E code. You, at this point, are . . . superfluous to my investigation, and your constant attempts to make me leave this office indicate that you are unlikely to provide me with any meaningful assistance."

"My attempts to make you leave?" *Meaningful assistance!*

"I see no another explanation for your kissing me."

He certainly had none to provide.

"And while you might be accustomed to women swooning in your dazzling presence, I simple don't have the time. You see, I have a code to decrypt." The lass stood, straightening the papers on her desk and then her ugly skirts. "As a matter of fact, I have just thought of a line of inquiry to which I must attend. So, if you would be so kind as to excuse me."

The lady left the office and Seamus was still staring at the door when Mister Habernathy walked into the office carrying his morning coffee.

"No coffee today, James." Seamus waved off the black libation. "I believe I shall work from home."

"Everything all right, sir?"

"Grand," Seamus said, feeling anything but. "However, there is nothing more for us to do here until the newspapers are published Monday next."

Nothing he could think of, anyway.

Seamus took one step toward the door when James asked, "Is Lady Juliet expected in today?"

Feeling a flash of guilt, Seamus glanced at the small desk and stared at the spot where they had been standing when he had kissed Juliet Pervill.

Seamus shook his head, dumbfounded, as he racked his brain for a possible line of investigation that he had overlooked.

"I've no idea where the lady has gone," he finally admitted to his secretary . . . and himself.

Juliet stood on the chilly front steps of the Foreign Office and attempted to breathe.

It had taken a great deal of determination for her to re-main in that room after Seamus McCurren had kissed her. Juliet had sat in her chair lest she fall down and only prayed that the man did not notice her hands shaking like leaves in a stiff wind.

But she would be damned if she was going to run out of the room as he wanted her to do.

Mister McCurren had no idea, of course, that she had no other place to go, had no idea that his exquisite kiss was all she had at the moment to occupy her muddled mind.

Still, she wished that he had not kissed her. Now, she would have to sit in that office day after day, knowing how marvelous the man felt. How delightful his warm power had felt beneath her hands.

Damnation!

Restless, she walked down the steps and onto the crowded walkways of Whitehall. "A line of inquiry!" Why on earth had she told him that? *To get under his skin . . . as he had hers.* The only problem with her little act of vengeance was that she had nothing new to investigate.

Idiot!

Felicity's carriage was not due back until four o'clock that afternoon and she really should return to the safety of the Foreign Office. But she could not bring herself to do it. Juliet would rather die at the hands of a footpad than admit to the breathtakingly arrogant Seamus McCurren that she had no "line of inquiry" to pursue.

"Come on, Juliet! You're a clever girl," she muttered be-neath her breath.

She could go anywhere in London. *But where?*

Juliet stared at the low-hanging winter sky for several contemplative moments and then called for a hackney, say-ing, "The *London Herald*, please," as the driver assisted her over a steaming pile of horse manure and into the hired black carriage.

The interior of the hackney was old and worn, but

thankfully clean. Juliet leaned back against the squabs as the conveyance rocked her down the cobblestone streets of London, giving her a considerable amount of time to think.

The E anomaly appeared in specified publications on specified weeks. Therefore, if she were able to identify the last marker, it would stand to reason that Falcon would be able to post agents at the identified publication and wait for the French cryptographer to arrive.

It might take several weeks to identify the courier, but it was, as far as she could see, their only course of action.

Satisfied with her reasoning, Juliet sat back and tried to think of anything but Seamus McCurren. However, trying not to think of the man just brought him to mind, and the vicious circle was broken only when the conveyance blessedly rolled to a stop.

Juliet stepped from the hackney and handed her driver a generous amount of coin, asking, "Please, wait for me here."

The driver tipped his dusty hat, grinning from ear to ear, and Juliet tried not to stare at the forest of black hair peeking from his upturned nostrils like two burst caterpillars that writhed as he talked.

"I'll be glued to this very spot, my lady, never you worry."

"Yes, thank you." Confident that the hairy driver would not abandon her on these unfamiliar streets, Juliet turned toward the large building standing before her.

The red bricks were made even darker by the years of unattended soot, and the drab, square building boasted utilatarian function rather than architectural aesthetics. The only stylistic element she could see at all was the gold-leaf wording the *London Herald* painted on the glass panel inset of a battered wooden door.

Determined to show the Scot something for her efforts, Juliet pushed open the door to one of London's many daily news publications. However, the moment she stepped inside, Juliet instinctively put her hands over her ears, the sound of the printing press louder than she had expected.

Startled by the sight of a female in the print room, a young man covered in what appeared to be black ink ran toward her and silently pointed Juliet toward a door at the far end of the enormous room. She nodded her understanding and then walked to the distant door and turned the round knob, ruining her white glove with a mixture of grease and black ink.

Juliet pushed the grimy door open and, upon entering, removed her soiled glove as she looked about the hectic front office of the *London Herald*.

She was not impressed with what she saw.

A lone clerk stood behind the tall wooden counter while several older gentlemen sat behind him at well-used desks with their heads buried between mountains of papers.

Juliet had two men waiting in front of her as she proceeded to queue, thankful for the moments to formulate her questions now that she had seen a daily publication at full function.

The first man concluded his business and left with a nod as the elderly man in front of her shuffled forward to speak with the lanky clerk.

The older man, it seemed, was selling his home after the passing of his wife.

How sad.

Juliet looked at the elderly gentleman again, wondering if their marriage had been a happy one. She knew there were happy marriages. She knew, in theory, that her parents' disastrous union was the exception rather than the rule. Why then did she always view marriage with such overwhelming cynicism?

She contemplated the unfathomable question as the old man continued to speak with the clerk about the precise wording of his week-long advertisement and the fee that would be involved in printing it.

When they had finished negotiating a price, the elderly man hesitated and Juliet could see that she had been right.

As the man made the final decision to sell his home, his distress was clear to anyone who took a moment to look.

"Well?" the clerk asked with not one ounce of compassion. "Do you want to place the advertisement or not?"

Angry, Juliet smiled at the old gentleman and said, "They certainly don't give you much time to decide at the *Herald*, do they?" loud enough that the men at their desks glared in disapproval of the impatient clerk.

Appreciative of her kindness, the old man smiled back at her and then finally nodded to the clerk and paid the advertisement fee.

Juliet watched the elderly gentleman leave the lobby and then turned to the impolite clerk. She had just opened her mouth to speak when a long, bulky arm reached round her, holding up a thin brown envelope.

"Here you are, Mister Smith, same as last—"

"Pardon me." Juliet turned around to look at the insolent newcomer.

The enormous man with a ghastly scar across his left cheek looked down at her, his haunting brown eyes focusing through her as if she were not there.

"I'll just be a moment, madame." The large man lifted his envelope toward the clerk for a second time. However, the assent of the document was stilled by the exquisite Venetian fan Juliet placed against the man's muscular forearm.

"As shall I." Juliet smiled.

The clerk and the bulky man with the envelope exchanged a glance of irritation and Juliet ignored them both.

"Now"—she turned back to the clerk—"if you would be so kind as to answer some questions for me," she said with her most charming smile. "I would be most appreciative."

"Yes, madame," the clerk relented, although clearly annoyed.

"If I were to place an advertisement in your newspaper today, when might I expect that advertisement to appear in your publication?"

"Three days' time."

Juliet calculated, asking, "And if I were to place an advertisement today, what is the maximum length of time in which you would refrain from printing that advert?"

"Why indefinitely, madame." His smile was, at best, tolerant. "All one need do is place the date on which you wish the advertisement to appear."

"Like that one." Juliet pointed to the large man's brown envelope, having noted a date scrawled on the outside.

"Yes, madame. Now, if that is all?" the restless clerk asked.

"One more question?" The boorish man behind her grunted in protest, prompting Juliet to spin round. "Sir, I believe you are making the clerk anxious. Perhaps it would be best if you were to stand over there."

They stared at one another but Juliet held her ground until the man reluctantly took a step back. She then turned her attention to the beleaguered clerk.

"How far in advance do you receive the articles from your contributing writers?" she inquired.

"The day before publication."

Juliet burst into an exaggerated smile for the ill-mannered men, saying, "Thank you," as she gathered her reticule to leave.

The tall man with the scar barreled past her and handed the clerk his envelope while keeping his empty eyes fixed on Juliet.

"Same as last time," he said, then turned and walked out the door, making his rather discourteous point.

Nine

Viscount Dunloch sat in the chair opposite Seamus, after having closed his tall study doors to the outside world.

"Right, I've told my servants not to disturb us so that you might tell me what is so bloody important that you could not wait until tomorrow evening? You are still going?"

"I said I would." Seamus waved off the subject of the Duke of Glenbroke's ball, moving on to more important and perplexing matters. "And I've your word of honor that you'll not breathe a word of this conversation to anyone? Not our brothers—"

"Nor our parents . . . Aye." Daniel rolled his eyes. "Damn it all, Seamus, what's the difficulty?"

Staring at his older brother and closest friend, Seamus confided, "I think . . . I'm going mad."

"What?" Daniel chuckled. "What the hell makes you think that you—"

"I kissed a colleague today."

His brother sat back, stunned, then cleared his throat and reluctantly met Seamus's eye.

"Well, Seamus," Daniel began, uncomfortable. "I'm your brother and I hold a great affection for you and that will not change. We shall simply have to sit Mother and Father down and explain that you're a sodomite and—"

"What?" Seamus shot out of his chair and then, realizing his mistake, sat back down. "No, no, no. She's a woman. My colleague is a woman."

"A woman? Oh, thank God." His brother took a deep breath. "I was not sure how the earl would have taken to the news that his second son was a sodomite. Although, I suppose it is better than his heir being a sodom—"

"I'm not a sodomite!"

"I know, I know. But if you are not, then I don't understand the problem." Daniel's turquoise eyes were fixed on his, trying to comprehend the difficulty. "You're attracted to a woman?"

"I'm not attracted to the woman." Seamus lifted both hands to emphasize his confusion. "That's the bloody problem."

"What do you mean, you're not attracted to the woman? Did you kiss the lass?" Daniel's eyebrows were pulled together as he stared intently at his face.

Seamus gave a slight nod. "Aye."

"Then you're attracted to her," Daniel pronounced, as sure of himself as ever.

"I swear to you, I'm not attracted to the woman." Seamus was adamant. "The lady isn't my sort at all. She's very plain, with ordinary brown hair. She's got quite beautiful eyes, I'll give her that, but she's a wee thing." He held his hand parallel to the mahogany floor.

"No, the lass does not sound your sort at all. If I recall, you prefer blondes." Daniel grinned.

"Why the hell do I bother speaking with you?" Seamus

stood and Daniel followed, holding up his hands in a calming gesture.

"Very well, I'm sorry." His brother attempted to appear serious, but the blackguard was failing miserable. "I can see you're distressed and in need of my counsel."

He was at that.

So, despite his better judgment, Seamus sat down to hear his brother's judicious advice. "Go on then."

"Right." Daniel leaned forward, his bulky forearms on his knees. "What was the lass doing when you thought to have a go at her?"

"For God's sake." Seamus rolled his eyes. "I didn't 'think to have a go at her'!"

"When you thought to kiss her then?"

"Aye." Seamus nodded in agreement of the verbal hair-splitting. "She was talking."

"Well, that explains it then." Daniel chuckled, shrugging his shoulders. "Any man would rather kiss a woman than listen to her prattle."

"She was not prattling." Seamus shook his head.

"What was the lass doing then?"

"She was . . ." Seamus averted his eyes, his right knee bouncing up and down nervously. "She was explaining her theses on differential calculus."

Daniel threw back his auburn head and laughed so hard that tears flooded his eyes. Seamus clenched his jaw and stood to leave.

"My apologies, Seamus. Please, I'm sorry. Please, sit down," his brother begged as he wiped his wet cheeks of his amusement. Daniel sniffed to clear his head and then remembered, "You don't even like mathematics," on a peel of robust laughter.

Humiliated, Seamus turned then walked out of his brother's study doors, knowing there was nothing for it.

Unfortunately, for Seamus, there was no one else with

whom he would be willing to confide. He would just have to figure out on his own what the hell was wrong with him.

Mister Collin poked his scarred face through the door as he knocked, reporting, "Seamus McCurren is requesting a seat at your table."

"Back already?" Enigma smiled with satisfaction at the return of the intriguing Seamus McCurren.

Dante's Inferno had not become London's most popular hell merely for the quality of its whores. No, Dante's had rather ingeniously thrown down the gauntlet to gentlemen such as Mister McCurren. Challenging these men to beat the house if they could and allowing them to bring their own cards to prove that the owner of Dante's Inferno was simply superior in intellect to the gentlemen of polite society. And the gentlemen of the *ton* had accepted the challenge in droves.

The foolish pride of its eager victims and an understanding, by the hell's humble owner, of the mathematical odds against them had made Dante's the most profitable gaming establishment in all of London.

Therefore, it was with infrequent pleasure that Enigma played a gentleman worthy of combat, a gentleman as stimulating as Seamus McCurren.

Mister Seamus McCurren had wandered into Dante's two months ago with Christian St. John, who had begged a chair at the famous owner's table. After being beaten soundly, St. John had encouraged McCurren to have a go, and much to Christian St. John's surprise, the gentleman did.

It had taken all night for Enigma to win the hell's blunt back from Seamus McCurren, but it was worth the effort merely to experience the thrill of mental swordplay. Mister McCurren had enjoyed their skirmish, too, as evidenced by his repeated presence at the hell's main table.

"Give Mister McCurren his usual seat."

"Lord Harrington is sitting—"

"Move Harrington." Enigma stared at the obsequious bodyguard. "I shall be down shortly."

Irritated, Seamus glanced at his pocket watch then took another swig of scotch. He had been waiting three-quarters of an hour and had half a mind to leave Dante's without having played one blessed hand.

He had come to the hell to occupy his mind, to forget his incomprehensible lapse in judgment with Juliet Pervill. Yet here he sat with nothing to occupy himself but the inane chitchat of the five eager gentlemen who sat at the table as excited as five fillies at Ascot.

Bored, Seamus leaned back in his chair, stretching as he glanced over the hell's costly courtesans. Perhaps all he needed was a good rut to clear his head.

He had not been with a woman since sending his paramour packing and this was no doubt the cause of his transgression with the uninviting Lady Juliet Pervill. His body was aching for release and Dante's whores were renowned for their salacious talents.

But Seamus had never paid for it, preferring a woman's enthusiasm to feigned flattery. Still, he sipped the fiery liquid, perhaps just this once he could pay to have a whore—

"Mister McCurren," the owner of Dante's Inferno said, gracing the table with his undeniable presence. "It is so nice to see you again and so soon. Come to win back your losses?"

Seamus met the man's gray-green eyes and they smiled at one another in an antagonistic show of respect. "As I recall, Mister Youngblood, the scales ended very nearly even."

"Very nearly." The annoyingly handsome man grinned then took his seat as did the other gentlemen allowed at his coveted table. "As you gentlemen well know, there is a minimum bid of ten pounds with no maximum bid.

"Transfer of property must be handled by my solicitor prior to being given a line of credit equal to its appraised worth. Accusations of impropriety will not be tolerated when you lose." Two of the players chuckled with confidence. "And as always, you are welcome to furnish your own cards, provided that all parties at the table agree to their usage."

Seamus yawned, scarcely listening to the familiar rules when Mister Youngblood glanced to his right.

With a crystal glass in hand, the stunning bawd of Dante's Inferno ambled toward their table then sank into the chair closest her handsome lover. Youngblood gave a proprietary grin for the beautiful procuress who managed his bordello, but only offered herself to Youngblood himself.

Mister Youngblood lowered his head, his caramel-colored hair covering his sharp green eyes as he twirled his right forefinger in the scotch, lifting it. The forbidden fruit leaned forward, her décolletage in full view of the table as she suggestively sucked the spirits from Youngblood's forefinger.

"Of course, your winnings can always be exchanged for services which Madame Richard would be happy to arrange."

Seamus smiled, staring at the bawd's indigo eyes as he pictured the services the enticing woman would provide. She was tall and blond, just the way he liked them, and the carnal possibilities were as endless as her lovely long legs.

"Shall we get on with it then," a gentleman of middle years asked, clearly distracted by the erotic display.

Mister Youngblood chuckled, scooting his chair closer to the table as he asked, "Are you so eager to begin, Lord Harrington? You have already lost your town home to Lord Pervill and now you play with your estate."

Harrington?

Incensed, Seamus turned away from Madame Richard to look at the man who had maliciously ruined his young colleague.

The gentleman had once been handsome and thought that he still was. However, his features were weathered by drink, and years of inactivity had softened his sharp angles with a layer of fat.

"Have you come to counsel me, Mister Youngblood, or are we here to play cards?" Lord Harrington leaned forward, his gray temples flashing in the candlelight as he placed an unopened deck of cards atop the immaculate baize table. "I've brought my own this time."

Youngblood's icy gaze met Lord Harrington's as a warm smile spread across his elegant features. "Surely you're not suggesting that my establishment has cheated you, Lord Harrington?"

Harrington swallowed as he glanced at the large men discreetly positioned about the busy gaming room. A guard with an immense scar that transversed his left cheek stepped forward and Mister Youngblood lifted his hand, stilling the muscle's progress until Lord Harrington had the opportunity of answering the question.

The right side of Seamus's mouth lifted at the thought of Lord Harrington being thrashed by Mister Youngblood's treacherous troops.

However, he was disappointed when the cowardly bastard sputtered, "No, no, no. Of course I'm not accusing Dante's of any impropriety, Mister Youngblood."

"Good." Youngblood lifted his scotch and, before taking a sip, added, "Because if I intended to fleece you, Lord Harrington, I can assure you that your town home would now be in *my* possession, not Lord Pervill's."

Madame Richard laughed as if the entire affair were some great amusement and then reached forward and grasped Lord Harrington's sealed deck of cards.

The woman's breasts pressed against the table and Seamus's attention dipped to enjoy the burgeoning sight. He felt a chill and lifted his eyes only to meet the icy green gaze of Mister Youngblood.

"Enjoying yourself this evening, Mister McCurren?"

"Immensely." Seamus smiled, unrepentant, amazed that a man who displayed his lover so freely would then become jealous of another man's gawking. "Although I'd be enjoying my evening far more if we bloody well got on with it."

"Want Lord Harrington's estate, do you?" Mister Youngblood asked, shuffling the cards.

"I can't imagine that I would want anything once owned by Lord Harrington."

Harrington's brows furrowed at the insult and he glared at Seamus as if seeing him for the first time. "What the hell did you say your name was?"

"I didn't." Seamus reached for his cards, eager to add to Lord Harrington's misery.

The proprietor of Dante's Inferno chuckled at Seamus's rudeness then sorted his cards as his paramour elegantly draped herself against him.

"Whenever you're ready, old man," Mister Youngblood said to the blond dandy on his left, who then tossed the first card, launching their costly diversion.

Glancing down at his hand only after the first card had been thrown, Seamus determined that he had already lost. The remainder of the hand was tedious and he played with little enthusiasm.

Lord Harrington gloated as he picked up his winnings and Seamus would have moved away from the bastard if being seated next to the arrogant drunk did not give him such a considerable advantage.

"Well done, Lord Harrington," the confident Mister Youngblood congratulated the man. "At this pace, you might well win enough blunt to buy back your town home from Lord Pervill."

Seamus glanced at the greed simmering in Harrington's glassy eyes then gave a snort of disgust. He was sure that Lord Harrington had not given a second thought to the woman he had ruined, if he remembered ruining Juliet Pervill at all.

Leaning forward, Seamus eagerly scooped up his second hand. He would win this one. Mister Youngblood was the only man at the table capable of beating him, but not when Seamus held all of these cards.

He played the hand slowly, allowing the pot to build. Seamus watched Youngblood's features carefully as he played his final card and with a slight smile and a rush of satisfaction said, "Mine, I believe."

The gamester lifted his clear, mossy gaze to Seamus. "Yes, I believe this one is yours," Mister Youngblood agreed, the game now fully on.

They played for hours. The other men at the table provided ammunition for the true battle taking place before them, and when all was said and done, Seamus pushed away from the table, his demons momentarily silenced.

"If you gentlemen will excuse me, I believe I have finished for the night."

Unaccustomed to losing, the proprietor clenched his jaw, asking, "Will you not stay, Mister McCurren, and give the table the opportunity to win back our loses?"

Seamus rose, pulling out his pocket watch from his cobalt waistcoat, and verified his body's suspicion of the late hour. "I'm afraid not, Mister Youngblood."

Madame Richard snapped her long fingers and a small man appeared at her side. "Mister Matthews, please pay Mister McCurren his winnings and then call for his conveyance to be brought round."

Dipping his head toward the beautiful bawd, Seamus held her shimmering eyes as the tiny bookkeeper scribbled in a leather ledger before begrudgingly handing over the considerable amount that Seamus was owed.

"Good evening," Seamus said to his host as he stuffed the stack of currency into the right pocket of his jacket, his fingertips confirming the presence of the cold steel of his pistol.

He turned away from the table then walked to the front door, carefully avoiding the whores who were so very eager to help him celebrate his good fortune. Once clear of their temptation, Seamus rode home, all the while mentally preparing himself for yet another bout with polite society and another daunting week with the inscrutable Juliet Pervill.

Ten

It was two o'clock on Saturday afternoon and Juliet was reading in bed when the door to her bedchamber burst open.

Startled, she looked up, and her mother strolled in as if it were her home and not Lord Appleton's.

"So," the countess began, looking down at Juliet with both hands on her narrow hips. "You're alive."

Juliet rolled her eyes. "Don't be so melodramatic, Mother. Of course I'm alive."

Her mother grasped the cozy counterpane and snapped it back, exposing Juliet to the harsh winter air.

"What else was I supposed to think when you failed to come home last weekend?" Her mother raised a brow in what Juliet knew to be irritation.

"I never agreed to come home, Mother." Juliet leaned forward and yanked the blankets back to their rightful, and much preferred, position.

"And how was I to know that, as you never wrote saying you would *not* be home?" her mother inquired, pulling the counterpane off the bed entirely, thus forcing Juliet to get out of bed and don a heavy dressing gown or freeze to death.

"I'm sorry, Mother." She leaned over to pull on her slippers, but when she rose, Juliet was startled to see tears in her mother's beautiful blue eyes.

She had never seen her mother cry. Well, almost cry, and Juliet watched as her mother's hurt was once again masked by her elegant composure.

"I would have preferred it if you had written, Juliet. I would have come to town immediately instead of waiting for you at the estate."

"I apologize, Mother," Juliet offered with utmost sincerity. "It was inconsiderate of me and I can only tell you that I was not thinking clearly last week. Please, forgive my thoughtlessness."

"Of course, I forgive you, darling. I just . . ." Her mother swallowed and met Juliet's eye once again. "I would have been here . . . had I known you were not coming home."

"I know you would have come, Mother." Juliet had to stop herself from crying, too. "I'm all right, or rather, I shall be all right." She attempted to sound cheerful. "Being ruined will take some getting used to, I'm afraid."

"Yes, I'm sure that it will." The countess patted her perfect coiffure. "However, I refuse to allow you to lock yourself away with your books."

Juliet grinned. "I like my books."

"I have noticed that over the past twenty-two years, darling," her mother remarked, annoyed. "But if you do not remove yourself from this room on occasion, you shall end up as wide as the door with only me and your cats for company."

Juliet smiled impishly. "I shall always have Felicity."

"Felicity will marry."

Juliet blinked, never having truly considered their separation.

"Felicity has refused nine offers of marriage," she pointed out in a bit of a panic.

Her mother heard the alarm in her voice and smiled kindly. "You have seen your cousin with babes, Juliet. Mark my words, Felicity will settle within the next few years."

Juliet thought of her cousin's deepening sadness and knew that her mother was correct. Felicity would marry and Juliet would be alone, a ruined woman.

"I don't know what to do, Mother."

The countess hugged her and whispered in Juliet's ear, "Felicity will always welcome you in her home. I just want you to understand that it will be different once she marries." Her mother leaned back and wiped Juliet's frustrated tears from her cheek. "In the meantime, you are to get dressed in your most magnificent gown so that we might attend the Duchess of Glenbroke's ball."

"I really do not wish to—"

"You must, darling," her mother insisted. "You did an excellent job at the Spencer ball of putting doubt into the gossips' minds. Oh, how I wish I could have seen you slap your father."

Juliet laughed. "It was quite spectacular."

"I'm sure," the countess agreed, grinning. "But for the moment you must behave as if nothing untoward has occurred with Lord Harrington. The Duke and Duchess of Glenbroke are hosting this ball to influence the opinion of polite society in your favor. If you do not attend, you are as good as admitting your guilt."

"That's ridiculous," Juliet snapped.

"Yes, it is, but unfortunately, it is true. Now . . ." Her mother walked toward the armoire, throwing it open to find something suitable for Juliet to wear. "Dear God, Juliet," she gasped, staring at the drab gowns Juliet had commissioned from Madame Maria's. "A scullery maid has been depositing her clothing in your armoire!"

Juliet sighed, knowing she would have to explain. "Those are *my* gowns, Mother."

"Oh, darling!" Countess Pervill fingered the dowdy fabric, aghast. "These are the most hideous gowns I have ever laid eyes on."

"That is their purpose, Mother." Juliet tightened the sash to her dressing gown and walked toward the countess, who was holding a gray gown as if it were a child's soiled nappy. "Those are my vocation clothes."

"Must you use that word, Juliet?" Countess Pervill dropped the deficient gown on the floor.

"Vocation?"

Her mother groaned. "Yes."

Juliet smiled at her mother's snobbishness.

"You always know how to lift my spirits."

"It is not your spirit which needs reviving, Juliet, it is your reputation. Now"—her mother pointed toward the washroom—"go and bathe and I shall find something suitable for you to wear to the ball."

Resigned, Juliet walked toward the door, knowing that defying her mother would only increase the duration of her own suffering.

"As you wish, Countess Pervill, and might I assume that I can expect the continued pleasure of your company?"

"You can," her mother said simply, unscathed by Juliet's sarcasm. "However, you shall have to wait to enjoy it as your bath water is getting cold."

Juliet rolled her eyes and shut her mother out of the small washroom. The sound of pouring water welcoming her as she walked through the warm steam to the side of the tub.

"Thank you, Anne." Juliet nodded to her lady's maid, who curtsied before leaving the tranquil room.

The instant the door closed, Juliet untied her sash and stepped tentatively into the deep tub. The water was the perfect temperature, and as she sank down, the warmth continued until it had reached her scalp. She moaned with pleasure, thinking there was nothing better than a hot bath on a cold day.

Winter in London was dreadful and it seemed as though she was never truly warm until the sun reluctantly returned in spring. Juliet swept her long, chestnut hair over the rounded edge of the bathtub and leaned back.

Perhaps she should marry an Italian, now that she was ruined. She could live year round in a warm home with the added benefit of a husband with all that lovely caramel-colored skin. But would her Italian lover taste as good as her favorite sweet?

Yes, she was quite certain that he would.

Juliet took a moment to formulate a picture of her very tall, very muscular, and very swarthy Italian husband.

Grinning with the pleasure of her own daydream, Juliet sank beneath the surface to wet her hair in preparation for washing, the heat of the bath water seeping into her very bones.

I could never live in Scotland, it's far too cold.

The caramel of her lover's skin faded and Juliet bolted upright as her mind's eye stared at the likeness of a nude Seamus McCurren. Stunned, Juliet grasped her lavender soap and scrubbed her licentious thoughts away as she mercilessly washed her unruly hair.

Seamus McCurren? Juliet snorted. With his angular features and exceptional body, the man was well out of her reach.

Those eyes, my lord, those golden eyes could tempt a woman to bed without him ever uttering a seductive word. And the words would be seductive when uttered by those lips . . . Juliet stilled and her eyelids drifted closed so that she could feel his lips again.

Her heart began to race as she pictured kissing him back, kissing that beautiful jaw, the subtle cleft, the pulse of his throat as it led down to that beautiful—

"Juliet, are you all right?" A loud thud brought her back to her senses as her mother spoke through the door.

"Yes," she shouted, flustered. "I've just dropped my soap in the tub."

"Well, do hurry, darling. We must dress your hair."

Mortified, Juliet quickly dried herself, emerged into her sitting room, and immediately crinkled her nose.

"What is that horrible smell?"

"Your gowns." Countess Pervill tossed one of Juliet's drab gowns on the fire.

"I need those gowns!" For protection against men, against her love of men.

"Too late, darling, that was the last ghastly gown."

"Mother!"

"As for this evening's attire," Countess Pervill continued, completely ignoring Juliet's protests, "Anne and I have selected a lovely ball gown and we will pile your hair in a chignon to make you appear taller than you are."

"Oh, a chignon will make me appear six foot at least."

"How I wish I had given birth to a simpleton," the countess lamented.

"As do I." Her mother raised a brow, surprised at Juliet's docile agreement. "So that I might not know the extent of the humiliation I am about to endure."

"I did not raise a coward, Juliet," her mother observed. "So, why were you hiding in bed like one?"

Juliet gave an exaggerated *tsk.* "My hiding in bed has nothing to do with being ruined . . ." she began, before realizing her mistake and falling silent.

"Juliet?" *Damn!* Her mother walked over and stared her down. "Why were you in bed?"

Juliet stared back, not about to tell her own mother that a colleague had kissed her, not about to admit the crushing truth that he had done it only to ruffle her feathers and get her out of his precious office. Not about to admit that she had just spent far too many delightful moments picturing that colleague nude.

"I didn't feel well."

"And now?"

"Fine."

"Excellent." Her mother's maneuvering was flawless, giving Juliet no avenue of escape. "Then go have Anne set your hair."

Juliet turned to see her lady's maid dutifully standing at the vanity with a mother of pearl hairbrush at the ready.

"Very well," she said, refusing to be coerced by her resolute mother. "I shall attend the ball because Sarah has generously given it."

"Yes, the duchess has been quite generous." Her mother's eyes sparkled, frightening her. "She even provided you an escort."

"Please"—Juliet's face was contorted by trepidation— "tell me you are joking."

"I would not jest about something so significant as this, darling."

"Who is he?"

"I've no idea." Her mother shook her dark head. "However, when the gentleman arrives, I shall express my gratitude for his willingness to escort a woman of questionable reputation."

It was rather good of the man. "Please, don't, Mother," she begged.

"Very well."

Her mother sighed and Juliet raised a brow, wondering who this chivalrous gentleman might be and wondering more if he might expect some form of gratitude from a "woman of questionable reputation" in return.

Eleven

❦

"*Bloody* cold tonight." Christian St. John stamped his feet as his older brother, Ian, knocked on the Appletons' black lacquered door.

"I told you to wear your heavy coat," the Marquess Shelton said with not one ounce of sympathy.

"I couldn't," Christian explained. "My greatcoat clashed with the color of my jacket."

Ian glanced at Christian's blue jacket and his blond brows furrowed with distaste.

"You're a bit of a dandy, aren't you, little brother?"

Irritated by the condescension in his arrogant brother's voice, Christian fired back, "Not all of us dress to impress Parliament, Ian. Some of us prefer the notice of women."

"And some of us," the marquess said, looking down his nose, "prefer the notice of ladies."

The door opened and Christian was spared from yet another lecture on the unsuitability of his many paramours.

"Good evening, Marquess Shelton," Lady Felicity's butler said, expecting them. "Lord Christian."

Christian nodded, appreciative of the butler's courteous acknowledgment of him while in his illustrious brother's company.

"If you would be so kind as to wait in the drawing room, I shall inform Lady Felicity that you have arrived."

"Thank you," Ian replied, prompting the butler to bow deeply to the future Duke of St. John before withdrawing from the foyer.

"He never bows for me like that." Christian plopped into his favorite chair of the familiar drawing room.

"Well." His brother removed his beaver skin top hat and set it on a round side table. "You are only the spare after all."

Christian adjusted his white gloves, noting the grin that his brother attempted to hide. "You're quite the blackguard, aren't you, big brother."

"Better a blackguard than a wastrel." Ian walked to the fireplace.

Christian laughed, ending their brotherly barbs. "Good of you to do this, Ian."

"Not at all." His brother waved his gratitude away as he warmed himself in front of the fire. "I needed a break from Parliament."

"I would put a bullet through my head if I were forced to bang the political war drums," Christian muttered to himself more than to Ian.

"The work I do is imperative, Christian. Many would vote to withdraw from the Peninsula, giving Napoleon free rein over Europe. What they fail to comprehend is that our isolation will only give Napoleon the time and resources he needs to invade England."

"I know, I know." Christian stretched both arms over the back of the settee, having heard the speech a hundred times before. "I'm in complete agreement, remember?"

Ian chuckled, placing an elegantly positioned elbow on the mantle. "My apologies. Force of habit, I'm afraid."

"Well, do quail the habit when the ladies arrive. I know you are a bit rusty when it comes to women." His brother shot him a glace that conveyed forbearance.

Lady Felicity swept into the room, looking as beautiful as ever.

"Marquess Shelton, it has been far too long," she said, offering Christian a polite nod before turning back to Ian. "I shall just go and retrieve Lady Juliet. However, I did first want to thank you for doing this for my cousin, for me." Felicity put her right hand to her chest.

"It is purely"—Ian bowed, lifting her hand to his lips—"my pleasure, Lady Felicity."

Felicity curtsied and Ian met Christian's eye over the lady's lovely head, raising his left brow.

"We will be but a moment."

Christian bowed as Felicity left the room and then looked at his brother the instant the door closed.

"What was that?"

"What?" his brother asked innocently, but Christian knew him far too well.

"Don't bloody well fob me off. That look . . . with the eyebrows." Christian pointed to his brother's irritatingly handsome face.

The marquess shrugged, shaking his head. "I had forgotten how beautiful Lady Felicity was."

Christian's jaw dropped, stunned. "When is your birthday, Ian?"

"Next month and thank you for remembering."

"I knew it! You'll be thirty next month," he accused his brother.

"You really are quite strange, Christian," Ian said, turning away from him. "Perhaps we should consult with a physician specializing in—"

"Don't change the topic of conversation." He walked

toward Ian, peering into his brother's eyes. Ian was a master at hiding his thoughts but Christian had spent his life digging them up. "When you were twelve, you told me that you planned to marry by thirty and have two heirs by age thirty-five."

"What do you care if I wish to marry?"

"Oh, I pray you marry, Ian." Christian was nodding adamantly. "If only to keep Father off my back. However, you will *not* court my friends so that you might adhere to some self-imposed schedule."

"Thank you for the advice, Christian. I shall consider it as much as I ever do."

"I'm quite serious, Ian."

His brother raised a brow, looking him up and down. "Are you?"

"Yes." Christian held his ground as the door to the sitting room opened.

"Good evening," Juliet offered, forcing Christian to turn away from his obstinate older brother.

"Good evening, Lady Juliet. You look enchanting," Christian said and this time he happened to be telling a woman the truth. "You'll be the talk of the ball."

"That's what I'm afraid of, Christian."

Lady Felicity threw him a look of admonishment as Ian swept forward, the epitome of gentlemanly sophistication as he offered Juliet Pervill his arm.

"Your beauty will most assuredly occupy the minds of the *ton* for weeks to come."

Both ladies smiled at his brother's chivalry and Christian objected, "Isn't that what I just said?"

"No, it was not." Lady Felicity took his arm, which he had thus far failed to offer, and then led them out of her home.

The brothers assisted the cousins into the marquess's exquisite carriage, and as the foursome sat, Christian could see Juliet's anxiety increasing.

"Countess Pervill wished to convey her gratitude for your escort. She would have come herself but I convinced her that we were late." Juliet grinned at Christian, knowing how uncomfortable he was with her mother's probing into his marital ambitions and then she turned to Ian. "I myself wanted to . . . thank you, Marquess Shelton, for . . . offering yourself as escort."

Christian's heart constricted. Juliet Pervill had never been one to ask for help and she absolutely abhorred pity.

"It is I who should be thanking you, Lady Juliet," his brother said. "I do not attend functions frequently enough, and when I do, the mamas of the *ton* descend like a pack of ravenous wolves. However, tonight you will provide my protection from the most dogged of pursuers."

They all chuckled and Christian met Felicity's eye, both of them thankful to Ian for making tonight tolerable for Juliet.

"A winning situation all the way around," Lady Felicity said with a quirked brow.

"Quite." Ian smiled, full of charm, as their carriage rolled to a stop. "And I shall expect to be saved as many dances as you can spare."

"Oh, I believe my dance card will be rather open," Juliet observed dryly.

Felicity turned to her cousin and Christian watched as she discreetly squeezed her hand. "You have many friends attending this evening's event, Juliet."

"I myself wished to reserve a cotillion," Christian asked his dear friend. "As you are the only lady of my acquaintance who enjoys a cotillion without concern for what the *ton* thinks of you while dancing it."

It had sounded better in his head, but fortunately Juliet understood his meaning.

"I would be delighted to dance with you, Christian." Juliet smiled, amused. "As I know I could do no more damage to your reputation than you have done yourself."

His brother burst into laughter at Lady Juliet's brutal and unerringly accurate honesty.

"Quite true," Ian agreed, adding a condemnatory, "Regrettably."

Lady Felicity pulled the loops of her reticule around her delicate wrist, but Christian could see Felicity's embarrassment at the veiled reference to his many indiscretions.

The door to the landau opened and Christian changed the subject, quite relieved to do so. "Ah, we're here."

Seamus arrived at the Duke of Glenbroke's ball late. His valet had taken longer than expected to dress him. He was now bathed and clean shaven, his black jacket setting off the dark green of his waistcoat and enhancing the gold of his eyes.

Not that he gave a damn about his appearance, but if he was going to find a new paramour this evening, he thought it best to display his wares in the most flattering light.

He glanced about the ballroom, the corners of his lips turning upward when he saw the *ton*'s most eligible widow and his night's goal. She was young and beautiful and, if the gentlemen at White's were to be believed, insatiable in bed.

Seamus walked toward the lady but a movement to his left caught his eye. He turned and sighed at the sight of his brother's large arm waving him over toward his small group.

He hesitated, deciding in the end that he would dance with his brother's wife and then spend the remainder of the evening wooing the lovely widow, unmolested.

"My lady." Seamus kissed his sister-in-law's hand with just enough rakishness to annoy his taxing brother.

Daniel took a step back to make the introductions to the other members of their party. Christian St. John stood next to a slightly shorter, slightly more muscled gentleman who resembled Christian so closely that he could only be his older brother Ian, the Marquess Shelton.

The elegant marquess inclined his head then reached back to assist his companion to her feet. "May I introduce to you, Lady Juliet Pervill?"

It was the second time Seamus had seen Juliet Pervill wearing a ball gown, but the first time that he was paying attention.

"How do you do?"

The lady wore a pale blue gown of the finest silk and her face had been lightly powdered to conceal the freckles decorating her nose. Her burnished brown hair was piled atop her head in ringlets secured by a lovely sapphire comb. As Seamus bowed, however, it was her surprisingly full décolletage that drew his discreet scrutiny.

"And may I introduce, Lady Felicity Appleton," Christian was saying and he turned away from Juliet Pervill in favor of her beautiful cousin.

"How do you do, Lady Felicity?" Seamus bowed again, smiling charmingly.

"Very well, thank you, Mister McCurren." The lady smiled back, her pink gown and fawn-like eyes adding to the ethereal aura surrounding her.

"Well," Christian chimed in. "This would be my dance, I believe, Lady Felicity."

"Oh." Felicity Appleton glanced at the card dangling from her wrist as the opening cords of a gavottes were struck. "Is it your dance already?"

"Yes," Christian insisted, hurrying her away.

The group watched the pair leave and then gathered closer so that they might hear one another over the soft murmur of the crush.

"And what have you been up to, Seamus?" his sister-in-law asked. "It has been an age since I've seen you outside of a ballroom."

Seamus smiled at the marquess and touched, only briefly, on Lady Juliet's clear, blue eyes before answering, "I've been quite occupied with my latest acquisitions."

"My brother studies ancient tomes," Daniel explained for the benefit of Ian St. John and, he believed, Juliet Pervill.

"Ah." The marquess nodded, politely interested.

"Well, that makes two scholars then." His brother's wife glanced at Juliet Pervill, and Seamus felt the instant paralysis of dread. He watched his sister-in-law's beautiful lips, willing her to speak no more, but she did. "Lady Juliet is quite the scholar herself."

Uncomfortable, the lass fiddled with her already perfect curls as all eyes settled on her.

"I'd no idea, Lady Juliet," Daniel said, truly surprised as the Marquess Shelton looked at the lady with renewed interest.

"Nor I. What is your area of expertise?" the marquess asked graciously.

Unable to witness the inevitable outcome, Seamus turned his head to watch the dance floor, praying that the lady would have the decency to lie.

"Differential calculus."

Damn!

Seamus groaned to himself when Daniel choked on his champagne.

He avoided his brother's questioning eyes as Daniel coughed then asked with a devilish grin, "Differential calculus, you say?"

"Yes." Juliet nodded, embarrassed. "It is really rather tedious."

"It sounds quite interesting," Ian St. John remarked, but Seamus was too busy tossing back his champagne to notice.

"*Quite* interesting," Daniel echoed, the words directed at Seamus.

Seamus met his brother's gaze, silently telling Daniel to sod off.

"If you will excuse me, I am expected for the next dance." Seamus lied.

"Certainly," his sister-in-law said. "But I shall expect you for the seventh."

"I look forward to it as always." Seamus bowed toward the group as a whole and shot Daniel a warning glare before making his way toward the lovely widow.

She was encircled by dandies, pups, and rogues but Seamus was undeterred.

"Our dance, I believe," he gambled.

The widow smiled at his audacity and gave him her hand. "Yes, I believe it is."

Seamus swept her into his arms as the next dance began, noting how pretty her pale skin looked in contrast to her black hair.

"Are you residing in town permanently, Lady Everett?" he asked seductively, pulling her slightly closer than was advisable.

"Yes, I am, Mister McCurren." The experienced woman fluttered her lashes. "Although my town home is in desperate need of updating and lord only knows how long that will take. My late husband had absolutely horrid taste when it came to décor," she added, making it clear that she was a lonely widow in need of companionship.

"Thank goodness I was able to secure the services of Mister Ferguson." Seamus had the distinct impression that he was supposed to be impressed. "Mister Ferguson has already begun to refurbish the ground-floor parlor, choosing a palette of vermillion and gold. I am quite pleased with the outcome thus far and hope to host a musicale as soon as the ground floor is complete.

"Unfortunately, my bedchamber will not be refurbished until the common areas have been finished." The widow smiled, invitingly grazing his thigh with hers as they held one another in their sensual dance. "However, that should not interfere with the overall function of the room. Do you not agree?"

"I shouldn't think that it would," Seamus said, suddenly not interested in finding out.

The widow laughed suggestively and Seamus danced with her until he was able to return the worldly woman to her adoring hordes.

Juliet turned her head at the strident sound of a lady's laughter as an attractive woman spun the length of the room in Mister McCurren's experienced arms.

She stared and, much to her annoyance, found Seamus as elegant on the ballroom floor as he was eloquent in his academic suppositions.

Yet, as arrogant as he was, Juliet had to admit that the man was beautiful—stunningly, breathtakingly, ruggedly beautiful—and the woman in his arms obviously thought so, too. The lady was absolutely simpering and Juliet was sure that they would end up in bed together. The idea was somehow . . . disheartening.

A widow could do as she pleased, bed any man she wanted, and as long as she was discreet . . . the *ton* looked the other way. Yet polite society was not so blind when it came to virtuous ladies like herself . . .

"So, what have you been doing with these studies of mathematics, Lady Juliet?" Daniel McCurren asked and Juliet all but groaned aloud at her continuing interrogation.

"Nothing as of late," she fibbed, wishing she had her cousin's ability to mask her mood behind a polite smile.

"My God, Daniel!" Lady Dunloch came to her rescue, piercing her husband with her violet eyes. "Do stop badgering Lady Juliet and come dance with me."

The Marquess Sheldon turned to Felicity and offered her his arm, saying, "Shall we," with all the grace of an experienced politician.

Dipping her head as if immensely honored, Felicity conceded, "Yes, thank you."

Sighing at her perpetual solitude, Juliet leaned back in

her chair in the corner of Sarah's massive ballroom, swinging her feet beneath her voluminous skirts. She was not a shy woman, by any means, but neither did Juliet enjoy the idle chitchat so prevalent at society functions.

And what on God's green earth was the matter with Daniel McCurren? At one point, Juliet was sure he was going to ask her to present her mathematical papers at this very ball.

Regardless of the viscount's annoying prodding, Juliet was relieved that the evening seemed to be going so well. Not a single person had given her a second glance, no doubt because Sarah's husband would toss them out on their ear if they did.

Still, it was a relief, and Juliet was grateful to both the Duke and Duchess of Glenbroke, not only for this evening, but for their unwavering support of her. Juliet was contemplating ways in which to show her gratitude when someone entered the circle of chairs.

Thinking Christian had finally wandered back to the fold, Juliet looked up, smiling at her friend. "Nice to see you again, Christi . . . Oh, it's you."

"Your enthusiasm for my companionship is overwhelming." Seamus McCurren glared down at her like a handsome laird.

What was it about a dark man that made him more masculine, more sensual, more utterly . . . appealing?

Flustered by just how appealing the man was, Juliet offered him her right hand, saying tartly, "My enthusiasm is directly proportionate to the quality of my companion."

The Scot brought her hand close to his lips and then dropped it, taking the seat to her immediate left.

"You've quite an acid tongue, Lady Juliet," he said, his golden eyes cold.

"How would you know, Mister McCurren, as you have only tasted my lips?" Juliet ignored the sting of his assessment and focused on her anger.

His full lips compressed into two thin lines. "I came to offer you my apology."

"For your kiss?" Juliet raised both brows as Seamus McCurren glanced about the room, clearly not wishing the *ton* to know that he had kissed the notorious Lady Juliet.

The Scot met her eye, refusing to answer, and she sharpened her aim on the one thing men valued above all else . . . their pride.

"Yes, it was rather a sloppy kiss, now that you mention it." His spine stiffened and she continued to torment him. "Do you apologize to all the women you kiss or just the women not in your employ?"

His eyes flashed and Juliet was pleased to have shocked him. She lifted her left eyebrow and grinned at her bawdy implication, both of them knowing that she had managed to bring him to a heated simmer.

His already impressive chest was made broader as Seamus McCurren took a calming breath before allowing himself to speak.

"I merely hoped to assure you that my . . ." He sought the appropriate word. "Actions of yesterday were not motivated by a desire to see you resign your commission at the Foreign Office."

"Then what was your motivation for your 'actions of yesterday'?" Juliet asked, her heart jumping from a trot to a canter.

Seamus McCurren blinked his beautiful eyes once and then said, "My 'actions of yesterday' were motivated by an admiration . . ." Juliet could not breathe, her heart now at a gallop as embarrassment passed over his perfectly proportioned features. "For your books."

Her heart faltered and she sputtered inelegantly, "My books?" as if the man were not adding up.

Seamus McCurren nodded. "You have read my papers. You know that my research involves the analysis of ancient texts."

Juliet could not believe what the man was implying. "Are you suggesting that you kissed me yesterday out of some peculiar sense of . . . appreciation?"

"I have never seen a book of that . . . age written in Mandarin. I suppose if you had been a man, I would have . . . embraced you. But as you are a woman . . ." He shrugged his flawless shoulders. "I . . ."

"Kissed me." She nodded.

"Quite." The Scot inclined his dark head, saying, "Therefore, I offer you my most sincere apologies and wish to assure you that my enthusiasm for my work shall never again interfere with our assignment."

Dumbfounded, Juliet had no notion what to say to the man. She understood to some extent having passion for one's work, understood the thrill of intellectual discovery. But this . . . "enthusiasm" for old tomes seemed a bit beyond the pale.

But then again, the man was a Scot and they tended to be people of passionate sensibilities.

"Would it be easier for you if I removed my books from the offi—"

"No." The unflappable Seamus McCurren actually blushed. "I am confident that my enthusiasm will *never*," he said with such emphasis that she felt a twinge affronted, "be repeated."

Juliet paused, knowing she had but two options. One, she could resign from the Foreign Office, or two, accept Seamus McCurren's somewhat offensive apology.

"Very well." Juliet chose the latter, shaking her head as she shrugged. "I accept your . . . apology." She looked at the man, and upon seeing his considerable relief, her mouth opened of its own accord. "It is not as though anything remarkable—"

"Excellent." Seamus McCurren turned, interrupting her discourteous assessment of his amorous abilities. "I shall see you Monday morning?"

She only wished that the insulting appraisal were true.

Twelve

❦

Seamus sat in his carriage wondering why in the hell he had touched the obstinate woman. It was humiliating enough that he had behaved like an ass, only to have to kiss her hand for the pleasure of that humiliation.

He sniffed his white glove for the twentieth time, knowing that the glove was ruined. It smelled so strongly of lavender that Seamus was sure the girl had a bar of soap tucked beneath her stylish chignon.

His carriage rolled to a stop in front of his home and Seamus jumped down. He scarcely looked at his butler as he walked into the entryway.

"Put these in the rubbish bin, they smell of lavender." Courtesy of an irritating little woman with a freckled face and larger breasts than he'd given her credit for.

Before he had the opportunity to hand his butler the tainted calf-skin gloves, the man announced, "You have a guest, Mister McCurren. I have taken the liberty of placing him in your study."

"Who is it?" Seamus asked, stuffing the gloves in his jacket pocket.

"His lordship Viscount Dunloch."

Seamus opened the door to his study, rolling his eyes. "What the hell do you want?"

Daniel rose from a chair in front of the fire, grinning like the blackguard that he was. "Can't a man visit his beloved brother merely to—"

"Not this man." Seamus sat behind his desk. "Now, cut line, Daniel. I've not got all night."

"Need to brush up on differential calculus, do you?" His brother laughed outright and Seamus could have murdered the handsome bastard.

"If you wish to leave my home with our relationship intact, I suggest you stop right there."

Ignoring him, Daniel resumed his seat then lifted his black Hessians to rest on the ottoman.

"I just wanted to discuss your problem now that I know the identity of the lady you're attracted to."

"I'm *not* attracted to Juliet Pervill!"

"Very well," Daniel conceded. "The woman you desire, but are not attracted to."

Seamus thought about it and decided that after two such incidents he would just have to live with that humiliating assessment. "Discuss away."

"First of all, what in hell gave you the idea that Juliet Pervill was homely?" Daniel's brows were furrowed with confusion.

"I don't know," Seamus admitted after seeing her tonight. "The first time I saw the lass was the evening she confronted her father. Initially, my attention was on Lady Felicity." Daniel nodded, fully understanding that any man's attention would be on Felicity Appleton. "And then my mind was on the scene, not the lady. If you take my meaning?"

"Aye, but Seamus, you've been working alongside the lass for the past . . . what? Three days?"

Seamus ran his fingers through his disheveled hair. "She's been wearing these gowns . . ."

"What the hell are you talking about? I hope to God the lass has been wearing gowns. What else would she wear to Whitehall? Breeches?"

"Christ Almighty, would you just leave my house."

"Not until we discuss the matter fully. Right." His brother blew out a thoughtful breath. "You say you were not attracted to her, but you desired her. Was she kind to you?"

Seamus scoffed. "Uh, no." Being long acquainted with the lady in question, Daniel snickered. "Although to be fair, I was not the most chivalrous of gentlemen when she first arrived at my office."

"You said Lady Juliet was speaking of differential calculus when you kissed her?" Daniel eyes narrowed to turquoise slits.

"Aye, I was bored to tears. Mathematics is not my area of interest."

His brother's back suddenly stiffened and his eyes grew wide as he nodded, smiling. "I know what ails you, Seamus."

Daniel rose and Seamus lifted himself from the edge of his seat. "Do tell, brother of mine," he said sarcastically, desperate to know what his brother understood that he did not.

"No." Daniel shook his auburn head. "I don't think I shall."

"What?" Seamus gave up all pretense of disinterest.

"You're a clever man, Seamus, but at times you're a bloody idiot. This, dear brother, is one of those rare times."

"You pronounce me a fool and then just leave me to behave like one?" Seamus was furious and more than a little frustrated.

"Aye." Daniel nodded, explaining, "Your admiration for Lady Juliet is something best determined by you."

Seamus shook his head, uncomfortable. "All I need is a new paramour."

Daniel laughed, clasping him on the shoulder. "Good night, little brother."

Seamus let the blackguard leave, sure that his desire for Juliet Pervill was simply a result of her close proximity.

Seamus kicked off his boots and removed the lavender-scented gloves from his pocket, smelling them one last time.

"Damn!" he cursed, catching himself.

Thirteen

Enigma slid off the black stallion, having finished her survey of the newly acquired estate.

The vast lands had gone on for miles and with proper crop management could be converted into a very profitable acquisition. Yet its arrogant and indolent owner had left the ten-thousand-acre estate virtually uncultivated and its tenants resentful of their indifferent landlord.

The lord of the manor had foolishly chosen to spend his money and his time on improving his gardens and manor house, neither of which brought in any income.

God, but these men were stupid.

"Perhaps now you should give me the tour of the manor house, Lord Harrington?" Enigma said, smiling with satisfaction for filching everything from the fool in a single night of gaming.

"Yes, of course." The obsequious man swept his arm toward the enormous front door, which had been carved with gruesome and garish scenes from Greek mythology.

Enigma walked through the hideous door and looked up at the impressive foyer, which led the eye up a grand staircase to the chandelier hanging from the second-floor ceiling.

"Shall we begin the tour in the parlor, Madame Richard?"

Enigma nodded and they were shown into the large parlor before making their way around the ground-floor rooms in a clockwise rotation.

"When was the estate built?" she asked.

"The estate was built in 1751 by my great-grandfather, Lord Henry Harrington. That is him just there." Harrington pointed to a stupid-looking man as they climbed the staircase and Enigma glared at Mister Collin, who had thought to laugh at the gentleman in the portrait.

"How is the hunting on the estate?" Enigma asked, estimating the value of the paintings hanging from the brocade-covered walls as they walked up to the first floor of her new country house.

"Harrington Hall has the best hunting for ten counties," Lord Harrington boasted as if he still owned the estate.

"Mister Matthews," Enigma called to the other man following them and put Harrington in his place. "I would like you to inventory the furniture, paintings, jewels . . . so on and so forth throughout the entire house," then turning back to the previous owner, inquired prettily, "You've not removed anything from the estate, Lord Harrington?"

"No." Lord Harrington shook his head, blatantly wishing he had thought to do so before her unexpected visit. "Of course not."

"Good." Enigma nodded and Matthews left to begin the extensive process. "Now, shall we discuss the ways in which you might retain your estate?"

Harrington's puffy eyes went wide at the mere possibility. "Yes, anything." The greedy man stopped at the head of the stairs and she could see that he thought to outwit a mere woman. "Anything you ask."

Enigma smiled, enjoying bringing the *ton*'s arrogant fops to their knees.

"I want you to begin by hosting several events at the estate." Harrington's brows furrowed in confusion, a reminder of how stupid the man was. "You will invite the gentlemen I tell you to invite and then you will ply them with drink and women," Enigma said, spelling it out.

"Yes, certainly, Madame Richard, but might I ask why, when you would make more blunt if these men were entertained at Dante's?" he asked with the tone of a man teaching a woman about trade.

"Information is a powerful thing, Lord Harrington," she said, the chill in her voice unmistakable. The pudgy man paled. The implication of blackmail was finally sinking in. "And you will acquire as much information from these gentlemen as possible while they reside under my roof." Enigma swept an elegant hand over the deserted hallway as they stood at the head of the stairs.

Lord Harrington visibly winced at the reminder of his status as pauper.

"As you wish." The gentleman lowered his head, defeated.

"The first thing you will do is dismiss your butler."

"What? Foster has been with my family for over thirty years," Harrington protested.

"Very well." Enigma nodded sympathetically. "If you do not wish to see your butler let go, then perhaps you should call him over so that we might explain the transfer of ownership."

"Yes," Harrington said, relieved. "That would be much better." His condescension grated. "Foster," he shouted down the hall and his butler walked to where they stood.

The elegant servant bowed and Enigma smiled, asking, "How long have you been in Lord Harrington's employ?"

"Thirty-four years," Mister Foster said with pride.

Enigma met Mister Collin's eye over the butler's head, saying, "A lifetime of service, how quaint," then watched as the bodyguard twisted Mister Foster's head round with a distasteful crack before pushing him down the winding staircase.

Lord Harrington gave a throaty yelp and several footmen came running from different directions.

"Call for a physician, the poor man has fallen," Enigma ordered as Mister Collin glanced at Lord Harrington with dark eyes void of remorse.

Mister Matthews appeared at the foot of the stairs and stared at the butler's body. After a moment, he pushed his spectacles up his upturned nose then lifted his head to meet Enigma's watchful eye.

"How tragic," Matthews said to her, visibly swallowing his fear.

"Yes, it was," Enigma agreed. Lord Harrington looked first to Mister Collin and then at his dead butler, whose head lay awkwardly against the third step of the staircase. "However, I have always found it better to get on with things, back to business so to speak."

"Y-y-y-yes." Harrington nodded, clearly terrified. "Best t-t-to get on."

"Now, shall we retire to your study until the physician arrives." It was not a question as Enigma led them down the winding stairs, lifting her skirts, and stepped over the dead butler with the assistance of Mister Collin's powerful hand.

Fourteen

$Monday$ morning was clear but cold and Juliet tensed the moment she set foot outside Felicity's front door. However, the bite of the winter wind was nothing in comparison to the constriction in her chest when she saw Lord Robert Barksdale standing beside her carriage.

She stared through the dim light then lowered her chin and focused on the icy stairs in front of her. Juliet lifted her skirts several inches to avoid tripping, ignoring the persistent Lord Barksdale completely.

"Juliet," he begged. Her footman bowed and opened the carriage door, but Robert stepped between them. "Please, Juliet." Lord Barksdale stared down at her. "Five minutes, I swear it. Please."

Five minutes.

What could Robert possibly wish to say in five minutes that would justify his waiting for her in the cold this early in the morning?

"Very well." Juliet met his eye for the first time and unable to help herself said, "Wouldn't want to make a scene that Papa may catch wind of."

Juliet spun on her heels and avoided treacherous patches of ice as she made for Robert's elegant landau. She accepted the assistance of Barksdale's footman then stepped into the familiar conveyance.

"You sit there." Juliet pointed to the opposite corner of the luxurious coach as she herself settled on the burgundy velvet squabs.

"Hyde Park," Barksdale called to his coachman before reaching up and drawing the matching velvet curtains lest they be seen together. "It's a bit cold."

Hurt, Juliet met his eye. "Do get on with it, Robert."

Juliet stared at him, annoyed that he looked so well, so beautifully turned out.

"I wanted to apologize to you, my darling Juliet, for the manner in which last we parted. I was . . ." Robert met her eye and then looked down, penitent. "Distraught by a difficult situation and spoke precipitously of a possible solution to the problem in which we now find ourselves."

"Damn right you spoke 'precipitously.'" Juliet's anger grabbed her tongue and refused to relinquish its hold. "Not to mention offensively."

"I know, darling." Robert shook his head and sat next to her, tentatively testing the waters.

She allowed him to remain and Juliet could see that Robert wanted to kiss her. The damnable thing was that Juliet was not sure that she did not want him to.

"I came to ask"—Robert got down on one knee and took her right hand—"no, beg you, my darling Juliet, to be my wife."

"What?" Juliet jerked her hand away, stunned by his newfound sense of propriety.

Robert smiled and then resumed his seat next to her. "Marry me, Juliet?" he asked, looking down at her.

Now, it did occur to Juliet that she should be overjoyed,

elated, but as she stared into Robert's midnight blue eyes, she could not help remembering the manner in which he had drawn the conveyance curtains.

He took her lengthy silence as consent and then bent his head to kiss her. Juliet was trapped against the squabs when he swept into her mouth, eagerly circling her tongue with his own.

"Oh, Juliet." His hand caressed her right shoulder. "I cannot wait to make you my wife."

"Robert, darling?" Juliet's eyes narrowed and she allowed his hands to wander, curious to see where they would roam.

"Yes?" He was kissing her neck, his hand descending to the bottom of her skirts.

"When shall we announce our engagement?" She stared at the curtains.

"No need to rush, don't you think? Best if we wait a month or so." His right hand was traveling up her bare calf. "Let the scandal die down."

Juliet let his hands get as far as her knee before she stopped him.

"You are most likely correct." She handed him a rope with which to hang himself. "However, I do think we should stop being alone with one another until our wedding night."

"I love you, Juliet," Robert whispered in her ear, his hand gliding above her knee as if she would not notice. "What is the difference if I make you mine now or on our wedding night? We are engaged after all."

His large hand grasped her backside, pulling her hard against his erection, and Juliet was so hurt that tears welled in her eyes. Robert Barksdale had no intention of marrying her. She had known him long enough to see the truth behind his heated gaze.

With promises of marriage, Robert would take her virginity and make her his mistress.

But why? Why if he loved her, and she believed that he did, why would he not try to change his father's mind?

Robert pushed his hips against hers insistently and grunted with pleasure and possession. Possession, that was his motivation.

After all, Robert knew firsthand her weakness with men. Juliet had allowed him to kiss her, and wanton woman that she was, she had even kissed him back.

But she had been in love with him.

Hadn't she?

"Stop it, Robert," she said, knowing him well enough to be sure that he would. "Take me home."

Juliet opened her mouth to tell him that he could make love to her on their wedding night, that she would give herself to him body and soul once they were legally wed. But as she stared into his lust-filled eyes, feeling not an ounce of desire as his body pressed against hers, Juliet knew they were finished.

In the weeks since her ruination, Juliet had come to realize that Robert Barksdale was a weak man and not what she wanted in a husband.

She needed a man whose will was as strong as her own. Juliet needed a man able to match her mind and, on occasion, win an argument or two.

She needed a man like Seamus McCurren.

Seamus climbed the front entrance of Lady Felicity Appleton's town home, his brown Hessians pounding the marble steps in a brisk, controlled rhythm that betrayed his exhilaration.

He lifted the heavy brass knocker and banged three times, then was forced to wait an eternity.

"Come on, come on," he caught himself muttering beneath his breath.

In the end, the black door opened and Seamus offered the

requisite card and polite smile to the poised butler. "Mister Seamus McCurren to see Lady Juliet Pervill."

The older man bowed, standing aside to allow Seamus to enter the vast entryway decorated with alternating squares of brown and white marble. "If you would be so kind as to wait—"

"Mister McCurren," a wholly feminine voice called from a doorway to the right. "How kind of you to call."

"Lady Felicity," Seamus said, bowing toward the stunning creature, who broke into a radiant smile. "I've come to consult with Lady Juliet. We were expecting her at the Foreign Office this morning." Hearing a touch of irritation in his own voice, Seamus added, "She is well, I trust." Felicity Appleton continued to stare, making him decidedly uncomfortable.

Lady Felicity's warm eyes glowed and she smiled more fully. "Oh, yes, Juliet is quite well. So well, in fact, that she chose this morning to ride in the park with Lord Barksdale rather than deal with the confinements of the Foreign Office."

Barksdale?

"How nice," Seamus observed with considerable annoyance.

He had spent the morning identifying the last marker of the E code while Juliet Pervill gallivanted about Hyde Park with the gentleman who had abandoned her the moment that scandal erupted.

The spineless prick.

By all rights, Seamus should return to the Foreign Office and inform Falcon of his progress. Yet for some indiscernible reason, he wanted to share his find with Juliet first. He felt as though she was one of the only people who would understand his intellectual excitement at the discovery.

"She is out then?"

"Oh, no. I believe she has returned and is having tea in her sitting room." The lady turned to her servant and spoke as though the man were doing her a kindness rather than his duty. "Alfred, would you be so good as to escort Mister McCurren to Lady Juliet's sitting room."

"Will you not join us, Lady Felicity?" Seamus asked, surprised that he would not be accompanied by a chaperon.

"Nonsense, Mister McCurren." The lady smiled brightly. "Why, you are practically family."

Seamus nodded in gratitude for the lady's faith and understanding of their need for privacy then followed the butler into the depths of the town home.

The butler led him up a wide, jade-colored staircase and Seamus glanced at the portraits of Lady Felicity's ancestors, noting that with each passing generation the lady's family had enhanced not only its holding, but also its physical beauty.

When they had reached the first-floor landing, Seamus glanced down the corridor, which was decorated with welcoming plants set atop Ionic pillars. The elegant décor screamed of Lady Felicity, once again reminding Seamus that Juliet Pervill was but a guest in her cousin's home.

His escort knocked on the second door to the right and a familiar female voice bellowed, "Come in," as if irritated at being disturbed.

The older servant lifted his hand to the doorknob and Seamus felt his curiosity rising as the man turned it. He smiled to himself as the butler entered a room as dramatic as the woman who lived here. The vibrant colors were tempered by lush textures.

He did not at first see Juliet Pervill, but as his escort turned to his left, so, too, did Seamus. The diminutive lady lay outstretched on a gold damask chaise with her face obscured by a leather-bound book. Her long, chestnut hair spilled over her pillow and she twisted a shimmering strand around her delicate forefinger as she continued to read.

His chest tightened instantly as Seamus recalled the women he had thusly positioned in far less intellectual pursuits, lovers whose hair had hung over him, caressing his chest as they made love.

The butler cleared his throat to make their presence known, announcing, "Mister Seamus McCurren to see you, my lady."

The lady's twirling finger stilled and her book dropped below her chin. She looked toward the door with her delicately arched brows pulling down over her bright blue eyes.

"What on earth are you doing here?" Lady Juliet Pervill asked ungraciously and the butler stood his ground as if Seamus had come to the woman's sitting room to accost her.

Overlooking her rudeness, Seamus did not hesitate to explain, "As you failed to grace the Foreign Office with your presence this morning, I have come to consult about the matter which has been of interest to us both."

The girl sat up and he cringed as she tossed the fragile book next to the others that already littered the sitting room floor. "You've found something pertaining to the code?"

"Yes," Seamus said with considerable satisfaction. "I have . . . found 'something' as you so eloquently put it."

"Thank you, Alfred, you may go."

"Very good, my lady." The butler was clearly uncomfortable leaving them alone. "Would you like some tea brought—"

Lady Juliet shook her head, her long hair brushing her breasts. "I've had tea, remember? You brought it not half an hour ago."

The butler's eyes slid to Seamus in obvious embarrassment and then the man recovered, saying, "As you wish, my lady," before withdrawing from the sitting room altogether.

The instant the door closed, Juliet Pervill looked Seamus directly in the eye.

"Well?" she asked with a shrug of her pretty little shoulders. "What have you found?"

"The last marker," he said triumphantly as he walked toward the lass, reaching into the inner pocket of his russet jacket. He withdrew the clipping from the *London Herald* and handed it to Lady Juliet as he sat at the far end of the chaise longue.

"Of course you found the last marker," she snorted as though he were an idiot, and handed the article back to him, unread. "It's the third week of the code."

Seamus felt a flash of irritation punctuated by a sense of disappointment. It was inevitable that they find the last marker, but his subsequent observations of those markers would be significant only to those who understood the intricacies of mathematical sequencing.

"You found the marker in the *London Herald*," she said, confirming rather than asking.

Seamus stared at the lass's features, her perfectly sculpted nose and smattering of freckles. "Then you've read the article?"

"I can't say that I have."

Busy with Lord Barksdale, no doubt.

"Then how did you know I found the marker in the *Herald*?"

The lass rose and walked across the room, picking up a leather-bound book from atop a rather cluttered desk. She smiled, pleased with herself, then sat on the settee and invited him to sit beside her with a pat of her right hand as if he were a dog.

Begrudgingly, Seamus sat, his curiosity overtaking his pride. He looked down as she opened the book resting on her lap, revealing that it was not a book at all but rather a journal.

However, unlike any other journal he had seen before, this one consisted entirely of numbers—hastily written figures and symbols, most of which were quite foreign to him.

"Those are mathematic formularies?"

"You're as clever as everyone says that you are, Mister McCurren. Yes." She smiled like a proud parent. "I analyzed the information gathered from the code thus far, frequency of occurrence of the code in each publication, circulation of the newspaper, distribution areas, so on and so forth . . ."

Seamus followed her tiny little finger down the unusual journal to the dramatically circled figure at the bottom of a page.

"Determining with a seventy-nine percent probability that the *London Herald* would be the next publication in which the marker would appear."

As she sighed with satisfaction, Seamus just stared at her, his heart racing . . . with anger? "Why did you not bring your finding to the Foreign Office first thing this morning?" *Instead of gallivanting through the park with your lover.*

"Do you really want to know?" she asked, holding his eyes.

"Yes." He did.

"I did not go to the Foreign Office this morning because I went for a drive in Hyde Park with the man I thought to marry." *Thought to marry?* He waited for her to explain. "Yes, you see Lord Barksdale made me quite an offer this morning."

Seamus was stunned. "Uh," he blinked, "congratulations, Lady Juliet."

She snapped the leather journal closed, her silky hair swishing from side to side as she walked back to her desk.

"None required, I'm afraid," she said with the casual air of someone declining to have sugar in her afternoon tea. "Robert merely asked me to be his mistress. Again."

Seamus's head jerked back in disbelief and then his jaw clenched. "Lord Barksdale asked you to dishonor yourself before today?"

"Yes." She spun round, looking into the air as if she were contemplating the question. "But to be fair, Robert was kind enough to offer to marry me at some distant point and only *after* I become his mistress."

"Well, we must be fair to Lord Barksdale." Seamus

couldn't contain his sarcasm as he felt the heat of anger burning in his chest.

"You did ask why I was not at the Foreign Office."

"Yes, but I thought you would inform me that you had a lame horse, not that Barksdale had ... asked you ..." Juliet looked so lovely standing by the desk that Seamus had the overwhelming urge to go to her, to press his lips to her throat. Taken aback by the depth of his inclination, Seamus tensed markedly. "To become his mistress."

He quelled his own lustful thoughts and watched the petite woman set the journal on her desk.

As Juliet Pervill returned to the sitting area, he watched her walk toward him with the anticipation of a spider watching a fly. He knew then that he should go—quickly.

"Well, if you are already aware of the article," he said, beginning to rise. "Then I shall see you—"

The lady placed her hand on his shoulder and he sank back onto the chaise, shocked by the jolt of her touch.

"You can't leave." Juliet Pervill was looking down at him, which wasn't very far, considering her stature. "I haven't read the article and as you're here ..." she said, her delicate brows pulled over her striking blue eyes.

"We can discuss the matter tomorrow at the Foreign Office."

"Oh, I see." She resumed her seat next to him, nodding. "I made you uncomfortable when I spoke of mistresses?"

"Yes." Seamus echoed her nod, jumping on any excuse to avoid thoughts of making her his.

He leaned forward to rise, and being a clever woman, Lady Juliet anticipated his attempt to leave. She placed a hand on his right thigh and his lungs collapsed in on themselves.

"Forgive me, Mister McCurren," she asked, her hand lingering longer than it should have, but less than he wanted it to. "I speak too freely. I just thought as you are an . . . experienced gentleman and, well, you did ask." She sounded irritated.

"I shouldn't have." What the hell was wrong with him? He had never been a man to lose control with women. But as Juliet Pervill continued to touch him, Seamus knew that he was so very, very close. He met her eye, willing her to understand his attempt at chivalry. "I really . . . need to leave you, lass."

"Why? You've just gotten here."

Could she be so naive? Yes, an innocent girl would be blind to a man's need.

"Because if I don't go, I'm going to kiss you," he said, intentionally blunt.

She jerked her hand from his thigh as if he were made of fire. "Why?"

Her curiosity was killing him.

"Why would I kiss you?" He laughed.

"Yes." She nodded as if he were one of her equations.

"Because men enjoy kissing women," he said, knowing that an innocent lady would not understand a man's desire for a particular woman.

Hell, he did not understand his desire for this particular woman.

"Perhaps I want you to kiss me," she whispered, her honest eyes revealing a tentative spark of lust that sent his heart racing.

"Why?" Seamus needed to know and he knew also that this woman would tell him.

Juliet shrugged shyly and her long, dark hair shifted over her lovely bosom.

"I like your company." Her simple confession caught him off guard. "And I like the complexity of your eyes."

She reached up and caressed his cheek with her hand then moved down to catalog his other attributes, and bastard that he was, Seamus just sat there and let her.

"I like the way your sideburns emphasize your jaw." Her fingers traced that line and his heart began to pound.

His mind screamed warnings of the dangerous waters she was wading into, but his body took hold of his tongue, silencing him.

The lady leaned closer, the tip of her forefinger brushing his bottom lip as she whispered, "I like the way you kiss me." She stared at his lips, adding, "And I liked the approach you took in determining commonalities of sequencing in ancient languages."

Seamus's breath became shallow but he managed to whisper back, "And I quite enjoyed your article on volume displacement. Your conclusions will prove very useful to British shipbuilders."

She gasped, clearly shocked by his knowledge of her work. "Yes, I thought so, too."

They stared at one another and the glistening of firelight against her moist lips was more than Seamus could take. He bent his head, closing the last few inches separating them, and kissed her soundly, unable to stop himself.

His hands slid around her tiny waist and her arms curled around his neck, both pulling the other closer, deeper into the sensual embrace.

The lady's lips parted and she sought his warmth as eagerly as he sought hers. Their tongues intertwined and she gave a soft mewling of approval that sent a wave of lust straight to his shaft.

She tasted of inquisitive inexperience and an intellectual potency that all but brought him to his knees. Seamus kissed her more deeply, with more sexual purpose, but she pulled her head back and stared at him.

Her eyes were filled with desire. She glanced at his face, his neck, and finally at the exposed flesh of his chest, confessing, "I like the way you feel."

Bloody hell!

The lass bent her head to kiss his throat and Seamus gritted his teeth as her soft breasts brushed his chest. He took his hands off her hips and clutched the edge of the chaise until his knuckles turned white.

"Juliet," he protested weakly as she untied his cravat, pressing her eager lips on his newly exposed flesh. He should stop her, stop this from going . . . *Oh, God.* His fingers speared her lush strands as she kissed him just below the ear.

"I even like the way you smell of leather and . . ." Her nose nuzzled his neck to confirm his scent. "Masculinity," she breathed in his ear.

"Stop, Juliet."

But she wasn't listening. She was too focused on tasting his throat as her hands explored the rest of him.

"Juliet." He held out for as long as he could, but when she began unbuttoning his shirt, he lost the battle.

Seamus lifted her onto his lap, moaning at the feel of her backside against his length. He bent his head, needing his turn, needing a taste of her, finally kissing the feminine line of her throat.

His right hand was caressing her breast before Seamus knew what he was doing and they both moaned in appreciation. He lifted his head, eager to press his lips to the succulent mounds when a flash of light drew his attention to the near empty glass of scotch sitting atop her side table.

The lass was foxed!

The boldness of her kiss, her blatant desire, he should have guessed. But he was too damn caught up in his own need to notice her liquid courage.

Bloody hell!

Seamus slid her off his lap as he rose, distinctly dissatisfied. "I have to go," he said to himself.

He had no notion why he desired Juliet Pervill. Something about her drove him mad.

She was shorter than was his taste, and her face was

flawed by freckles that emphasized her innocence when he preferred the sophistication of experienced women.

"No, you don't." She looked up at him.

But those eyes.

His stomach flipped with a ripple of wanting as those clear, blue eyes continued to peruse him.

Lady Juliet Pervill might be an innocent woman, but the lass sure as hell admired the male form. Seamus could see it in her gaze, had felt it in her fingertips, and he wondered what such a clever woman would do if those hands were given free reign.

Seamus blinked, his breathing erratic.

"Trust me, lass." He nodded adamantly. "I do."

He thrust both his hands through his hair then turned his back on her to ease his lingering sensual thoughts.

And his thoughts were wicked, but Seamus was a clever enough man to know that the real question was . . . why? Why out of all the beautiful women the *ton* had to offer did Juliet Pervill drive him to distraction?

He had no damn idea but one thing was for sure. Now that he had touched her, seen her desire for him, he would not soon be able to forget it.

Fifteen

≈≈≈≈

Enigma stared at Seamus McCurren over the large gaming table, decidedly disappointed.

"Having a bit of bad luck this evening, Mister McCurren?" her front man asked.

Mister McCurren's play thus far this evening had been dismal and was providing her absolutely no challenge at all. Indeed, if the gentleman continued on this way, he would lose everything he had won upon their last meeting.

"It would seem so, Mister Youngblood," McCurren replied apathetically, his eyes dull, distracted.

Something was clearly occupying the man's mind. But what?

She stared at the delicious Seamus McCurren and then placed her hand on Youngblood's inner thigh. Youngblood was an exceptional card player, which along with his good looks, was the reason she had hired him. But even with his exceptional skill, Youngblood was nowhere near capable enough to deal with Seamus McCurren on his own.

With the possible exception of this evening.

"Are you unwell, Mister McCurren?" she asked, searching for any explanation for his appalling play.

"No." He grinned halfheartedly, understanding her fully. "Although I wish I were so that I might offer you some form of explanation."

"No explanation necessary." Youngblood dealt, drawing McCurren's attention away from her. "Dante's welcomes your money."

After making mince meat of the Scot yet again, Enigma left Youngblood to run the table. She crooked her finger for Mister Collin to walk upstairs with her while calculating McCurren's considerable losses.

"Where are we in our dealings with Lord Harrington?" she asked Mister Collin when they arrived in her office.

"We've set up our man as butler," he began, closing the door, "And arranged for two of our whores to work as chambermaids at the Harrington estate."

"Are they trained domestics?"

He nodded.

"Clever girls, are they?" Enigma asked, sitting behind her desk.

"Yes, Mira has already sent along information and I've just left her reports on your desk."

"Anything of import?" she inquired, reaching for the missives.

"Not particularly, but the girl did manage to bed a member of the House of Lords, asking him what 'they was goin' to do about that bloody Napoleon' and the fool revealed several possibilities being discussed."

"Excellent, double the girl's fee." Enigma sighed, changing the subject to more interesting matters. "Now, what have you learned about Seamus McCurren?"

"Nothing more than I've already told you." The body-guard bristled. "He is a scholar and the second son of the Earl of DunDonell, wealthy in his own right after investing the funds his father gave him."

Enigma nodded, having known similar men, mesmerizing gentlemen who had taken advantage of her intellectual thirst by taking her to bed.

She had been a poor girl craving an education and they had certainly given it to her. But she had gotten their money in the end. When her naïveté and innocence were finally vanquished, she had been the clever one.

Smiling at the memory of her past triumphs, she turned to Collin. "I want Seamus McCurren followed."

"Why?"

Because Seamus McCurren was different from those gentlemen—he was clever, noble, and stunningly handsome. Her old weakness for brilliance troubled her and Enigma reprimanded herself.

"If you question me again . . ." She shot Collin a glance that bore through him as if it were a ball of lead. "It will be the last question you ask."

"My apologies," he offered wisely.

Still, she sighed, there was something about Seamus McCurren that demanded investigation.

"I want to know everything about Mister McCurren; where he goes, who he speaks with, everything. Am I making myself perfectly clear?"

"Very."

"Tell me about his women."

The bodyguard's eyes flared. "He kept a paramour for almost a year but he recently threw her over."

"For whom?"

"I've not heard rumors of a new mistress, but he is reported to take to quality"—the man paused—"ladies of the *ton*. Particularly blondes."

"Blondes?"

"It was bandied about town some years back that Mc-Curren frequently entertained the widow Lady Catherine in the same bed with her twin sister, Lady Rebecca."

"Really?" Enigma smiled with admiration for Seamus McCurren's prowess.

"But then again, he was eighteen at the time and now is six-and-twenty."

"You don't think the gentleman still up for the job?"

"Not now." Mister Collin shook his head and stared at her. "McCurren's not the sort to keep two lovers."

Enigma walked toward Collin, pressing her breasts against his chest.

"You mean like me?" she whispered seductively.

Her bodyguard's breathing was becoming shallow. The more he lost control, the more she wanted him to.

"Yes," Mister Collin ground out. "Like you."

"Now, Jack." Enigma fluttered her lashes, caressing his cock with her right hand. "You must admit that Mister Youngblood is damn beautiful."

Mister Collin remained silent, knowing that she was intentionally taunting him.

"Do you really . . ." She pushed his jacket off those deliciously broad shoulders. "Want me to choose between the two of you?" she asked, discouraging his stupidity. "Or would you rather take me to my desk and plow me?"

Her bodyguard made a primal grunt and began stripping her of her clothes by way of an answer. And when she was nude before him, Jack laid her atop the desk and stared at her body while he himself undressed.

Enigma teased him while she waited, drawing his attention to places she wanted touched, caressed.

Mister Collin's body was itself beautiful, larger and far more muscular than Youngblood's. His arms bulged into rounded mounds of muscle as he worked diligently to remove his stubborn trousers. He stepped forward, his chest broad and so captivating that her eyes descended to view more of him. She stared at his erection and smiled up at him, provocatively spreading her thighs. His dark eyes flared and he grasped her around the waist, yanking her to the edge of the sturdy desk.

"Please let me ride you," he asked, knowing the rules.

"Youngblood is far more skilled a lover," she said, inciting his anger. But this time he grinned, confident of her desire, then leaned over so that her tight nipples brushed his hard chest.

He stared down into her eyes, his thick arms on either side of her head when he whispered, "We both know you don't want Youngblood's skill, you want my power."

"Yes," Enigma admitted and he impaled her.

She cried out at the sheer force of the man over her, in her. It was so rare that she was able to be dominated, and as his intoxicating power moved against her, Enigma allowed herself to be overcome. With each masculine thrust, Mister Collin was becoming more aroused, more demanding.

He grabbed her backside and drove deeper, groaning, "Can you feel how deep I am inside you?"

"Yes."

He smiled, his lean stomach contracting as he thrust into her. "Am I a better lover than Youngblood?"

She did not reply and he squeezed her nipples, causing her to shiver. "Am I better?"

She nodded once, so close to finding her pleasure that she could hardly speak.

"Say it," Jack whispered, holding her eyes. "Say I make you tremble harder and longer than Youngblood ever has."

"Yes." She met his arrogant gaze and her bodyguard smiled, devoting himself to performing his duty. "Yes," Enigma said, encouraging him as his hips drove faster, deeper, and then she arched her back, spreading her thighs so that she could feel more of him, more of his power.

The instant he saw that she had reached her peak, Jack

grabbed her waist and gave one last thrust, spilling himself with a feral groan of sublime satisfaction.

Enigma came to her senses slowly, leisurely. She opened her eyes and licked her dry lips as he watched, still inside her. She gave him one last caress before pushing him away, and it was his turn to tremble before her.

She rose to her knees on the desk, slightly taller as she faced him and then looked into his possessive eyes.

Enigma made sure that her breasts brushed his rough jaw as she whispered in his ear, "You might have a bigger cock, but Youngblood is much prettier to look at." Mister Collin's eyes hardened in anger as she had intended. "And if you're very good"—she stroked his chin with the back of her fingers—"I shall let you watch the next time I ride him. Would you like that, Mister Collin?"

"No." Jack jerked his face away from her provocative touch.

"Oh, I think that you would." Enigma exerted her power over him. "Have you never lain in your bed when you knew that I was riding him and—"

"No!" her bodyguard growled.

"Wanting to watch what he did to me, wanting to know how he made me—"

"Does Youngblood know?" Mister Collin's eyes fixed on hers and Enigma felt a jolt of excitement at his rebellion.

"Know what, darling?" She slid off the desk and he followed her as she gathered her clothes to dress.

"Does Youngblood know that while he is downstairs charming your customers, you are upstairs screaming for me?"

"Careful, darling." She ran her finger over the scar she had given him, but he continued to speak in defiance.

"Mister Youngblood strikes me as the jealous type, but then you like to have men fighting over you." Jack pulled her hard against him. "Like two dogs with the same bone."

"One more word," she warned, "and I shall make Seamus McCurren my new dog." The idea was appealing. "And what do you think I will do with the old one?" Mister Collin released her, knowing full well what she was capable of.

"Now get back to work, and when I want you"—she made clear her other choices—"I will call." She slapped him on the tight, bare ass. "Now do as your told."

Sixteen

Annoyed, Falcon sat in his office on Tuesday afternoon and waited for his stubborn cryptographers to arrive.

He had, unbeknownst to the pair, seen them both individually earlier in the day and that was indeed the source of his current irritation.

"Lady Juliet, Mister McCurren, and Mister Habernathy," his secretary announced.

"Send them in."

Falcon hid his anger as the trio took their seats. Juliet and Seamus sat in the two wooden chairs, while Habernathy sat on a stool behind them.

"It appears to me as though we have a problem with the function of your office."

Seamus looked stunned, having not a half hour ago informed Falcon that he had identified the last marker of the elusive code. "What 'problem' are you referring to?"

Falcon leaned forward, his hands clasped together as his forearms rested on his desk.

"Were you aware, Lady Juliet, that Mister McCurren has already identified the remaining marker?"

"He mentioned it, yes—"

"And did you discuss his findings pertaining to the discovery of the final marker?" The girl's eyes darted to Seamus. "Or was that the day you chose to stay in the comfort of your home rather than travel to the Foreign Office?"

"I do apologize, my lord." The lady looked down, contrite. "I'm afraid I was not feeling well yesterday."

McCurren glanced at the girl, sympathy crossing over his handsome features, a sympathy that Falcon did not share.

"My agents are expected to send word of such inevitable occurrences, and had Mister McCurren not himself gone round to check on you"—the girl's head snapped up, surprised that he knew—"I would have been forced to send Mister Habernathy to divine your location."

"Yes, my lord." The lady nodded once then shook her head, adding, "It shall not happen again."

"See that it does not." Falcon turned his attention to Seamus McCurren. "And were you aware, Mister McCurren, that Lady Pervill had visited the office of the *London Herald* Friday last?"

The boy's jaw dropped a fraction but he refused to look at the diligent young woman. "No, I was not."

"Which is precisely why I have called this little meeting." Falcon glanced from one of his brilliant cryptographers to the other. "It appears to me that this collaboration of minds is at the moment anything but collaborative."

"Yes, my lord," they mumbled in unison.

"If we are to capture the Frenchman, we must first set aside pride and petty jealousies and work together. That includes sharing information!" Falcon was beginning to shout so he paused, calming his pounding heart. "You will go back to your office, discuss what you have learned individually, and then apply that knowledge toward breaking this code. Together!"

When he had nothing else to say, Juliet Pervill rose then curtsied a reticent farewell as Habernathy opened the door for her, reminding Falcon of his second reason for calling this meeting.

"Mister Habernathy, I would like for you to stay." Mc-Curren gave his secretary an encouraging nod then left the room, closing the door behind him. "I have a very important job for you, James."

"Yes, my lord?"

Juliet stormed down the main corridor of the Foreign Office, eager to put as much distance between herself and that Scottish scoundrel. She had been analyzing the last marker all blessed morning and not one word from Seamus to inform her that he had found something in the article!

As a matter of fact, he had not spoken to her at all.

"Good morning," a deep voice said and Juliet looked up at the face of an exquisite gentleman walking toward her.

"Good morning," Juliet replied, cursing her mother for burning her dreary gowns.

The man stopped before her, smiling rakishly as he asked, "Are you in need of an escort, miss?"

Juliet felt herself blush, unaccustomed to such forward, and decidedly handsome, young men.

"No, she is not." Juliet looked over her shoulder at the dull rumble of Seamus McCurren's deep voice as he caught up to her, grasping her upper arm from behind.

"I'm afraid we must get back to our office, good day," Seamus said, his tone anything but solicitous.

The young man bowed and let them pass.

Seamus pushed her forward but Juliet could not help looking back over her left shoulder. The rogue down the hall grinned as he gave her figure the once-over. Finding her to his liking, the blackguard winked. Juliet gasped at the young man's blatant assessment and was thankful when they had turned a corner and were out of the man's lecherous view.

"What do you expect when you walk around like that in a building full of men?"

"When I 'walk around like' what?" Juliet was incredulous.

"What happened to those gray gowns you wore when you first began working at the Foreign Office?" Seamus demanded, opening their outer office door.

"My mother burned them, if you must know." She wrenched her arm free and opened the door to their inner office, slamming it in his face.

Seamus opened the inner door with a violent tug. "Why?" he growled, then it was his turn to slam the abused door.

"She found them unsightly." Juliet sat at her desk.

"That was a mistake." Seamus was at his desk in three strides.

"Why?"

"Beautiful women in a building full of unmarried men will only lead to—"

"Temptation?"

Seamus turned to stare at her, apparently unsure if she was referring to *her* temptation or that of the men.

"Ruination." His eyes were cold and cruel and Juliet looked away from the sting of his censure.

There was a lengthy silence and Juliet swallowed the lump that had formed in her throat.

"May I read the *Herald* article? I had no idea you gleaned any information from it bar the finding of the last marker." Juliet glared at him, her tone accusing him of conspiring against her.

"Aye, you can read it." He walked the short distance to her desk. "If you tell me why you went to the *London Herald* in the first place."

Juliet did not look up, but she could feel him staring down at her. "It occurred to me that if I knew the amount of time it took from the submission of an article to its publication date—"

"Falcon could have his men wait for the French cryptographer to submit the next code." Seamus finished her thought, unimpressed.

"Yes, then I went home with my new information and made calculations to determine in which publication the anomaly was most likely to next appear." Juliet looked up and, having nothing else to say, asked, "Why didn't you tell me of your findings?"

"I did." Seamus held her eyes.

"You most certainly did not." She would have remembered, but then again she had forgotten quite a lot of that particular conversation the moment Seamus kissed her. Juliet rose, uncomfortable with him standing so close to her, remembering his kiss.

"I told you about the marker yesterday." He waited and then turned his back to her. "However, you might not remember as you were a bit indisposed."

Juliet stared at his back in disbelief. He thought she had been inebriated during the encounter. She knew that he had seen her tumbler of scotch, had realized after he was gone that it was the reason Seamus had left so abruptly.

Because he believed no lady would behave as wantonly as she had unless her judgment had been soaked in whiskey.

And he was correct, most ladies would not. But there was some quality to Seamus McCurren that sent her mind on holiday. Touching the man was so incredibly . . . Her eyes drifted to his alluring backside.

And having him touch her . . . She bit the side of her lip.

"Yes, I had just returned from the park," she offered as a feeble explanation, deciding it better that he believe her to have been "indisposed" than to know the humiliating truth. "Will you show me your findings now?"

Seamus shrugged with a touch of embarrassment. "Aye."

"Thank you," she said, so mortified she could hardly think.

"It would be easier if you came to my desk," Seamus said, pointing as if she'd no idea where his desk was located. "I found the last marker in the *Herald*, and once I did, I examined the papers as a whole as you did last week."

Juliet smiled, feeling validated. "Yes?"

"The four publications in which the markers appeared are the *Herald*," he held up the latest paper. "The *Gazette*, the *Times*, and the *London Post*." She nodded and he continued. "The first marker was found in the *Gazette*. The second marker appeared in the *Herald*, the third . . ." Seamus stared at her but needed to go no further.

"The stupid frog put the markers in alphabetical order?" Juliet laughed and he smiled brilliantly, nodding.

"Rather stupid."

"Rather," she agreed, momentarily dazed by his masculine beauty. "Did you, uh, find anything else?"

"This cryptographer covets order."

"Yes." To the point of foolishness.

"So, with that in mind, I looked at the articles again and found another pattern."

Her jaw dropped and she hit him on the shoulder with the back of her hand. "That's fantastic, Seamus!"

He chuckled and Juliet looked down at his elegant fingers as they spread out the five E code clippings. She could not help remembering the feel of his hand splayed across her breast.

"Initially, I thought the E placement was random until I found the last marker. But look at this." Seamus pointed. "The E appears in the second paragraph twice, the fifth paragraph once, and the sixth once. I think the paragraph in which the E marker appears denotes the retrieval site location."

Juliet turned toward him, her eyes widening with comprehension. "Then there are at least three retrieval sites."

"At least three." Seamus stared down at her, his eyes

dancing with intelligence. Juliet could not help herself. She rose on her tiptoes and kissed him.

Hard.

Seamus stumbled backward, not expecting her weight, and Juliet followed. She closed her eyes and pressed his back to the office wall then leaned against him, needing the stability, needing her feet on the ground as her mind wandered the length of his beautiful body.

Her arms slipped around his neck, and much to her surprise, his arms snaked around her waist as Seamus pulled her flush to his exquisite form. Her breasts were crushed against his chest and Juliet moaned. She felt a rush of embarrassment, which dissipated as Seamus ardently returned her awkward kiss.

He turned her head to make it easier to sweep into her mouth with his tongue. She closed her eyes and focused her mind entirely on the pleasure of kissing the brilliant Seamus.

His lips were supple but insistent, and his tongue glided around her mouth, beckoning her to follow. She did, pursuing him into the very recess of his mouth as she pressed herself more firmly into his arms.

He gave a masculine moan of approval, the sound of which sent a stab of desire that began in her belly before radiating through what was left of her body. Then the kiss intensified and Juliet began to panic, never having felt such passion, such power from a man, from herself.

"I'm sorry." She pushed away. "I . . ." Juliet made the mistake of looking up at him. "Perhaps the Foreign Office does provide too much temptation."

And then she realized what she had just said, what she had just admitted.

"Good afternoon," Juliet mumbled as she left her reticule, her hat, and her winter coat, fleeing out the office door.

"Heading home so soon, Lady Juliet?" Mister Habernathy caught her in the corridor.

"Yes, James."

"I trust you reconciled matters with Mister McCurren."

"Oh, yes, we shared everything there was to share and a bit more."

Much more.

"Glad to hear it." Mister Habernathy's smile was full of relief. "See you tomorrow morning."

Juliet stilled, wanting nothing more than to curl into a ball and die on that very spot.

Seventeen

It was all Seamus could do to wait until the opera's intermission before walking into the box of the Marquess Shelton, looking for Christian.

"Good evening," Seamus said as he parted the curtain to the marquess's coveted box.

Christian was already standing and Ian St. John turned around to see who had been so presumptuous as to invade their privacy.

"Good evening, McCurren," Christian St. John said, his grin amiable. "Might I introduce to you, Baroness Petrovna?"

"How do you do?" Seamus bowed and the woman inclined her head, no doubt pulled forward by the weight of the enormous diamonds encircling her lovely neck.

"Very well, thank you," the baroness said, her accented English harsh on the ear.

However, the lady was far from harsh on the eyes. Her strawberry-blond hair was flawless, and her face looked as though it had been painted from a man's sensual dreams. Seamus had no doubt that the woman knew how to warm a man's bed, but there was something decidedly cold about the Russian baroness.

"You are acquainted with Shelton and Lady Felicity, of course." Christian's jovial voice warmed them all as they exchanged greetings.

Seamus then said to Christian when the niceties were out of the way, "Might I have a word?"

"Certainly." Christian smiled and then looked at his older brother. "I'll just go down and have another bottle of champagne sent up, shall I?"

Ian agreed with a nod and they left, diving into the crush of operagoers seeking refreshment.

"So what did you think of her?" Christian asked with wide eyes.

"I like Lady Felicity ver—"

"Not Felicity, you blackguard." Christian shook his head, irritated. "The baroness?"

"She's stunning."

Christian stopped and looked directly at Seamus. "You don't like her."

"I saw her for all of five seconds."

"And in those five seconds you have determined that you dislike her?"

Seamus shrugged, not one to lie. "Aye."

"A bit cold, don't you think?"

"Like a Russian winter."

"Not her, you!" Christian sighed. "She's fantastic in bed."

"I've no doubt that she is, Christian."

"You think I should get rid of the lady? My father and brother do," he mumbled and then grabbed a passing footman and two glasses of champagne. "Would you send a bottle of your best champagne to the box of the Marquess Shelton?"

"Right away, my lord."

"Now," Christian turned and looked at Seamus. "As to your problem. What is it and how can I help?"

Seamus looked around and then walked to an empty alcove, drawing the thick velvet curtain. "I kissed Lady Juliet today."

"You kissed Juliet! Are you stark raving mad?" Christian's blue-gray eyes gleamed with irritation. "You know how hard we've been working to restore her reputation."

"I know." Seamus closed his eyes against his guilt. "Perhaps it will ease your sensibilities to know that the lass kissed me first."

Christian took a step back. "You're joking."

"I'm not."

"That little hellion." Christian was shaking his head. "Juliet has been mad about men for as long as I've known her."

Seamus felt a sharp pain in his chest. "Really?"

"Thank God, most men were too intimidated by the woman to go anywhere near her. But to thrill seekers like Lord Barksdale, Juliet was an irresistible challenge. Still is, no doubt."

"Yes, I had heard that they were . . . connected," Seamus said, his voice brittle.

Christian looked up. "Mind you, Barksdale fell hard once they began seeing one another. Absolutely besotted ever since and was truly crushed by the whole Harrington business."

"Don't feel sorry for the bastard just yet." Seamus smirked. "He's since asked the lady to become his mistress."

"What?" Christian tightened his grip on his champagne flute and it shattered in his hand. "Damn it all!"

"Here." Seamus retrieved a handkerchief from his pocket as Christian set the jagged stem on the nearest windowsill.

"Thank you." Christian wrapped the handkerchief around the gash in his right hand and was looking down when he asked, "Is that why you kissed her, because she was crying about Lord Barksdale? I've never been able to deal with a woman's tears either."

Seamus laughed. "Oh, Juliet was not crying about Robert Barksdale. She was right furious with the man."

"Sounds like Juliet, much more capable than most women." Christian's grin held a deep affection. "So, why did you kiss her then, Seamus?"

"I don't know, that is why I'm coming to you. Daniel has been useless, thinks my kissing Juliet Pervill is bloody amusing."

"You are behaving rather oddly." Christian nodded. "But why come to me, of all people?"

Seamus gave a frustrated sigh. "I have to see the lass to-morrow, and with the amount of lovers you've had, I knew that you would have run into this situation once or twice."

"Oh, I see." Christian grinned. "Best thing to do when encountering an old lover is ignore it. Don't ignore her, just pretend that nothing has happened between you and avoid the subject at all costs."

"That does not seem a mature way to handle the situation."

"I find maturity highly overvalued." The bell rang for the start of the third act and Christian turned his head in the direction of the reverberating noise. He lifted the curtain to the alcove then stopped, looking back at Seamus. "You never did tell me why you kissed Juliet."

Seamus shook his head. "Proximity?"

Christian laughed. "Good luck, Seamus. But if you do anything more than kiss Juliet Pervill, I will be forced to call you out."

The curtain fell and Seamus stared at the folds of the shifting chartreuse, unsure if Christian had been jesting.

"Stop picking at your food, Juliet." Her mother had been ordering the same instruction for as long as she could remember.

Juliet sat up and sighed, making her decision.

"May I ask you both a question?" She looked at her mother and cousin, thankful that her uncle had gone out for the evening.

"Leave us," the countess told the six footmen posted around the dining room. When the doors had closed and they were alone, her mother stared at her. "What is it you wish to ask, Juliet?"

"In your experience . . ." She spoke to them both as they had far more dealings with men, varied though those dealings may be, but primarily because she was desperate for an answer. "Why would a gentleman who is wealthy, handsome, experienced, and a renowned bachelor kiss an innocent young lady?"

"Someone has kissed you?" Felicity asked, sounding as though she already knew the answer.

"Yes." My God, was she so easy to read? "The first time I thought he did it to ruffle my feathers, but today—"

"The first time? Today!" The countess was appalled. "This man has kissed you twice?"

"Well, to be fair, I kissed *him* today."

"You kissed this gentleman today?" Juliet was cut off by the force of her mother's accusation.

"Yes." She felt a growing weight in the pit of her stomach when her mother's demeanor turned flippant.

"We are all clever women." The countess smiled, pushing her dinner plate forward and placing her elbows on the table, her hands bound together in exaggerated contemplation. "Let us see if we can come up with a reason why a handsome, wealthy, experienced gentleman of the *ton* would welcome the favors of a woman reported to give them away."

Tears moistened Juliet's eyes and she glanced at her mother. "I take your point."

However, Felicity was shaking her head adamantly. "No, Seamus McCurren is a true gentleman. He would never take advantage of an innocent lady."

Juliet looked across the table, shocked. "How did you know I was referring to Seamus?"

"I sent him up to your sitting room. Remember?"

"Juliet?" Her mother always knew when there was more to any given story. "You allowed this man in your sitting room?"

She turned to face her mother. "I saw Robert Barksdale that morning, and being . . . distraught, I did not feel up to going into the Foreign Office, so Mister McCurren came to me."

"Yes, I've heard." Her mother stared at her. "But explain to me how your discussion of matters political turned into his kissing you?"

"I'm not sure." Lady Pervill raised a brow and Juliet confessed, "Well, perhaps I was a bit more open in my admiration of Mister McCurren's academic abilities than perhaps I should have—"

"How could you allow a gentleman into your cousin's room?" Her mother was staring at Felicity, who paled with the weight of responsibility. "You know how much she enjoys them."

"I don't 'enjoy' men." Juliet was indignant.

"I am speaking of enjoying them intellectually, not physically, although it sounds as if you are venturing quite willingly into that carnal realm."

"I . . . Mister McCurren wanted to discuss matters at the Foreign Office so I thought it best, given their positions, that they were given some privacy." Felicity turned to Juliet, begging forgiveness. "I never would have left you alone with Mister McCurren if I for one moment thought you were in any danger."

"I wasn't in any danger. He barely kissed me," she lied.

"Oh." Felicity's eyes went wide. "I thought . . . Well, with his cravat—"

"His cravat?" The countess kept Felicity on point.

"Mister McCurren must have . . ." Felicity blushed. "Retied it upstairs as it was different than when he arrived."

Juliet dropped her head in her hands, unable to picture a more shameful scenario.

"Well." The countess held up a glass of wine. "I think we've just discovered why a wealthy, handsome bachelor of the *ton* would *continue* to kiss a ruined young lady. A lady we have all been trying so desperately to bring back into favor."

"Oh, I don't think Mister McCurren would speak of Juliet's lapse with anyone," Felicity assured her aunt.

"You didn't think the man would kiss an innocent girl either."

Come to think of it, his kissing her was not very gentlemanly. Even if she wanted him to, he should never have done it.

What if he did mention their encounter to someone? Juliet's heart sped up. Not that Seamus would intentionally try to ruin all the work her friends had done to restore her reputation.

Oh, God.

"I just . . ." Felicity was still shaking her head, "I just don't believe Seamus McCurren would take advantage of Juliet."

"The question, Felicity dear"—her mother took a sip of sherry—"is whether you believe Juliet would take advantage of him."

"May I speak with Mister McCurren, please?" Juliet smiled prettily at the impressive butler.

"I'm afraid Mister McCurren has retired for the evening." The man's demeanor was pleasant and he clearly did not expect his announcement to be challenged.

"Well, resurrect him," Juliet said, pushing past the flustered man.

"I . . . I'm afraid that that is not possible." The butler made the mistake of glancing at the first door on his left. "Mister McCurren is unavailable."

"Really?" Frantic, Juliet walked to the tall mahogany doors and knocked loudly. "Mister McCurren, you will remember me, Lady Juliet Pervill? I very much need to speak with you and fear that I am making your butler very distressed."

Seamus yanked open the door and smiled caustically. "You do seem to have that effect on people, Lady Juliet."

McCurren ushered her into his study and only then did she see that he was in his dressing gown. He really had retired? Rather earlier than she would have thought.

"Do you recall coming to my home Monday last?" Juliet asked, cutting to the chase.

"Yes, I seem to recall a thing or two about that visit." Seamus poured himself a brandy, his broad back to her.

"You didn't tell anyone, did you?"

"Tell anyone what?"

"That you kissed me?" Juliet held her breath, waiting for him to answer.

"I'm surprised you remember." He smiled charmingly. "You were a bit . . . indisposed at the time. Brandy?"

She blushed and tried to sound convincing when she asked, "Was I?"

"Yes. Scotch, if I recall your preferred poison." He lifted his snifter to his lips.

"Felicity knows."

"Knows what?" He shrugged. "That you kissed me in your bedchamber?"

"You kissed me!"

"So you do remember?" He leaned forward as if imparting some great secret. "I was beginning to think I was losing my touch."

Oh, how Juliet wished to tell him that he was, but even she was not that convincing.

"Felicity noted that you left her home sporting a different style of cravat than when you had arrived. What I would like to know is if anyone else is aware of . . . our encounter."

Seamus raised his left brow at her decidedly accusing tone. "Ask me politely and perhaps I'll tell you."

"Perhaps?" Juliet cast him a withering glare. "I am attempting to rebuild my reputation!"

"Then, my dear Juliet, I suggest you refrain from kissing men in your bedchamber." His golden eyes met hers, void of remorse.

"You kissed me!" She was furious.

"And you liked it well enough to remove my cravat."

As Seamus continued to stare at her, she remembered just how much.

"As you've said"—she blinked—"I was 'indisposed.' "

"After yesterday's lapse . . ." He smiled. "I'm beginning to wonder if you had taken a single sip."

"Well, I had. Loads, in fact," she lied.

He sipped his brandy. "And yesterday?"

"The excitement of discovery." She shrugged the kiss off. "Like you kissing me for my books. My God, it's boiling in here," she said, desperate to change the subject and he let her.

"I'm afraid I was not expecting company."

Juliet glanced at his silk dressing gown and his partially exposed chest.

"Yes, I can see that. So, if you will just tell me if you told anyone of our . . ." Juliet looked away from his perceptive gaze. "Lapse, then I shall be on my way and you can get back to . . ." *Lounging in your study nude.* "Reading."

Seamus grinned, both of them knowing this was as close as she had ever come to a man in his altogether. For all she knew, he had a widow waiting in the next room, eager to take Seamus to bed.

"You're just angry that Felicity found out about your . . . lapse."

"Don't be stupid," she protested, knowing that this man was anything but. "Have you told anyone that you took advantage of me?"

Seamus burst into laughter and then walked to his chair, sitting as she followed. "I took about as much advantage of you in your home as I did yesterday."

She gasped and would have defended herself, but all thoughts vanished when Seamus's silk robe slid a good four inches away from his right thigh as he set his feet atop the black ottoman.

Juliet stared, never having seen a man's bare leg, so long and powerful, so utterly beautiful . . . and hairy. But for some inexplicable reason that was rather nice, too.

Wait, he was saying something.

"What do you mean?" she asked, having no clue what they had been discussing. Her mind entirely focused on the thought of running her hands down his muscular thigh, wondering what the dark hair would feel like against her skin, her body.

"We both know that you wanted to kiss me yesterday." He finished his brandy and she watched the cords of masculine muscle surrounding his neck as he swallowed.

"Do stop messing about, Seamus," she said, less forcefully then she had hoped. "Did you tell anyone about our . . ." she conceded as he rose. "Indiscretion?"

"You mean, about our *indiscretions*?" he said, looking down at her with that amused grin that turned her brain to mush.

"Stop it, Seamus."

"Stop what?" He shrugged, drawing her attention to his beautiful broad shoulders.

Juliet closed her eyes and the heat in the room became oppressive as she felt him standing mere inches in front of her, around her.

Seamus repeated his stipulation.

"Ask me nicely." His voice fell over her like a silken sheet.

She was becoming light-headed, and in the interest of self-preservation, Juliet acquiesced to his demand.

"Very well. Please," she breathed, "tell me if anyone else . . ." She tilted her head back and looked him in the eye. "Knows that I . . ."

"Kissed me," he whispered, his head bent, his breath on her lips.

"Yes," she hoped she said before standing on her tiptoes and kissing him again.

Juliet placed her hand on his bare chest as he pulled her flush against his powerful body.

With half of her mind on the moist heat of his mouth, she allowed the other half to explore his exceptional body. Her hands slid around his ribs and then descended down the silk covering his muscular back. The subtle curve of his taut backside was irresistible, and Juliet could not help giving him a squeeze as she pulled him closer.

He moaned and it was then that Juliet felt his hardening length against her belly. Her nipples tightened to sensitive peaks and the feel of his heavy chest moving against her breasts was wonderful. She closed her eyes as they continued to kiss and she felt her passion gathering momentum between her thighs.

All the mental restrictions drilled into ladies of the *ton* disappeared when Juliet suddenly remembered—

She was a ruined woman.

Juliet reached up and grasped the burgundy silk around Seamus's shoulders and yanked the robe from his enticing body.

Seamus stared down at her in complete shock and then smiled with a seductive heat in his eyes, asking, "Disappointed?"

Breathing heavily, her eyes scanned the muscled curves

of his chest, noting his nipples so deliciously different from her own. She bit the side of her lip, looking lower at the lines that crisscrossed his flat belly, at the trail of dark hair that disappeared beneath . . . *Damn!* His drawers.

"Yes," she said truthfully. Seamus threw his head back and roared with laughter, causing her to blush.

"Well, lass, I would not want you to leave my home unsatisfied." Juliet watched his hand go to the drawstring of his drawers before she closed her eyes, humiliated that she wanted very much to see more of him.

"I'm so sorry to have disturbed you," Juliet whispered on the verge of tears, sure that this was quite amusing for a man of Seamus McCurren's ilk.

She turned, rushing toward the study door, but it would not open, and then she felt his heat against her back.

"I'm sorry, Juliet," he breathed in her ear. "I was just teasing, lass."

His lips pressed against her neck and then Juliet did cry, overwhelmed with her want of him.

"Despite what you may have heard, Mister McCurren, I have no experience with such . . . games. Good night."

Seamus let her go, knowing now was not the time. There never would be a time for them.

Juliet was an innocent, as overcome by her awakening sensuality as was he. When she had ripped his robe from his body, Seamus had very nearly done the same to her gown.

He was still shaking from the need to make love to her and he knew that something had to be done. He could not go on like this, working side by side, all the while wanting something he could not have.

"William," Seamus shouted to his butler as he opened the study door. "You are never to allow that woman in my home again."

"Yes, sir."

Now, if he could just keep her out of his office.

* * *

A hairy little Welshman clung to the warmth of the brick walls across the street from the house he had been paid to watch. He snuffled and reached for his gin, taking a small swig then putting the half-empty bottle back in his overstuffed pocket. The man took out a scrap of paper and a pencil and huddled under the lamppost so that he could note the time.

Mister McCurren had arrived home late from Whitehall. What the hell Seamus McCurren did at Whitehall he had no notion, nor did he care. He and his brother were being paid to watch the fancy and nothing more.

The job had been a right bore until the lady arrived. She was young, fresh, and angry when she pushed her way into McCurren's home. She hadn't stayed long, and by the look on her face when he watched the lady being helped into her carriage, she had left more troubled than when she had arrived.

"Who's the woman?" He saw his brother's pipe burning on a slow draw before he saw his ugly face.

"Don't know. First time I've seen her." He looked his brother in the eye. "I'll follow the lady. You stay here and watch McCurren," he suggested, his elbow aching at the first sign of a freeze. "Did you bring some blankets? It's gonna get cold tonight."

"Never you mind about me." His brother smiled around the bone of his ever-present pipe. "Just remember that you'll be the one freezing tomorrow night."

"True," he chuckled, rubbing salt into his brother's wound. "But tonight I'll have a warm bed at Dante's and an even warmer whore."

"As long as you get me money from Mister Collin, I don't give a damn what you do with your evening."

"Don't forget to write down everything McCurren does." He jerked his head toward the fancy's house. "And the time he does it."

The Welshman jumped atop his horse as the lady's carriage rolled forward.

"I have done this before, you know," his brother said, looking up at him.

"Not for these people you haven't."

The brothers stared at one another, aware of the consequences for failing people such as these.

Eighteen

"*I'm* afraid that I am no longer able to work with Lady Juliet and am therefore forced to resign my commission at the Foreign Office."

"Resign?" Falcon stared at Seamus McCurren, who had sought him out at his home.

"Yes, I'm afraid so." He nodded. "Now that the Foreign Office has commissioned a cryptographer as capable as Juliet Pervill, I feel comfortable in returning to my prior research."

Falcon was by now familiar enough with Seamus to know that something else was bothering the man. "Has the lady—"

"It really has nothing to do with Lady Juliet, I assure you." McCurren looked at him with regret. "Rather the fact that I prefer . . . That is to say, I am far more effective when working in solitude."

"Ah, so you have not found the lady's insight . . . useful?" Falcon watched the boy carefully for insight of his own.

"Quite the contrary, the lady is eminently qualified to decrypt French code. I just find it difficult to concentrate when . . ."

Falcon watched the scholar search for the proper word.

"Challenged?" he suggested helpfully.

The poor lad jerked his head back to look at him then blinked several times before he could manage, "No! No, not at all. I merely find it difficult to concentrate when a variety of methods are being applied to the information gathered by this office."

The boy had a point, he supposed.

"Mmm," Falcon mused. "You know, I often have this difficulty with the gentlemen in my employ."

"What difficulty is that?" McCurren appeared truly perplexed.

"When I hire a new man, my agents inevitably feel . . . threatened, feel that I find the work they are doing somehow lacking."

McCurren's dark brows pulled over his golden eyes, and Falcon could see that he was mulling over the never-before-considered possibility of his feeling threatened.

"No," Seamus concluded. "I do not believe that to be the difficulty in this particular situation."

"Which implies that you do know what the difficulty might be?" McCurren held his eyes and in the complex depths Falcon found the answer. "Perhaps the difficulty is that you are unaccustomed to working with women?"

"Yes." The man's tense shoulders were eased by relief. "As I've said, I concentrate much more effectively when working . . . in solitude."

"You seem to concentrate quite well with the assistance of Mister Habernathy."

"Quite true." Seamus glanced down, clearly embarrassed, and Falcon felt a twinge of guilt. "And I am quite sure that Lady Juliet Pervill will work with Mister Habernathy equally well."

"Thank you for informing me of your intention to resign in person." Falcon took pity on the lad. "I shall speak with Lady Juliet first thing tomorrow morning and inform her of the new arrangement."

"Thank you, my lord. It has been an honor working with you," Seamus said, leaving Falcon to wonder what would become of the brilliant Juliet Pervill when he dismissed her from his employ.

Juliet arrived at the Foreign Office at ten o'clock and, as she walked toward her office, told herself repeatedly to pretend as though nothing happened last night between her and Seamus.

To pretend that he had not kissed her . . . or rather that she had not kissed him, to behave as though she had not ripped his dressing gown from that magnificent bod—

"Morning, James." She forced a smile and then swept into the inner office.

"Morning, Lady Juliet," Mister Habernathy called after her.

But she stopped cold when she saw that the large Scot was not there. "Has Mister McCurren come in today?"

"No, Mister McCurren has yet to arrive." He looked up then shook his head, smiling. "Perhaps he is out making inquiries?"

"Oh, excellent," Juliet said, being the coward that she was. "Then we are sure to make some progress today."

"Undoubtedly," James agreed, always the optimist. "Also, his lordship wished a word with you the moment you arrived in the office."

"All right." Juliet removed her reticule and pelisse. "While I'm gone, would you be so kind as to brew me some coffee?"

She had not slept well.

"Certainly."

Juliet made her way down the maze of halls, wondering

why in the world the old man had chosen such a tiny office. Surely, his position within the Foreign Office required more room, if not recognition.

"Good morning," Juliet said to Falcon's pleasant assistant. "Is his lordship available?"

The man did not quite meet her eye. "Yes, he is awaiting you, as a matter of fact."

"Thank you," Juliet said simply, not wanting to disturb the gentleman further.

She walked to the door of his lordship's inner sanctum and knocked. The old man cleared his throat and called, "Come in."

Juliet smiled politely at Falcon's secretary, but when she met his eye, the man dropped his gaze. Confused, she pushed open his lordship's door, her attention focused entirely on the old man himself.

"You wanted to speak with me, my lord?"

"Yes, Lady Juliet." Falcon took a shaky moment to rise to his feet and then swept his hand over the set of familiar chairs in front of him. "Please, have a seat."

Juliet's brows furrowed, sensing that it was Falcon who would be handing out the information today, not the other way round.

"Thank you," she said, taking the same seat that she had the last time she had been in his office . . . with Seamus McCurren.

His lordship smiled and Juliet felt an immediate foreboding, which was confirmed when he began by saying, "Lady Juliet, your work with the Foreign Office over the past several weeks has been quite commendable."

"I am so glad that you think so." She stared at him, wary.

"However . . ." Juliet started to panic. "I'm afraid that your continued presence at the Foreign Office is no longer possible."

"You disappoint me, my lord." Her chin quivered and

she bit her bottom lip to stop it from shaking. "I would have thought you of all people able to deal with having a woman of questionable reputation in your employ."

"That is unwarranted, Juliet," the old man admonished. "If it were up to me, you would still—"

"If it is not up to you, your lordship, then who the bloody hell is it up to?"

She was near to crying now, not sure what she would do if she did not have the Foreign Office to come to every day.

The old man ignored her outburst.

"I was forced to make a decision." Falcon looked at her with great regret. "Seamus McCurren has resigned his commission at the Foreign Office if you continue on, and I cannot afford to lose you both."

"Then lose him!" Juliet shouted, her hand thrust upward as if by her logic. "Accept his resignation and keep me on as sole cryptographer."

Falcon shook his head, denying her. "That is impractical, I'm afraid."

"Why?" Juliet demanded, furious. "Because I am a woman?"

"Yes." The old man nodded, unrepentant. "You have been a distraction for several gentlemen at the Foreign Office but that is not the only reason you are being dismissed."

"Is Mister McCurren a better cryptographer than I?" Tears flowed so freely down her cheeks that Juliet did not even try to stop them.

"No," the old man admitted. "Mister McCurren offers different talents than you do, my dear. However, Seamus has been with the office longer and he is, as you so correctly point out, male."

"But why would he resign from—"

But before the words came out of her mouth, Juliet knew.

"Mister McCurren says that you are a distraction to his work."

Juliet nodded. It was true—she had kissed him several

times, and last night . . . last night she had practically assaulted him. The poor man was probably protecting his virtue from such a wanton woman.

"I understand," Juliet whispered, rising. "I'll just gather my things." *And my dignity.* "Thank you so very much . . ." She began to cry again and then forced herself to look her former employer in the eye. "For the opportunity that you have given me, your lordship."

"No, my dear." Falcon took her hand in both of his. "Thank you for the work that you have done for us . . . for Britain."

Juliet nodded, unable to speak, and then she left the old man's office for the last time.

"It has been an honor," his secretary said as she left, finally meeting her eye. "Working with you, Lady Juliet."

"Thank you." Her tears started up again and she pressed her gloved fingers to the corners of her eyes to quail them.

Juliet opened the door and stepped into the corridors of the Foreign Office, praying that no one noticed the redness of her nose. She arrived at their outer office, but it was empty, and she took a deep breath before opening the inner-office door.

"I've brought your coffee, my lady," James said, setting the steaming cup on her messy desk.

"Might I take it with me?" she asked, and hearing her distress, James Habernathy turned around.

"Take it with you?" The secretary handed her his handkerchief.

"I've been dismissed."

"You have not." He said the words as if they could change the outcome.

"Yes, I have." Juliet nodded, relieved that she was not the only person who thought her dismissal a shock and entirely unwarranted, not to mention unfair.

"They would not dare dismiss you after all you have

done with the E code." Mister Habernathy was indignant. "What on earth is his lordship thinking?"

Juliet walked to her chair and yanked on her pelisse, furious. "It was not his lordship who had me dismissed."

"Who else even knows you collaborate with the Foreign Office?"

Juliet raised a brow and Mister Habernathy looked at Seamus's desk, gasping. "He did not."

"He did! Sort of." Juliet slipped her reticule on her wrist and then began gathering her books from atop the desk. "He told his lordship that he would resign his post if I continued on."

"Why would Mister McCurren do such a horrible thing? You were making such progress."

Juliet shrugged as if she did not know, and the books in her arms started to fall to the side. "Ask Mister McCurren."

"Oh, do let me pack your things for you, Lady Juliet," Mister Habernathy offered, so gently that she just nodded. "Send them to Lady Felicity Appleton's home, if you please, and thank you for everything, James. It has been a pleasure working with you."

Mister Habernathy smiled and Juliet walked to the door, glancing back at her secretary and then at Seamus McCurren's very empty desk.

Nineteen

Embarrassed, Seamus returned to the office late that afternoon, praying that it was empty so that he might pack up his desk in peace.

But it was not.

"Afternoon, James," he said to Mister Habernathy's back as the secretary packed the contents of Juliet's desk into a small wooden trunk. "What are you doing?"

"Good afternoon, Mister McCurren." His amiable secretary's tone was curt and far from welcoming. "I spoke with his lordship this morning," James continued, having yet to turn round. "And I am emptying Lady Juliet's desk as per his request."

"Lady Juliet's?" James had gotten it all wrong. "No, it is not Lady Juliet who is leav—"

The trunk was slammed over his words and James Habernathy walked directly in front of him, eyeing him with a look of immense disappointment.

"I must say, I found the news disturbing as I have seen

firsthand the strides Lady Juliet has made in decrypting this most recent French code."

Seamus felt as though he had been struck in the gut, but he could not explain his motives for removing himself from this office, from removing Juliet from his reach.

"As have I, which is why I offered *my* resignation to his lordship," Seamus explained, trying to sound reasonable.

"You resigned?"

"Yes!" He nodded, angry. "You're packing the wrong desk."

"But I don't understand." James stared at the trunk on Juliet's desk as if he had no idea how it had gotten there. "His lordship said that Lady Juliet would be leaving the Foreign Office and returning to a life more befitting her station."

Oh, damn! Falcon had gotten rid of his reason for resigning.

Stunned, he sank into Juliet's chair as James continued to talk. "But I must say, Lady Juliet did not look as though she wished to return to a life of leisure. She looked absolutely murderous."

Mister Habernathy held his eye and Seamus tried not to flinch.

"Let's just get on with it, shall we," Seamus sighed. He had done the honorable thing. "Falcon has made his choice." And Seamus would do his best to convince the old man that he'd made the wrong choice.

"Yes, Mister McCurren." His secretary's cool formality punctuated the growing distance between them.

Seamus spent the remainder of a very long afternoon arguing with Falcon and then looking over the E markers. His "distraction" had been removed and the old man refused to reinstate her, leaving only Seamus to decrypt the code.

It was blackmail, pure and simple. He should bloody well tell the old man to stuff his commission, but he knew if he did that, it would be British troops who would pay the price.

At six o'clock, Seamus gathered his greatcoat and walked to the stables, angry and distracted. He called for his horse and rode through St. James's Park to clear his muddled head.

It seemed as though Juliet's absence throughout the day had caused him to think of nothing but the lady herself.

His lordship was correct, of course. She was back where she belonged, in the arms of the *haute ton*, protected from such ugly things as war and death . . . and him.

He closed his eyes, knowing how easy it would be to seduce her and how much he wanted to do just that.

Frustrated, Seamus slid off his horse, climbed the stairs to his home, and headed straight for a hot bath. But it was no good; every time he closed his eyes, he saw her face, felt her lips pressed to his. He sat down for dinner, and in the silence, he heard her voice.

He placed a piece of lamb in his mouth and chewed, confused.

He did hear her voice!

Seamus pushed his chair back from the table and walked silently to the door, concentrating on the ruckus in his entryway.

"I'm afraid Mister McCurren is unavailable this evening, Lady Juliet," his beleaguered butler explained as per his orders.

Seamus pressed his ear to the door so that he would not miss a word of what the lady had to say.

"I'm sure that if Mister McCurren knew I was here"— Juliet sounded angry—"he would gladly see me."

Nothing could be further from the truth.

"I am sorry, my lady."

"You mean to say . . ." Seamus could almost see the fire billowing from her nostrils as she spoke. "That you are refusing to notify Mister McCurren of my presence in his home."

"As I've said"—the brave butler held his ground— "Mister McCurren is unavailable this evening."

"I know Mister McCurren is in residence, I can smell his dinner!"

Seamus glanced at his plate of traitorous lamb and then walked on tiptoes to resume his seat lest the wee woman hear him and barge into the dining room with his footmen attempting to hold her at bay.

"Perhaps, if you were to come back tomorrow . . ."

There was a long silence and Seamus stared at the brass doorknob just waiting for it to turn.

"No," Juliet said. "I don't think I will come back tomorrow."

The front door closed and Seamus sat back in his chair, relieved. It had been a long, difficult day and all he wanted to do was finish his meal and go to bed.

Seamus was just lifting his silver spoon to enjoy his dessert when a painted white brick came flying through the window. It slid the length of the new mahogany table, scratching it the entire way, before coming to rest three inches from his custard, which was still jiggling from the shaking of the now ruined table.

Seamus looked through the shattered window at the madwoman in the street, as she shouted, "If you are going to behave like a child, then so shall I."

"William! Let her in," he ordered, sure that the other window would be next if he did not.

"Yes, sir."

Seamus gazed at his custard, knowing he would never eat it, then pushed himself up from his chair. He stepped into the entryway, offering a polite smile to his insistent guest.

"Lady Juliet." Seamus bowed with great exaggeration. "What a pleasant surprise."

"Mister McCurren," she countered with a deep curtsy. "How lucky to find you at home." Her eyes were ablaze and Seamus knew that he was in for it.

The lady took a long, deep breath, ready to unleash hell

when Seamus held up his index finger. "We should do this someplace else." *Not the study. Not the study.* "The parlor, perhaps?" He swept his arm in that direction and followed at a safe distance.

"Perfect," she agreed.

The footmen opened the door and Seamus looked at them both, saying, "For your own safety, I suggest you clear the area. William, you also."

"Is the lady unstable?" one of the lads asked in earnest.

"Oh, she's mad, all right," Seamus said, closing the parlor door like a man about to die.

Juliet was shaking as she stared at the parlor fire, she was that angry.

How dare he have her dismissed from the Foreign Office! Who in God's name did he think he was?

"Well." Seamus's rich baritone brogue skittered down her back. "Say what you've come to say so I can finish my dinner."

Juliet turned, smiling as she said, "I've not come to say anything," before slapping him across the face.

Seamus turned his head slowly to the left, rubbing his jaw as he stared down at her. "I suppose I should have expected that."

"You had me dismissed!" Juliet shouted.

"I resigned!" Seamus protested. "It is not my fault that Falcon dismissed you."

"You gave him an ultimatum!"

"I did no such thing." He shook his head as he walked toward the parlor door. "What do you care anyway, it is not as though we work well together, as evidenced by this little exchange."

"We made great progress, Seamus."

He turned toward her, giving her a shimmer of hope.

"You made progress, I made progress. 'We' "—he

motioned with both hands—"just happened to be seated next to one another."

"But we could make progress," Juliet reasoned, knowing that Seamus was the only person able to have her reinstated at the Foreign Office. "Together. You and I?"

"Lass." His beautiful eyes were kind, soft. "What happened last night was not . . . good. It's distracting us both from our work."

"Yes, and I apologized." Juliet was so frustrated that she was about the cry. She swallowed hard, pressing back the lump in her throat. "If I promise never to kiss you again—"

"No, lass." He wiped an errant tear from her cheek and Juliet felt as if she had been branded by the wet heat of his fingers. "I can't work in the same office as you. I would be happy to keep you apprised of the progress we—"

"It's not the same." Juliet could see that he was trying to understand. "I'm a ruined woman, Seamus. There will be no teas, no musicals or balls unless hosted by my friends. I'll never have a husband or children."

"Surely, somebody will marry you." He sounded as though she were a day-old selection of meats.

"Never mind," she said, wounded and unwilling to expose herself further.

Juliet walked toward the door but Seamus gently grasped her arm. "I am trying to understand you, lass. Truly, I am."

"This is all I have!" His beautiful lips parted, but he said nothing. Juliet pressed her advantage. "Please, let me work with you, Seamus."

"I can't." He shook his head, letting go of her.

"You can't or you won't?" she spat, furious and frustrated.

"Don't do this, Juliet." He opened the parlor door and made for the staircase. "I'm going to bed."

She watched him retreat from the foot of the staircase, his thighs flexing with each step, and then she laughed, desperate.

"You're scared of me, aren't you?" Seamus was very near the first-floor landing and she had to run to catch up to him. "Aren't you?"

He rolled his eyes and turned down the wide corridor with her at his heels.

"You're scared that I will break the code before you do." Juliet was sure she saw fear in his eyes. "That is why you had me dismissed."

"I resigned!"

Seamus opened a door to their right, and when she tried to follow, he stopped, filling the doorway with his presence. He grasped her around the waist and lifted her, placing her in the corridor.

"That's why you 'resigned' then?" Juliet demanded and he attempted to slam the door shut, but she barreled past him.

Juliet glanced around his bedchamber, his inner world. The deep burgundy drapes that hung from the canopy of his large four-poster bed would have dominated the room if Seamus had not been standing in it.

"Get out of my bedchamber!" He pointed to the door.

"Not until you admit that you're scared of my abilities and that is the true reason you presented your ultimatum."

"All right, lass," Seamus said reluctantly. "I'm scared of your intellectual abilities and that is the true reason why I resigned from the Foreign Office. Might I go to bed now?"

It sounded rather silly when he said it, but at least he had admitted it and she should leave. Juliet watched him remove his shirt, his muscled chest as beautiful as she remembered. "You don't mean what you just said."

"Aye, I do." Seamus was popping the buttons of his buckskins as he spoke to her. He was trying to intimidate her just as he had the first time he kissed her. "I'm bloody terrified of you, Juliet. Now go home!"

But she wasn't intimidated and she did not want to go home. "Say, 'I'm afraid you will break the code before me.'"

"Christ Almighty, Juliet." Seamus snapped his coverlet

down and then placed both hands on his trim waist. "What do you want from me?"

Juliet walked over and looked up at him, pleading, "I want my position at the Foreign Office back, Seamus."

"I can't give it to you."

"Then speak to Falcon."

"I did. He refused to accept my resignation or reinstate you."

"Then tell him you changed your mind."

"No." Seamus was shaking his head, not even considering the possibility.

"Why not!"

"Because I can't work with you, Juliet." His jaw was clenched and he was breathing heavily.

She was hurt, and her chin began to quiver, but she had to know. "Am I that difficult to work wit—"

"No." He sounded frustrated as he shook his head.

"Is it because I'm a woman?"

"Aye." Juliet looked down, disappointed, but he lifted her chin and stared into her eyes. "I can't work with you, Juliet, because every time you stand near me, I want to throttle you." She seemed to have that effect on people. "Or kiss you."

Juliet stared at him, stunned, and then managed to whisper, "I prefer being kissed."

Seamus chuckled and Juliet kissed him, forgetting the topic of their conversation. All she could think about was his bare chest, his heat pressing against her. Her hands caressed his muscular shoulders and she smiled at the feel of his thick arms sliding around her waist. His head was bent as he kissed her and Juliet felt completely surrounded by his strength.

And then she remembered their work.

"I forgot to tell you that I've begun a statistical analysis of—"

"Stop talking, Juliet." His breath was ragged as he spoke.

"But this is quite pertinent to the code." Juliet leaned back so that she could look up at him. "I've been formulating an equation based, ironically enough, on a French mathematician's recent findings—"

Seamus scooped her up in his arms and carried her to the bed.

"Juliet." Seamus stared down at her as she lay on the coverlet, his eyes a hot flash of gold. "I really need you to stop speaking, lass."

"Am I boring you?" she asked. "I sometimes forget that the majority of people have no interest in mathematical theories but I thought that perhaps you were differ—"

Juliet inhaled sharply as he yanked at the bodice of her gown, exposing her breasts. The cold in the room hardened her nipples into pink peaks.

Nervous, she licked her lips, trying to concentrate on something else.

"Perhaps I could help you with the sequencing portions of the code. Have you tried the Cavelli method, although finding the correct combination of . . . Oh, God."

His mouth was covering her left nipple, sucking in rhythm while his right hand traveled up her stocking-covered leg. Seamus was so gentle, so sure of where he was going, that Juliet found her body turning toward his large hands, trusting him to find his way.

She moaned at the feel of his mouth on her body and his attention turned to her other breast. Her right hand rose to caress the back of his neck then descended to the power of his naked back.

Encouraged, he lifted his head and settled on top of her, the heat of his hard chest pressing against her bare breasts. He tried to look at her, but then his beautiful eyes drifted closed and his arms tightened around her as Seamus pulled her closer into his body. He gave a masculine sigh that she would have missed if his mouth were not caressing her ear.

Her stomach flipped at the sound of his satisfaction and

then she felt his lips on her neck. Oh, my. She could not think, could not remember what she had been so determined to tell Seamus about the code.

"The commonalities . . ." Juliet said to the world in general and he looked up. "Are rarely . . . found . . ."

She had to stop talking. She could not breathe from the pure pleasure of having Seamus McCurren lying on top of her, looking down at her. His large right hand closed over her breast and he searched her face, gauging her reaction to his touch, to him.

She was shaking, her mind unable to contain her own desire while staring into his eyes. His muscular thighs were heavy and Juliet spread her legs to accommodate his larger frame.

The moment she moved, his golden eyes closed and he gritted his teeth, but it took Juliet a moment to realize why. She had seen pictures of the male form, had even felt his erection against her. But not until his length was pressing her into the mattress did she understand the enormity of the situation.

Juliet felt a moment's panic and then Seamus kissed her and her legs turned to jelly, making the entire endeavor much more plausible. She lifted her shaky legs, wrapping them around the strength of his abdomen, and the feel of him between her thighs sent a moist heat to her very core.

"Oh," Juliet said, lifting her hips so that she could lock her ankles at the small of his back. "That's much better."

"Good God, woman," Seamus whispered over her head, forcing Juliet to arch her back so that she could look up at him.

He groaned again and Juliet could feel him shaking as he braced himself on his forearms. "Are you all right?" Juliet asked, concerned.

"Stop . . ." Seamus looked down at her. "Moving, lass," he finished with considerable effort.

Juliet stilled until he recovered, watching as the muscles

of his chest expanded with each heavy pant of discomfort. And then he was pushing himself off her, coming to settle on the side of his bed. He ran his finger through his dark hair and stared at the floor.

"Go home, Juliet," Seamus said, closing his eyes.

Juliet had never seen a man struggling with temptation before and the thought that she was the source of that struggle made her feel . . . exhilarated.

"All right, Seamus," she said to his beautiful back as she slid the sleeves of her gown up over her shoulders. "I will speak to you at the office—"

"No," Seamus turned to her, shaking his head. "You will not speak to me at the office." He stood, the flat plains of his stomach taut with tension. "I meant what I said. I'll not work with you, Juliet."

"Because I'm a threat to you?" She was furious.

"Because you distract me!"

They stared at one another and she had to admit that he was a bit distracting himself. However, they were both full grown and certainly able to control themselves for the security of their country. Tonight might not be a good example, but surely in the office . . .

"Surely—"

"No." His mind was set. She could see it in his striking eyes as he looked down at her.

How could a man who was so handsome be so cruel?

"Go to hell, Seamus McCurren," she spat, devastated.

Twenty

On Saturday morning, Juliet lay in bed thinking.

She had been thinking about Seamus McCurren for hours when she should have been thinking about the code.

Men were dying in battle and she dreamed of the man who had gotten her dismissed from the one place where she could help them. She should be furious with him, but after last night, seeing him . . . feeling him on top of her, touching him . . .

What was she going to do with herself now? Do needlepoint until her fingers bled, paint until her eyes crossed? Of course, she could always go to the theater and be ignored by every member of polite society.

Oh, that would be enjoyable.

So, if she could not work on deciphering the French code what was she going—

Wait! Why couldn't she work on the code? Why was it necessary to work on decrypting the code at the Foreign Office at all? Could not a private citizen investigate suspicious activities and report them to the Foreign Office if any information came to light?

Juliet swung her legs over the side of her bed and stared at the intricate pattern of her carpet.

And wouldn't it be wonderful if her investigation yielded information before his? Excited, Juliet jumped out of bed and called for her lady's maid, writing out her instructions.

"I want you to have a footman run out and buy these publications." She handed her lady's maid the list of the four newspapers that had printed the markers. "Every day."

"Yes, Lady Juliet." Anne curtsied and began to turn when Juliet thought better of it.

"And don't tell anyone," she said. "Particularly my mother. Just bring the papers straight to my bedchamber."

Determined, Juliet got dressed and went down to the conservatory to meet her mother and cousin for luncheon.

"Good afternoon," Juliet said, the last to arrive.

"You're looking very bright-eyed this morning, darling," her mother observed before placing a napkin across her lap.

"Yes, I am in fine spirits today." Juliet smiled, not about to tell her mother why.

"I'm so glad." Felicity smiled back at her, having listened to Juliet's angry rant for half the night. "I was actually quite concerned for your safety when you were at the Foreign Office. So, I am rather pleased that you shall be spending your days at home with us."

"Mmm." Juliet nodded and her mother looked at her with suspicion in her eyes.

"Yes, I thought you would still be very angry about your dismissal." Her mother watched her carefully, thoughtfully.

"I thought I would be, too," Juliet said, having learned a thing or two about dealing with her mother. "But after speaking with Felicity, I realized that working at the Foreign Office was getting a bit"—Juliet looked at the glass ceiling—"boring, really."

"And was Seamus McCurren getting boring?" her mother asked, still suspicious.

"No," Juliet said, in too good of a mood to be bothered by the reference to her kissing Seamus. "Just insufferable."

"Oh, I quite like Mister McCurren," Felicity said to the room, adding, "He is a bit dark, though. I seem never quite able to determine what he is thinking."

"Yes, dark, brooding, and mysterious is loads of fun, Felicity," Juliet quipped. "No, I would much prefer a gentleman as easy to interpret as Christian St. John."

"Christian?" Felicity asked, "I'd no idea of your interest in him."

"Nor I." Her mother met Juliet's eye, knowing damn well that she was not interested in Christian St. John.

"Yes, well, something to think about if I get desperate for a husband." Juliet sighed. "Somehow I don't think Christian would mind if his wife were ruined. In many ways, I think he would prefer it."

"Oh, my darlings." The countess grinned at their naïveté. "Don't be fooled into thinking that what a gentleman says he wants is what he really desires. It is true the majority of the time. I grant you, but not when it comes to women, nor children for that matter."

"This is a pointless conversation." Juliet shook her head. "As no gentleman bar Christian would marry me."

"I'm not so sure about that." Felicity raised both delicate brows. "There will be many eligible bachelors at Lady Dunloch's ball, which we have all been invited to attend."

"Oh, how lovely." Her mother took a sip of tea. "It will be the perfect opportunity to further your cause."

"And another perfect opportunity for me to look a desperate fool."

"That is not at all true, Juliet." Felicity shook her head. "All the ladies of my acquaintance do not believe for one moment that Lord Harrington . . ." Felicity blushed.

"Dishonored you," Lady Pervill finished, coming to her niece's aid.

"Felicity, none of the gossips are going to gossip to you, now are they?" Juliet argued.

"No, I think Felicity is correct. None of my friends believe the charge either and they would most certainly gossip to me or rather they would hound me until I told them the truth of the matter."

Juliet smiled, seeing a ray of sunshine behind the dark clouds of her ruination. "Perhaps in a few weeks this will all be behind us."

And in the meantime, she would dedicate every waking hour to breaking the E code before Seamus bloody Mc-Curren.

Twenty-one

⟨❧⟩

Madame Richard sat at her desk eating an apple as she read the morning newspapers. She read the papers in the quiet hours of the mornings while her whores still slept and before the afternoon customers began to arrive.

This was her time to be alone, to think, to plan her future. She had amassed quite a large fortune and was beginning to feel the itch to move on, but not just yet.

She still had unfinished business in London.

And increasingly that unfinished business took on the stunning appearance of Seamus McCurren. She stared at the pages of the newspaper and pictured the one man in all of England with the ability to match her, best her mind.

No doubt, that was why she lingered in London longer than she should, to be bested by a man as capable and alluring as Seamus McCurren.

Enigma turned to the second page of the *London Times* and skimmed the article she had written to verify that her marker had appeared as scheduled. But as she continued to read the innocuous commentary, Enigma rose to her feet, furious with what she saw.

"Collin!" she shouted, and hearing her anger, her body-guard quickly opened the door. Enigma looked up at the man, forcing her temper beneath her smile. "Have a seat, Mister Collin."

He did as he was told and she walked to his side dropping the newspaper atop his large lap.

"Mister Collin," she began softly, "did you deliver the article I wrote to the *Times* last week as I requested?"

"Yes." He nodded warily. "I delivered it exactly as I always do. Was there a problem?"

Enigma pulled a dagger from the sheath on her right ankle as she stared down at the man. "How many markers were to appear in the article?"

Mister Collin's forehead creased with confusion. "One marker, same as always."

"Mmm." She tapped her chin with the fingers of her left hand. "One. Yes, that's right. One marker. But shall we count the number of times that an E *actually* appears in the article I entrusted to you?"

"Yes." Mister Collin nodded, knowing there was no other possible answer.

"One." Enigma stabbed at the first E with the tip of her dagger and he grunted as the knife pierced his right thigh. "Two." She stabbed again. "Three," she whispered in his ear before the dagger dropped. "Four." She jabbed. "Five, six." She let the sixth linger in his leg, the newspaper crinkling as she moved it from side to side. "Now, how many markers were scheduled to appear in the article?"

"One," her bodyguard said, his teeth clenched in pain.

"And how many markers did appear?"

"Six."

She removed her dagger from his thigh and pressed her breasts against his back.

"How do you suppose Napoleon's currier will retrieve

all that lovely information I have worked so diligently to gather if he does not know where to go to get it?"

"He can't retrieve it." Collin breathed through the sting of his wounds, crimson slits turning his brown trousers black.

"That's right, he can't retrieve the information, which means that I . . ." she ground out. "Will not receive all that lovely money the French pay me."

"I'll go to the *London Times* straight away and have a little talk with the man who—"

"Damn right you'll find out who is interfering with my code." She walked in front of him, dragging her index finger along his shoulder as she did. "But first, I'm afraid you will have to be punished."

"Yes, Madame Richard," he said. Enigma knew just where to hit him.

"Now, call Mister Youngblood to my office, will you."

Jack Collin met her eye but he knew better than to voice his complaint. He walked evenly from the room and she admired his ability to hide the pain his leg must be causing him.

A few moments later the door opened and Youngblood strolled in. "You wanted to speak with me?" her front man asked, his roguish smile firmly in place.

"Oh, I don't want to speak with you, darling." Enigma laughed, slapping him on the backside while meeting her bodyguard's dark eyes. "Mister Collin, do wait at the door to keep us from being interrupted."

The door closed and her smile was solely for Youngblood. The key to keeping his interest was to give the man an occasional taste, leave him wanting her all the more. It had been two weeks since she had taken Youngblood to bed, but Mister Collin did not need to be made aware of her preference.

No, what Mister Collin needed to know was that he was not the only bull in the pasture. He needed to learn his place and his duty.

Enigma stared at the handsome Youngblood, at his pretty green eyes and beautifully masculine features.

"Get undressed, darling," she ordered and his eyes flared, his excitement increasing the more she ordered him about.

He grinned, taking his time in removing his shirt so that she might better view his bare chest and flat stomach. Youngblood did like to perform.

"Oh, but you are pretty." Enigma looked him up and down, meaning every word. "Now, hurry up with your buckskins so that I can see all of you."

Youngblood striped himself of everything and waited for her next order. She walked up to him, still fully clothed, and pressed her silk gown flush to his nude body. His eyes drifted closed at the feel of her hands on his chest as his erection settled against the folds of her soft gown.

"Sit down," Enigma ordered, making him sit in the chair where Mister Collin had been. "Now, darling," she said, lifting her skirts and settling on his lap, facing him.

"Yes," Youngblood breathed.

"You know how much I like to hear you beg?" She kissed his neck, rubbing her body against his erection. "How much I like to hear you moan?"

"Yes." Youngblood nodded, so very eager to be ridden.

"Louder, darling."

"Yes." He could scarcely talk.

Enigma lifted herself and teased him as she stared into Youngblood's eager green eyes. "Yes," he begged.

"What do you want me to do?" she asked, sure that Collin was listening.

"Ride me, I want you to—" Enigma sank down on his rod and Youngblood groaned with the pleasure as she did. "Oh, God, yes."

His hands cupped her backside as she moved up and down him, shifting her hips to prolong each stroke, each masculine moan of anticipation.

"How do I feel?"

"You feel so . . . damn . . . good," Youngblood said and Enigma smiled, watching the shifting shadows beneath her office door.

"So do you, darling." She closed her eyes to concentrate on her own satisfaction and rolled her hips, taking him deeper.

"Oh, yes, ride me. That's it." Youngblood stopped speaking and just grunted with each delightful thrust and then with a declaration of intent, he screamed, "I'm peaking," loud enough for all of Dante's to hear, let alone Mister Collin.

Enigma felt him go rigid and she looked down at him, increasing her carnal pace. The man was beautiful, and as she watched Youngblood climax, she ran her hand along his pretty cheek.

She closed her eyes and felt her own burgeoning satisfaction cresting. But as Enigma thought of Jack Collin standing in the hall, her fulfillment was altogether disappointing. Youngblood was indeed handsome, but he in no way compared to the raw power of Collin that excited her so.

However, Mister Collin still had to be punished.

"Oh," she moaned, imitating her level of excitement with Collin, and then let out one last feigned whimper of gratification that made Youngblood smirk with masculine conquest.

"Did you enjoy that?"

"You're an excellent ride, Mister Youngblood," she said, leaving him with the notion that she had reached her pinnacle. "But perhaps you should get dressed and welcome our afternoon customers."

He smiled, strutting like a peacock as he retrieved his garments, and she enjoyed watching him put them on.

"Right away, Madame Richard." He swept her a bow, opening the door and looking back at her as Mister Collin watched. "Is their anything else I can do for you?"

"Oh, you've done quite enough already, Mister Young-blood." They stared at one another as if her bodyguard were not standing at the door. "But rest assured that I will call you if I want more of you."

Youngblood grinned before going downstairs to play the part she had hired him to fulfill.

"Come in, Mister Collin," Enigma said, the room still lingering with the scent of lovemaking. Her guard walked toward her, his jaw set in angry granite. "How is your leg?" she asked, caressing the outside of his wounded thigh.

"How do you think?" he said, his eyes meeting hers.

"I would imagine that it hurts," she whispered seductively. "Shall I make it feel better?" Her hand moved to caress his cock and Enigma could see the he was resisting her. But as she continued to stroke his long length, she could see his chest expanding more fully, more frequently.

"Now, go find out who is interfering with my code, Mister Collin." He nodded, his eyes closing. "Or shall I send Youngblood to do that task for you, too."

Collin's large hand wrapped around her wrist and he pulled her hard against his chest. "Why send Youngblood when we both know that you prefer my work to his."

Enigma felt a stab of desire that conflicted with her pecuniary need to control her bodyguard.

She grinned. "I might prefer your work, Mister Collin, but don't delude yourself into thinking that I did not enjoy riding Mister Youngblood. Or," Enigma added, "that there might be a third man I would prefer even more."

Jack glared, his jealousy evident. "Perhaps I should bend Chloe over your desk."

A flash of fury shot through her but she hid it.

"Chloe knows that I will slit her throat if she takes you."

"Jealous?" He grinned.

"No, Mister Collin." Enigma laughed as if he had the mind of a child. "I would slit Chloe's throat for doing something she was not told to do, just as I would slit her throat for failing to complete a task I had given her." His grip on her wrist eased and she let it fall to her side. "Now, go and find out what happened to that article."

Twenty-two

◦❧§❧◦

*J*uliet began her own investigation in the only place she could think to look.

"That's him." She nodded at the clerk of the *London Herald* and watched her footmen approach the man as he locked the office door.

The three men had words and then the clerk was being guided to Juliet's waiting carriage. No doubt lured by the money Juliet had instructed her footmen to offer the man if he joined her.

The thin clerk stepped into her conveyance, followed by one of her footmen.

Juliet smiled at the man, asking, "Do you mind if we drive while we talk?"

"Your coin, isn't it," the greedy clerk said.

"Quite." Juliet tried to ignore the smirk on his smarmy face, ordering the carriage forward. As they began to move, Juliet stared at the clerk and chose her words wisely.

"I have noticed that your publication during the last month or so has made several printing errors."

The clerk shrugged, smiling with condescension. "Happens all the time, miss a letter here—"

"Add an E there."

The man stilled and Juliet knew that she had him. "I don't print the papers, my lady."

"But you do give the articles to the printers."

"Who did you say you was?" the clerk asked and Juliet lied.

"I am a representative of Whitehall who is interested in the identity of the man who paid you to print the E error in those articles."

The clerk went white. "I don't know what you're talking about."

Juliet leaned forward, surprised by her anger, and said through clenched teeth, "May I remind you that we are at war and that you can be hanged for what you are doing."

"Hanged?" The man looked at the two footmen. "For printing a bloody E in me paper!"

"For selling British military secrets to the French."

The clerk swallowed, his eyes reflecting his shock. "I didn't know what he was doing, I swear it."

"Who?" Juliet hid her excitement.

The clerk looked around her carriage as he thought, considered. "No." He shook his head adamantly. "I don't know his name. No."

Juliet could see the fear in the clerk's eyes and she tried to reason with him. "This man may be dangerous but he is nowhere near as dangerous as the full force of the British Empire."

Juliet watched the clerk, sensing how very close she was to learning the identity of the French cryptographer.

"No, I don't know his name." The clerk was shaking his head and Juliet knew that she had lost.

Damnation!

She smiled, frustrated, and quickly altered her plan. "I can see that you are afraid of this man," Juliet said, taking on the roll of the sympathetic lady. "I shall give you three days to think about what you have done. What this man is doing to the soldiers dying for our country."

"Three days?"

"Yes, I shall return next week and we can discuss what is to be done."

"Thank you," the clerk said, grinning as if he had just fleeced her without her knowing.

Juliet smiled back as they rolled to a stop in front of the *Herald*, having come full circle. "No, thank *you*, sir. For I know you shall make the right decision come Monday."

The clerk descended onto the walkway and they drove on. Juliet looked at her footmen, still sitting in the carriage.

"Stop at the corner and follow him," Juliet said. Knowing that this was well beyond their duties, she added, "And do be careful."

The footmen looked at one another and chuckled at her concern as they checked their pistols to verify that they were loaded. They stepped down from the landau and Juliet drove on, wondering if she should go to the Foreign Office and speak with Falcon.

And tell him what?

That a clerk at the *London Herald* might know the cryptographer's identity? No, better to have the man followed and see what became of her investigation.

It was a calculated risk to contact the clerk. In the end, however, Juliet had reasoned that the man would give up the name of the French cryptographer or lead her to him. Either way, she would be able to go to Falcon and his arrogant underling and inform them that she had found the Frenchman on her own.

Juliet smiled at the thought and walked to her sitting room the moment she arrived home.

"I'm back, Anne. How long until dinnertime?" Juliet looked at the stack of unread newspapers by her chaise.

"Two hours."

"Excellent, can you come back in an hour and assist me in dressing?"

"Of course, my lady." Her maid curtsied and left Juliet to her mountain of reading.

Twenty minutes into her research Juliet raised her brows to keep her eyes from closing. The fire was warm and all of this tedious reading was making her decidedly sleepy. She would just finish the *London Times* and have a quick nap before Anne returned to dress her for dinner.

She turned the page and yawned. Two pages and she would be finished. Juliet forced herself to keep looking for patterns when her drowsy eyes snapped open. She scanned the article she was reading and was shocked to find not one but six E anomalies within the same article.

Six!

Why on earth would the cryptographer place more than one marker in the same—

"McCurren!" Juliet groaned to herself.

Juliet grabbed her pelisse and gloves and left the house, dinner completely forgotten.

"Are you dim-witted?" Seamus heard from the study door as he read. He looked up, and upon seeing Juliet Pervill, he exhaled in disbelief.

"I'm sorry, sir." The butler lowered his head in shame.

Seamus rose from his favorite chair and just stared at the woman who shouldn't be there. "William, the lady is all of five foot and . . ." He looked at Juliet. "How tall are you?"

"Three inches."

"Five foot, three inches!" She waited patiently for him to finish dressing down his butler. "And she weighs all of seven stone!"

Juliet snorted.

"And still you cannot keep the woman out of my house?"

She began walking around his library, calmly examining his books and totally unconcerned by his ire.

"She threatened to—"

Seamus was only half listening, distracted by Juliet's leisurely wanderings. Her swaying hips, her meandering walk.

"I don't care what Lady Juliet has threatened to do." Seamus threw his hands in the direction of the study door, saying, "Toss her out."

"I think you will want to hear what I have to say." Juliet dropped into his favorite chair and placed the *London Times* in her lap as if his threat to have her dragged from the room were somehow boring her.

Seamus raised a brow, peering closely at the paper and seeing that Juliet had read his article.

"Leave us," he ordered his butler and then looked at the small woman. "Why did you inquire if I were dim-witted?" he asked the one person in London who could label him as such.

"Because, Mister McCurren," she began, "you have just placed six anomalies in the same article of the *London Times*."

"Did I?" Seamus smiled, enjoying her irritation. "How do you know that it was I who placed the anomalies?" He swept his eyes over her, curious as to her method.

"Mathematic probability."

"Explain?" he asked, sitting on the ottoman.

He looked at her if she were speaking Greek or rather one of the few languages that he did not understand.

God, but the lass was pretty.

"James Habernathy"—she held out one little finger—"you"—a second—"and I"—a third finger—"are the only people who knew in which order the markers were being published. Therefore," she reasoned, "we are the only three who knew which publication would be printing the marker this week."

"Did you ask James if he printed the anomaly?" Seamus inquired, enjoying their game and trying not to notice the elegant curve of her neck.

"No, I have not asked Mister Habernathy." The lass rolled her big blue eyes. "Nor have I asked the French cryptographer if he managed to muck up his own code."

"All right, yes," Seamus admitted. "I hired a man at the *Times* to read all articles submitted for publication. If he found one containing an E, he was to add an E to every paragraph of the article." He shrugged arrogantly, not seeing a problem. "Now that we know their method of relaying information, we can disrupt it."

"I need to know which anomaly is the Frenchman's so that I can analyze it against the other articles."

Seamus stared at her, furious. "You no longer work for the Foreign Office, Juliet."

"Thanks to you." The lass stared back and continued speaking as she rose. "And while your methodology of disrupting the code is extremely effective in the short term, the French will undoubtedly counter."

"How?" He stood. The intellectual in him had to know.

"As much as the Foreign Office would like to believe this cryptographer a stupid man, he is not." Seamus just stared at her. "The simplicity of his code rather brilliantly allows for variances of markers and retrieval sites.

"Therefore . . ." Juliet looked up at him, teaching him the error of his ways. "By disrupting his code just this once, you have effectively lost the opportunity for the Foreign Office to observe those four markers forever." His brows furrowed. "Seamus, you have just told the cryptographer that we are investigating his code and he will change all markers and retrieval sites as soon as is possible."

"I realized that, Juliet," Seamus said, annoyed by her condescension. "However, my main concern is with disrupting the flow of information."

"And if *I* were the cryptographer, I would find out who was disrupting it." She stared at him and for the briefest of moments he saw fear in her lovely eyes. "Promise me that you will be careful, Seamus?"

"The French will be forced to dispatch a man to the *Times* to investigate," Seamus said, ignoring her so that he might hide his sense of gratification for her concern. "I'll inform Falcon of the opportunity first thing tomorrow morning."

"I agree." Juliet nodded, distracted as she gazed at his lips, clearly remembering their last encounter. "I've also spoken with . . ."

The lass blinked, and seeing the look of a woman who had said more than she should have, he demanded, "Whom did you speak with, Juliet?"

"Falcon." They stared at each other, both knowing she was lying.

Seamus put both of his hands on her cheeks, fear clogging his throat. "Please tell me you are not investigating this code on your own, Juliet," he ordered more than asked.

"How could I?" She stepped out of his grasp. "I no longer work for the Foreign Office."

Seamus stared at her, too familiar with her mind to be fooled. "You did not answer the question."

"What if I am investigating the code?" Juliet shrugged, seeing no reason to deny it. "I am no longer working for the Foreign Office and therefore am not subject to its dictates." She met his eyes pointedly. "Nor yours."

"Juliet," Seamus said, his alarm cloaked by anger. "If you continue to investigate this cryptographer, I will have you arrested."

Her eyes turned to slits of blue ice. "You would not dare!"

"Oh, yes." Seamus lifted her chin with one finger so that she would see his determination to protect her. "I would."

They stared at one another for a very long time and Juliet called his bluff. "You don't have the authority to have me arrested."

"I would get it," he said. "You know that I can."

"How?"

"I would inform Falcon that you are interfering with the investigation. After all"—Seamus smiled—"you did just place these six anomalies in the *London Times*."

Her beautiful mouth fell open when she saw that he was serious. He would have kissed her if he was not quite certain that Juliet would bite straight through his bottom lip.

"That is not amusing, Seamus."

"It was not meant to be, Juliet."

It was meant to keep her safe, protected. But increasingly Seamus felt that he was the one who needed to protect himself from Juliet Pervill.

"Fine," she said and turned toward his study door.

"Fine?" Seamus repeated on a rush of air. "What the hell does that mean?"

She shrugged her pretty shoulders dismissively. "I'll not investigate the cryptographer." Her eyes gleamed with defiance and he knew instantly that she had something else in mind.

"Juliet!" Seamus growled at her. "What are you planning to do?"

"Good evening, Mister McCurren."

The Welshman watched the lovely Juliet Pervill leave Seamus McCurren's home, her head lifted in defiance as the Scot glared at her from his front door.

He smiled as he watched Lady Juliet's lithe little body climb into her carriage. She looked every bit the lady, fresh and innocent. But her continued visits to McCurren's home led one to conclude that the innocent young lady was not so innocent.

His cock jumped at the very thought.

He kicked his horse in the side and followed the lady's carriage, propelled more by his increased fascination than by his fee.

The carriage rolled to a stop in front of Lord Appleton's town home and the Welshman steered his horse across the street. He watched as Lady Juliet got out of her carriage and climbed the front steps. But then she stopped and turned in his direction.

The lady stared into the dark and he smiled, wanting her to see him, to know that he knew what carnal acts she was performing with Seamus McCurren. A burst of light bloomed, lighting up the left side of her pretty face as the front door of the house opened, drawing her attention away from him.

Juliet Pervill stepped inside and he looked up at the second floor of the house. The Welshman grinned as a light moved across her bedchamber window and he waited, picturing the girl as she undressed and then got into bed.

Aroused, he gave a regretful sigh and then turned his horse to go and watch the man who had just taken the lady to bed, all the while wishing that he were that man.

Twenty-three

꧁❦꧂

Mathematical columns were like music to Enigma, and she could spot a sour note quickly. She tapped her finger on the paper and said, "You made an error here."

The accountant glanced at the neat rows and stared at the miscalculation, terrified. "Yes, you're correct. I apologize and will—"

"Are you trying to rob me, Mister Matthews?" Enigma whispered in his ear so that he might feel her threat.

"No!" The accountant shook his head and swallowed. "No, I would never . . . that is to say, I fully understand the penalty for doing so."

"Very well, Mister Matthews." Enigma smiled, more from the profit Dante's Inferno had brought her than for the accountant's compliance. "I believe you. Now, finish balancing my books."

The man nodded and Enigma walked out of the tiny office at the back of the brothel, only to be intercepted by

Chloe. "The Welshman has just arrived. I put him in bed-chamber four."

"Where's Mister Collin?"

"Downstairs," Chloe said, never asking questions.

"Keep it that way."

Enigma walked into the brothel room and was stunned by the amount of anticipation she felt when she saw the little Welshman sitting on the well-worn bed.

"Good evening, Mister Jones. It is so nice to see you again," she said to her sometimes employee.

"Evening." He bobbed his graying head and looked around the room, nervous as a virgin in a roomful of rogues.

"It will be just the two of us tonight," Enigma informed him, not wanting Mister Collin with her when she received this particular report. "Is that all right with you, Mister Jones?"

The man paled. "Oh, yes. I . . . that's fine, just fine by me."

Enigma walked toward the Welshman, flashing a bit of thigh. "Just tell me what you have observed of Seamus Mc-Curren this past week."

"Well." The man swallowed when she sat next to him on the bed. "Mister McCurren keeps to a routine."

"Does he?" Enigma's left brow rose, fascinated with any insight she might gain into Seamus McCurren's interesting mind.

"Yes." The Welshman referred to his ever-present pad of paper. "He leaves his home at the same time every morning, early like." The man's beady blue eyes looked up to verify that she was following. "And he comes home at about the same time every afternoon. Excepting this one time when he was right late."

"And where does Mister McCurren go every morning?" she asked, envisioning the handsome Seamus McCurren's movements.

"Whitehall," Enigma stilled but the little man continued

to talk. "Mister McCurren goes to the Foreign Office, every day like clockwork."

"Tell me." Her heart was racing and she smiled to divert his attention away from the importance of the question. "Have you ever heard anyone call Mister McCurren by the name 'Falcon'?"

Her breathing was becoming shallow from trepidation and more than a little excitement as she waited to discover if the brilliant Seamus McCurren was also the elusive Lord Falcon the French were so keen to capture.

"No." The Welshman shook his head and then laughed. "Although he does have a ladybird, do you think she could be his Falcon?"

"Ladybird?" Enigma asked, annoyed.

"Lady . . ." The man looked down at his notes. "Juliet, that's right, Lady Juliet Pervill."

"I want to know everything." Enigma raised her forefinger to emphasize her point. "Everything about this woman." And then she remembered. "Is she Lord Pervill's brat?"

"That's the one." The Welshman nodded. "Got her reputation ruined a couple of weeks back when she was caught entertaining Lord Harrington. Guess the lady has moved on to Mister McCurren now."

"Lord Harrington?" Enigma thought of the middle-aged drunk and the stunning Seamus McCurren, sure that these men would never feed from the same trough. "What happened with Lord Harrington?"

"She were caught in her cousin's library with him. The girl denies it, of course, says Lord Harrington done it to get back at her father." Enigma smiled, remembering that Lord Pervill was now the proud owner of Lord Harrington's town home. "Pretty little thing, Lady Juliet Pervill, clean like."

Her nose wrinkled at the man's defining pretty as clean. "You've done very well, Mister Jones. Has Mister McCurren had any other guests to his town home?"

"His brother visits a lot and Christian St. John. Juliet Pervill, of course." Enigma felt a flash of irritation. "That's it thus far, but we ain't been watching him very long."

"Keep watching him." Enigma nodded as she thought of her profitable code. It would take a very intelligent man to detect it much less be able to identify the publication in which it would next appear and understand how to disrupt it. "Keep watching Seamus McCurren," she repeated with a slight smile.

Twenty-four

The Marquess Shelton held the invitation to the weekend gathering in his right hand as he made his way toward that very event. It was a two-day journey from town but something about the invitation had compelled him to go.

" 'Lord Harrington cordially invites you to Harrington Hall for a meeting of the minds,' " Ian read aloud. " 'Meeting of the minds'?"

He shook his head. From what he had heard of the man who had so maliciously ruined Juliet Pervill, Lord Harrington had very little mind to meet.

Why not then send out invitations for a hunting weekend or a fishing party? Even a musical gathering would seem more likely than a "meeting of the minds."

The invitation was decidedly odd and it was that peculiarity that had prompted Ian to accept the invitation. He had taken precautions, of course, two pistols as well as informing his butler of his whereabouts for the upcoming weekend.

No, if anything, the weekend might prove amusing, and

if not, he could always retire to his bedchamber and polish his upcoming speech to Parliament.

Committed, Ian stared at the garish gate as they rambled onto Lord Harrington's land. The parks of the estate were pristine and quite beautiful. Yet as they continued to travel mile after mile with no cultivation in sight, Ian began to wonder how the man sustained the estate.

He arrived at Harrington Hall at the same time as several other gentlemen. Men he knew and men he knew of. Well respected all. They were shown to their rooms and Ian stared out his first-floor window at the perfectly tended lawn, the sculpted hedges, and an impressive array of fountains.

The clothes in which he traveled came off first and he walked to the wash basin to refresh himself before he dressed for dinner. A half an hour later Ian joined the others in Lord Harrington's drawing room, sinking into the right side of a settee as he waited and watched.

"Thank you all for coming," Harrington began, "to the first of what I hope to be several weekends in which prominent members of society gather to discuss the difficulties facing our nation and the possible solutions to those problems."

"Forgive me, Lord Harrington," an earl drawled, "but isn't that the function of Parliament?"

Several men nodded, Ian included. He raised his finger toward a footman and asked for a brandy while he awaited Harrington's ineloquent answer.

"Yes, of course." Lord Harrington smiled at the earl. "However, Parliament is not conducive to extended conversations pertaining to these issues. Nor are the less influential members of the House willing to state their true beliefs or possible solutions in front of the entire body of Parliament for fear of reprisals."

"A regrettable fact, to be sure," the earl continued, "yet would not that same situation arise at this gathering?"

"Not if the members invited here for the weekend come

with a willingness to listen to the others," Harrington explained.

"It is my hope that these weekend gatherings will allow for an extended voice to those members who are rarely heard. And if not"—Lord Harrington held up his glass—"then we shall have a jolly good time hunting."

The other men laughed and Ian smiled politely at Lord Harrington, a man who had yet to show his face during the current session of the House of Lords.

"What shall we discuss first?" a young viscount from Bath asked.

"I suggest we begin with the most pressing problem our nation faces. Napoleon."

The group of English peers burst into a heated conversation, several maligning the lineage of France's peasant emperor.

"Bloody Corsican," one gentleman said, drawing Ian's attention. "We should sail to Calais then march to Paris while the bulk of his army remains on the Peninsula."

"You forget," an older man said, "the bulk of *our* army remains on the Peninsula with the bloody Corsican."

"I think we should call Wellesley back to England to guard our own bloody borders," the earl standing by the fireplace interjected.

Ian glanced at Lord Harrington, who sat in his chair like a proud vicar overseeing his parish.

"What do you think should be done about Napoleon, Marquess Shelton?" a younger man asked, deferring to the most senior man in the room.

Ian cleared his throat and spoke loudly enough for all the gentlemen to hear.

"My opinion is, of course, a matter of public record. I feel very strongly that Napoleon must be stopped before he has a chance to accumulate enough force to invade England," he said, choosing his words carefully.

"But do you not think our infantry would be put to better

use if they were left here in England," the earl continued to argue his point, "rather than losing our soldiers and the ships transporting them to fight in foreign lands?"

"No, I do not." Ian stared at the earl, trying to decide if he was merely playing the opposite side of the coin or if the man truly believed what he was saying. "If we wait until Napoleon amasses the armies of Europe, he will march through England as if it were Lord Harrington's lovely gardens."

The room erupted into debate, and Ian sat back and watched the others argue, keeping a sharp eye on Lord Harrington. The spirits were freely given and the debate became increasingly loud until finally, at midnight, Ian could take no more of it and excused himself in favor of bed.

He walked the deserted corridors of Harrington Hall, the masculine voices fading to a murmur. He fished in his pocket for several moments, admonishing himself for not having brought his valet. His hand closed over the cold key and Ian pulled it from his pocket and opened his bedchamber door.

However, he stilled when the first thing he saw was a very feminine backside as a chambermaid bent over his unmade bed.

"Oh, pardon, my lord." The pretty little brunette curtsied, her bright eyes shining with lingering surprise. "I was sent to warm your bed." Ian quirked a brow until the girl pointed to a bed warmer sitting on the hearth of his fireplace. "I tended your fire, too."

"Yes, thank you very much," Ian said, stepping to the side so that the girl might leave.

The chambermaid smiled and took one step toward the door and tripped on the edge of the carpet, crashing into his chest. His hands darted around her waist to keep the girl from falling to the floor. He steadied her but the chambermaid did not move from his arms. Instead she looked up at him, her breasts pressed firmly against his chest.

"Is there anything else I can do for you, my lord?" The chambermaid batted her lashes while rubbing herself against his cock.

Ian smiled down at the girl, asking, "What did you have in mind," curious as to where this would go.

She grabbed his right hand and lifted it to her breast. "Anything you can think of, Lord . . . What did you say your name was?"

"Shelton." Ian gave her his most seductive smile. "Miss . . ."

"Mira." She began unbuttoning his trousers. "Just call me Mira."

Twenty-five

※

The clerk walked into Dante's Inferno, wanting to speak with the man who had paid for his frequent visits to his favorite opium den.

The skinny clerk rubbed the corner of his eye and scratched his head as he scanned the room. Not seeing the big man, he walked to a little man leaning against the wall.

"You work here?"

"Might do," he said, a Welsh accent blanketing his words.

"You seen a man with a nasty scar across his face?" He dragged his finger down his right cheek.

The Welshman lifted his bushy black eyebrows and then looked him over from head to toe. "What do you want with him?"

Irritated, the clerk ran his fingers through his hair, white flakes showering down on his dark jacket like snow. "Never you mind. I need to speak with him is all, and believe you me, he will want to speak with me."

"Let's see then." The hairy plug of a man jerked his head, indicating that the clerk should follow him.

He turned to the bar on the right side of the narrow central corridor and smiled at the pretty whores who wiggled in customers' laps, convincing them to pay for more than their drinks. The men laughed and the whores laughed harder and the clerk wondered if he would be rewarded with more than money for his information.

Brushing the white flakes from his black lapel, the clerk glanced at the left side of the room. Not so much laughing going on there. Gentlemen sat at round wooden tables with a much larger baize-covered table sitting in the middle of them.

A gentleman as smooth as the devil was dealing cards to the other players, and the clerk blinked as he walked into a particularly thick cloud of cheroot smoke.

The sturdy little man placed his foot on the stairs and the low rumble of men's voices gave way to the feminine howls of whores plying their trade. He grinned as they turned to the right and the man knocked on the far door.

"Yes," a woman said and he was confused.

"I don't want a whore," the clerk said and the Welshman just stared at him, opening the office door.

He blinked against the bright lights that contrasted to the dim gaming room below and listened as the Welshman said, "This man says he has urgent business with Mister Collin."

The clerk nodded as he looked from his escort to the muscular man with the scar across his hard face. "How do, Mister Collin." He bobbed his head in greeting to the familiar face.

"What do you want?" a whore said and the clerk looked at her for the first time. She was beautiful. Blond with long legs and the perfect-sized breasts for a man to grab hold of.

"I've come about a lady."

The whore snorted, saying, "Get him out of here," to the short Welshman who had brought him.

"No, I don't want a whore. A lady." He scratched his right cheek. "A lady come to visit me at the *Herald*. Small and young with big blue eyes, sorta pretty."

The hairy man looked at the blond whore and pointed to a chair but asked him, "Chestnut hair?"

"Yeah, that's her." The clerk nodded, sitting.

"Sounds like Lady Juliet," the Welshman said.

"The lady invited me to her carriage and told me that she was from Whitehall and that them mistakes I've been putting in the *Herald* is something to do with the war."

The beautiful whore and Mister Collin glanced at each other and he knew what he was telling them was important.

"I thought I should tell you as I'm supposed to meet with her tomorrow."

"Where?"

"The *Herald* at closing time, six o'clock." The clerk sat up. "And there is something else, too."

"Yes," the whore said.

"I've been followed for the past few days."

"Were you followed here?" she asked and the clerk grinned.

"I give them the slip at Covent Garden and come here quick as I could. Thought Mister Collin should know about the lady."

"You did the right thing by coming here." The whore smiled and walked toward the hairy man at the door. "Go ask Mister Matthews to get this man ten pounds."

Ten pounds!

The clerk smiled as the Welshman left. "Thank you very much," he said to Mister Collin as he tried to picture the amount of opium ten pounds would buy him.

"I do have one more question," the whore said from behind him.

"What do you wanna know?" He scratched the side of his nose and then his ear.

"Why did you agree to meet with this lady in the first place?"

The clerk opened his mouth to answer but was startled by the sight of blood squirting across the room. His neck felt wet and then he felt the searing pain. His hands went to his throat as he tried frantically to close the slit she had opened across his neck. Thick liquid oozed between his fingers, spilling onto his dirty jacket.

His eyes grew wide and he looked at Mister Collin for assistance, but he and the woman just stood there, talking as he bled.

"Go to the meeting and bring Juliet Pervill to me. Take the Welshman to identify her but don't bring her to Dante's. Take her to the inn."

"Right."

The clerk sucked in a breath but it didn't make it to his lungs as it bubbled out of his gapping throat. The room was going dim. His eyes rolled back in his head, and as he lost consciousness, the clerk wished that he had made it to the opium den one last time before he died.

It was six o'clock and Juliet squinted against the darkening sky as several men emerged from the front entrance of the *London Herald*, none of them the traitorous clerk.

She forced herself to wait another half hour before she called to her footmen, "See if the clerk is in the office."

The older of the footmen bowed, eager to redeem himself after having lost sight of the clerk at Covent Garden. "Yes, ma'am."

The footmen looked from left to right on the sparsely populated walkway and then knocked on the door. Juliet watched anxiously, and the older man glanced at her before turning the knob. It gave and he signaled to the younger footman, who nodded, his hand at his waist, touching what she presumed to be his pistol.

She stared at the door, her heart pounding at the guilt pooling in her chest. Juliet reminded herself that her footmen were in no danger, that she had merely asked them to inquire as to the clerk's whereabouts within the newspaper's office. However, the longer she waited with no sign of her servants, the more Juliet felt that she should have gone with them.

She opened the door to her carriage and looked up at her coachman. "Wait here, I'll be back in just a moment."

The man nodded, thinking nothing of her request as he had no idea of their true mission at the *Herald*. Juliet had kept that information between herself and her loyal footmen, not wanting her mother to discover that she was investigating the code on her own.

She walked to the door and opened it, peering into the darkened lobby of the *Herald*. The smell of extinguished lamp oil still hung in the air and Juliet took a step forward, closing the door.

The hairs at the nape of her neck bristled and she turned to her right, catching a glimpse of her footmen lying on the floor the instant before a dark force looming over her grabbed her from behind.

She began to scream, but the man's hand clamped over her mouth so violently that her mind reeled with wild pictures of a very violent death.

"The clerk sends his apologies for not meeting you." The man gave a burst of breathy amusement, the note of cruelty raising gooseflesh on her arms. "But as my employer slit his throat, it is very unlikely that he would have spoken overmuch to a representative of Whitehall."

Juliet closed her eyes, berating herself for concocting such a dangerous lie. She jerked her head away from the man's hand, thinking to use his misconception to her advantage. "Whitehall knows I'm here."

She tried to turn to look at the man but he grabbed her chin so hard that she winced.

"We better leave then, hadn't we." He laughed, stuffing a piece of muslin in her mouth.

He pushed her forward and Juliet glanced at her footmen, looking for any indication that they were alive. She saw that one of them was breathing and Juliet prayed that her coachman would find them soon.

The man shoved her toward the back of the large building and then stopped. She tried again to turn her head to look at him but he grabbed a fistful of her hair, jerking her head back against his hard chest.

"Draw attention to us and you will suffer the same fate as the clerk."

Juliet nodded, hearing the cold indifference in his voice and knowing this man would not hesitate to kill her. He opened the door to the alley and propelled her to a waiting carriage. She stepped up and her brows furrowed at the sight of a small man that Juliet could have sworn she had seen before.

"Is this her?"

"That's her." The hairy man smiled as he reached up to tie a blindfold over her eyes and then she remembered. She had seen him riding just outside her house.

He had been watching her, she realized.

"Did you have to kill anybody?" the man asked with a distinct Welsh accent.

"Didn't have to," the larger man said, and Juliet sighed with relief.

The big man pulled her right arm back so roughly that Juliet grunted against the muslin gag. She felt a band of cold metal around her wrist and then he was yanking her left arm, causing her shoulder to crash against the squabs.

The manacles clamped closed and Juliet felt her panic rise at the finality of the ominous sound. She had to think, sure that she was safe until she met with the French cryptographer.

And then he would slit her throat.

Seamus!

Did they know about Seamus?

No, the clerk had not known about Seamus and she was sure that the Frenchman wanted information from her, indicating that he had little. But what information could she provide that would keep her alive?

She was still thinking when she felt the carriage had stopped. The Welshman pushed her up an outer flight of stairs as the bigger man spoke, ordering, "Put her in the first room. I'll leave you here while I inform Enigma of her arrival, but it might take a few minutes for us to get over to the inn."

Enigma. That must be the cryptographer and they were holding her at an inn. Juliet felt a ray of hope, sure that there would be guests in the other rooms.

"Right," the Welshman said and a door opened, blasting her with warm air.

Their footsteps echoed in what her senses told her was a narrow corridor and the small man came to a stop, opening a door and guiding her by the arm into what she assumed was the first room. She took small steps so as not to trip and then the Welshman turned her and Juliet's back hit a wall.

"Sit down." The left band of steel came off only to be fastened again.

He turned her so that her back pressed against something hard and then she felt the mattress and Juliet realized that her manacles had been strung around a bedpost.

"They'll be coming for you shortly," the Welshman said and Juliet stilled at the note of regret in his voice.

She heard him walk toward the door and Juliet tried to use the sound to orient herself in the room. The door opened and closed and then she knew that she was alone.

Juliet worked quickly, feeling up and down the bedpost and determining that she had but two options. Break the thick side rail of the bed or lift the sturdy wooden bed frame off the floor entirely.

Neither seemed likely.

Making her decision, Juliet pressed her back to the heavy wooden post, butting her heels against her backside. Her left hand was able to grasp the underside of the side rail, but her right hand was too small to hold the round wooden bedpost.

She took two breaths and held the last, pushing up with her feet. The bed lifted slightly from the floor, the manacles digging into her wrists as she strained against the weight of the wood. Juliet quickly dropped her arms and tried to slip the metal beneath the post, but the wood hit the floor before she was even close to getting out from under it.

Juliet began to cry, sure that she would never leave this room alive if she did not free herself. *Think.* She took a deep breath. *Think!*

Leverage. Use the bed against itself.

Juliet lifted the bed again but quickly turned, pressing the bedpost between her back and the wall. She pushed as hard as she could with her feet, sliding her back down the smooth bedpost, her arms stretching to get the manacles from underneath.

Her teeth were clenched against her gag, and her thighs burned from holding up the weight of the wood, but she only had a few inches to go. Her hands hit the floor and she was pulling them beneath the post when it slipped from between her shoulders, not enough of her back pressing against the post to keep it in place.

"No," Juliet whispered and then she realized that the post was resting on the metal bar connecting the right and the left cuffs of her restraints. Her heart stopped and she tried to slow her breathing. She would have nothing but her wrists with which to pull the manacles free.

Juliet leaned forward, closing her eyes as she pictured the post in her mind's eye. She could feel the bar scraping between the floor and the bottom of the bedpost and Juliet knew that she was making progress.

She stopped and took several breaths against the pain of her ripping flesh and then leaned forward again. The manacle gave and Juliet hit herself in the small of the back, she had been pulling that hard.

She gave one long sigh of relief before tackling the problem of her blindfold and cuffs. Juliet lay down, the manacles at the small of her back. She concentrated, thanking God for the first time in her life that she was small. She pushed against the floor with her feet, rocking back on her shoulders and wedging her backside between her arms.

Damn these skirts!

She rocked again, wiggling her small body between her arms until the manacles gave, hitting the backs of her knees. Juliet folded herself, dipping her right foot and then the left beneath her restraints.

Her shoulder ached as she ripped the blindfold from her eyes. She looked about the room, removing her gag, and then tilted her head to retrieve a hairpin. She picked the lock of her restraints as she thought.

She could scream, drawing the attention of the inn guests. But she would also draw the attention of her captors. This Enigma had brought her to the inn for a reason, and the best thing to do would be to slip out as quietly and as quickly as possible.

Her decision made, Juliet walked to the window and glanced down at the street below. She had no idea where she was and returned her attention to the manacles' lock. It gave and she moved on to her right wrist, which was far more difficult to unlock with her less dexterous left hand.

Finally, she gave up. She opened the window, making sure that the cuffs dangling from her right wrist did not break the glass. Then she heard it.

The door opened and she turned, standing eye to eye with the Welshman.

"Where do you think you are going?"

"To Whitehall," and then she remembered the note of

regret in the Welshman's voice when he had left her to die. "You know they intend to kill me."

The Welshman nodded and it was a shocking confirmation of her fears. Juliet just stared at the man, trying to read his mind as he closed the door. It was the way he looked at her, his head slightly lowered, that made Juliet raise her chin.

"I am the daughter of an earl and servant to His Majesty King George, and yet I am to die in my own country at the hands of a Frenchman."

His thick black brows furrowed and she realized that he had no idea whom he served. "What are you saying?"

"Your employer did not mention that he was selling secrets to France?" Juliet shook her head. "Whom did you think you were killing for?"

"I'm a blackmailer and a thief, but I've never killed a man."

"How about a woman?"

"Never!" The man lowered his eyes and Juliet suspected that he had become a thief out of desperation, but that did not excuse his current reticence.

"Are you willing to start now?"

The Welshman closed his eyes and she could see that he was struggling with his conscience.

"No." He walked toward her and Juliet held her breath, not sure what he intended to do. He pointed across the alley to the roofline on the other side.

"Don't take to the streets. They'll find you straight away, but they will never think to look for you on the rooftops. Stay up there as long as you can, Lady Juliet, do you hear me?"

"Yes," Juliet nodded. She started to climb out the window but the Welshman stopped her.

"Before you go, you must do one thing for me."

"Of course," Juliet said, willing to agree to anything.

"Strike me with the manacles."

"What?" Juliet was horrified.

"You must hit me with all your might so that they will find me without my senses."

"You're not going to stay here?" She thought of the cold man and of what he would do to the Welshman when he returned to find her gone.

"I have to until I can warn me brother. He's off on a job and will return in a few days' time."

"They might kill you."

"Better me than you." He grinned, resigned to his fate, and she touched his cheek as thanks. "Now, the harder you hit me, the more likely they will believe me when I wake." He turned his back to her. "Hit me here." The Welshman pointed to the crown of his head. "Hurry up."

Juliet took a deep breath and then swung the metal cuffs with all her might. He dropped like a sack of potatoes and she stared at the gash in his scalp, knowing that his pain would keep him alive.

Satisfied that the Welshman was still breathing, Juliet balanced herself on the narrow windowsill. She lifted her skirts and concentrated on the rooftop opposite her.

The alley was not wide but she would be dropping from a second-floor window to the roof of a one-story building. If she were to break her leg in the fall, she would be captured. Picking a spot least likely to kill her, Juliet bent her knees and hurled herself into the void.

She landed on the opposite roof, falling to her side, her right shoulder smashing into the chimney. Juliet glanced back at the window and began to run from roof to roof. She was four buildings away when she heard the shouts.

She flattened herself against the side of the chimney stack, straining to hear what the man was saying. She knew from the cruel tone of his voice that it was the same man who had kidnapped her.

Juliet could hear her heart pounding in her ears like a steady, urgent drum. Her mind moved quickly as she chose her path. She lifted her skirts, moving stealthily as she kept low to ensure that she could not be seen from the street, all the while repeating the Welshman's order in her head.

Stay to the rooftops as long as you can.

And then the rooftops ran out.

A ladder led to the ground below but Juliet hesitated, terrified that the cryptographer's crew would be searching the streets. And then she saw a hackney ambling down the road, looking for a fare.

Grabbing hold of her courage, Juliet ran down the stairs, her eyes sweeping the walkways for any threat. She darted across the street and looked up at the hackney driver.

"Belgrave Square," she said, jumping into the dirty conveyance before it had fully stopped.

"Right you are, my lady." The man tipped his hat.

The landau rolled forward and Juliet pressed her back against the squabs so hard that the wood supporting them groaned. She was shaking, but as the hackney picked up speed, Juliet began to believe that she would make it to the house alive.

Twenty-six

❧

Seamus was out of his mind with fear.

Countess Pervill had come to his home two hours ago to inform him that Juliet had gone to the *London Herald* and had not been seen since.

It was his fault, of course. He knew that she was planning a line of investigation pertaining to the code. He should have watched her; hell, he should have stood guard at her bedchamber door.

Seamus paced his study, not knowing where else to look for her. He had gone with Falcon's guards to the *Herald*, but she was not there. He knew the cryptographer had taken her. If he had been clever enough, he would have broken the code and Juliet would be safe.

Sinking into his chair with the weight of his guilt, Seamus put his head in his hands. His fault. If anything happened to Juliet, he would never forgive himself.

A knock sounded at the door and his head snapped up.

Seamus jumped to his feet, his heart racing, not sure he wanted to hear that she had been found.

Alive, please God, let her be alive.

And then the door opened and he closed his eyes, swallowing the lump in his throat.

"I'm sorry to disturb you, Seamus," Juliet said. "I don't know why I told the hackney driver to come here—"

He scooped her up in his arms and headed back to his study, shouting, "Get some warm water and then send word to Countess Pervill that her daughter is here." Seamus stared at her face, searching for confirmation that she was well. "Are you all right?"

She nodded and the dirty smudge on her chin began to quiver. "Yes," she whispered, barely audible.

Overcome with relief, Seamus pulled her to his chest then lowered her to the settee in front of the fire. He speared her hair with his fingers and pulled out the remaining pins as he searched her scalp for bumps and bruises. Her pelisse was next and Seamus took care to slide it off gently, noting that the right shoulder was torn at the seam.

"Did they touch you?" He held her eyes, both of them knowing what he was asking.

Juliet shook her head and Seamus closed his eyes, able to breathe again. She winced as she pulled her arms from the pelisse and he stared down at her wrists, feeling a rage deeper than anything he had felt before.

The long sleeves of her gown were soaked with blood, and with the depth of her cuts, it must have been terribly painful to have the lace rubbing over them.

"We need to remove your gown to see to these wounds, Juliet."

"All right." She nodded and his butler returned with warm water and a stack of clean muslin cloths.

Seamus glanced over his shoulder, not letting go of Juliet as he ordered, "Fetch a doctor."

When Seamus looked back, he saw that Juliet was trying to unlace her gown. "Here, let me."

"Thank you, Seamus," she whispered. "I really am sorry to be a bother."

"Stop talking nonsense." Seamus slipped her gown from her shoulders and then prepared her for what was to come. "Some of the blood may have dried to the sleeves."

"I understand," Juliet said and he could see that she did.

He peeled the sleeve away and it killed him to see her beautiful face contorting with pain. She let out several pants before the first sleeve relented, and when he grabbed the other sleeve, Juliet held up her right forefinger.

"Give me a moment, will you, Seamus."

He watched her face, amazed that she had not even made a sound to indicate her obvious discomfort. Seamus stroked her face and Juliet tried to smile as he whispered, "Take all the time you need."

He stroked her face two more times and then she nodded. "I'm ready."

Seamus grabbed the other sleeve, trying to decide if it would be less painful to yank the sleeve or move slowly as he had with the first.

Somewhere in between, he decided and pulled.

A rush of air escaped her when her arm was free and he could clearly hear her say, "Damnation!"

He looked down at the damage to her wrists, forcing himself concentrate on helping Juliet and not the urge to beat the men who had done this to her.

Seamus dipped a bit of cloth in the warm water and gingerly wiped at the worst of the blood.

"They tied your wrists?" he asked, now seeing that her wrists had been rubbed raw.

"Manacles. I left them in the hackney."

He met her eyes, his jaw clenched as he tried to calm himself. "Are you going to tell me what happened or am I to continue guessing?"

She looked down at her wrist as he continued to dab at them, all the while keeping his eyes on her downturned face.

"Well," Juliet began tentatively. "Do you recall that I had gone to the *Herald* to inquire as to printing practices?"

"Yes."

She looked at the ceiling, avoiding his eyes. "I had a suspicion, well, a feeling really, that the unpleasant clerk knew something about the anomaly."

"Go on."

She met his gaze and he could see that she was fearful of his reaction, fearful of upsetting him. "I questioned him, telling him I was from Whitehall and—"

"Oh, my God, Juliet." Seamus ran his hands over his head, not knowing what else to do with them. "You didn't tell them your name?"

"Of course not," she said, her charming nose wrinkled with offense. "How brainless do you think I am?" He lifted both brows as if speculating, and she rushed ahead.

"The clerk told me, in a roundabout way, that he had no idea what the misprint was for and he refused to tell me the cryptographer's name. I pressed him but he still refused so I told him I would give him a few days to think about the harm he was doing to his country.

"He left and I had my footmen follow him, thinking either he would tell me the Frenchman's name or tell the Frenchman that we were looking for him. Either way we would know his identity."

Seamus nodded, impressed with her logic. "So what happened?"

"My footmen lost the clerk." Seamus grinned at her note of irritation. "So, I was forced to meet him at the appointed time, hoping that he had changed his mind. But the clerk never showed and I sent my footmen into the *Herald*. When they didn't come out, I went in looking for them."

Seamus groaned, his heart thundering with something . . .

anger, he supposed. "Juliet, how could you have done something so dangerous?"

"I'm not an idiot, Seamus." Her brilliant eyes flared. "I didn't think the scrawny clerk would be a danger to my *armed*"—she emphasized—"footmen. I just thought the clerk was finishing some paperwork and I went into the office to question him inside rather than wait."

She paused, closing her eyes, and Seamus could see that she was still shaken by what had happened to her.

"I opened the door and saw my footmen on the floor." She met his eye. "They are all right, aren't they? The man said he hadn't killed them."

"Yes, they're fine." Seamus nodded and her shoulders relaxed. "Your footmen came back to the house and told the countess that you were missing. Now, tell me about this man who . . ." He couldn't say it, the fear of her abduction all too raw.

"He was big and cold and would not have hesitated to kill me."

The heavy weight in his chest returned. "How did you escape?"

"They took me to an inn and locked the manacles to a bedpost, but I managed to lift the bed."

"You?" Seamus looked down at the tiny woman.

"You would be surprised at how strong a person can be when someone is trying to kill you."

Seamus began ripping the muslin cloth into strips, the process very gratifying.

"I was just about to jump out the window of the inn—"

"Jump?"

"When the other man came back."

"What other man?"

"The Welshman. He helped me escape because he knew they were going to kill me. Before I hit him with my manacles—"

"You hit the man helping you?" His mind was reeling but Juliet just kept talking.

"I hit him so that it would not appear as though he had been helping me." Seamus nodded to her logic. "However, before I hit the Welshman, he told me to keep to the rooftops because they would never think a lady would jump to the next roof."

"No, they wouldn't, would they." Seamus was having a difficult time with the information himself.

"So, I jumped to the roof, hired a hackney and . . ." She blushed. "Came here."

Seamus wrapped the bandages around her wrists and then tore her bloodstained sleeve to make her more comfortable. "What part of town were you in?"

"No idea. I was so . . ." Juliet cleared her throat, embarrassed by her oversight. "Distressed that I did not think to ask the hackney driver where he had picked me up until he was gone. I'm sorry."

Seamus put her gown to rights and then gathered her in his arms. She rested her head against his shoulder and he whispered, "It doesn't matter, Juliet. All that matters is that you're safe."

Seamus stroked her back and kissed the top of her head while she recovered. He leaned down so that he could kiss her, take away the horrible ordeal she had just survived. But when he looked into her eyes, Seamus could see that she had been thinking while she leaned against him.

"You know what this means, don't you, Seamus."

Disappointed, he reached for the soiled rags and threw them in the water bowl, rising. "No, Juliet, what does this mean?" he asked, irritably.

"It means . . ." She stood, following him as Seamus opened the door and handed the bowl to a footman. She waited until he had closed the door and then looked up at him. "It means that we are getting close to capturing the cryptographer."

"We!" Seamus lost all control. "We . . ." He walked toward her and she walked backward, clearly intimidated. "Are not pursuing the cryptographer. I"—Seamus pointed to himself—"am investigating the code, while you"—he stabbed a finger in her direction—"will sit at home with a minimum of two armed guards at all times!"

Her brows were furrowed and her mouth hung open in shock at his tirade. It took several moments for Juliet to acquire the ability to speak. "You're overreacting, Seam—"

"Overreacting! You were kidnapped and almost murdered today, Juliet," he reminded her. Then he saw something in her eyes that prompted him to ask, "What have you remembered?"

"The Welshman called me by name."

"Oh, Jesus." Seamus rolled his eyes when a knock sounded at the study door, stopping his mind from considering the unthinkable implications. "Come."

Countess Pervill swept into the room and headed straight for Juliet, uncommonly composed. "Are you all right, darling?"

"Yes, Mother. I'm fine."

"What's happened to your wrists?" the countess asked, missing nothing.

"I'm fine, Mother." Juliet was shaking her head, her long hair making her appear younger and more fragile than she had before. "I merely scraped them when I escaped."

"Well, it is nice to have you home, darling." Countess Pervill hugged her daughter and Seamus watched as the countess closed her eyes in relief. "Thank you so much for seeing to my daughter, Mister McCurren. We shall forever be in your debt."

Seamus shook his head, having done nothing to protect Juliet. "I merely saw to her injuries."

"Nevertheless, thank you."

The countess turned, guiding Juliet from the room when he stopped her. "I'm sending you home with four of my footmen until proper protection can be arranged."

Countess Pervill turned, her dark brows furrowed. "Protection?"

Juliet *tsk*ed, rolling her eyes, but Seamus ignored her. "The men that kidnapped your daughter might try again."

"What?" The countess looked at Juliet. "Why?"

"Honestly, Mother, Mister McCurren is exaggerating the gravity of the situation. This was an unfortunate incident and I shall be much more cautious next—"

"There will be no next time, Juliet. Your work with the Foreign Office is finished." He turned to the countess, seeking an ally. "If you want your daughter alive, keep her at home and guarded at all times."

"Is she still in danger?" The countess looked at Seamus.

"No." Juliet shook her head.

"Yes." Seamus nodded.

Countess Pervill stared at her daughter. "We would very much appreciate your footmen as escort, Mister McCurren."

Seamus inclined his head, adding, "I'll send the physician to Lord Appleton's town home the moment he arrives."

Juliet glanced over her shoulder at the looming figure of Seamus McCurren. He watched her walk to her mother's conveyance as if she were incapable of making it from his front door to the carriage steps.

Her mother stepped in first and then the two footmen flanking her assisted Juliet into the landau.

"Oh, this is ridiculous, Mother."

She looked at Seamus, her guardian angel, as he stood on the landing of his front entry. His dark head was tilted and his eyes were fixed on her so intently that she felt somewhat disconcerted. The carriage started forward and she sat back, catching one last glimpse of Seamus as he spun on his heels, his jacket flaring as he swept inside his home.

Why did he have to do that? Why could he not just walk into a house like normal men? Why could he not just read a book instead of deciphering it? Or perhaps just stand in a corner rather than overwhelm an entire room? Or kiss her without consuming her?

"What's the matter?" her mother asked. "You look angry."

"I'm not a child, I don't need watching."

"When we get home, you will tell me precisely what happened today and then we will discuss how much *watching* you need."

Juliet had not even stepped out of the landau before Felicity was pulling her from it. She glanced at Seamus's four footmen as her cousin slipped her right arm around Juliet's waist then proceeded to walk her up the stairs as if she had two broken legs.

"Really, I'm fine, Felicity," Juliet said as they walked through the entryway. "I just need a bath and something to eat."

Felicity ran off to have the cook prepare some food and her mother stopped Juliet, saying, "Come to the parlor when you've freshened up."

Juliet nodded, too tired to do anything else as she made her way up the stairs. She was on the fifth step when she paused and turned round only to see four footmen nipping at her heels.

"Where do you think you are going?"

The most senior man stepped forward. "We have been ordered to keep you in view at all times, Lady Juliet."

"Like hell you will," Juliet snorted and turned to walk up the stairs but she stopped when she saw that the footmen were following. "Look," she sighed, "I'm home safe and sound and you can wait for me in the entryway if I need to go out, all right?"

"Mister McCurren said you would say that and wanted me to inform your ladyship that all four of us would be dismissed if we did not comply with his orders."

Juliet lowered her voice and wrinkled her nose, saying, "Well, Mister McCurren is not here, is he? And as I don't think any of you will tell—"

"He said you would say that, too, and wanted me to inform your ladyship that he would be calling on the house and, if we were not at our posts when he arrived, we would be sacked."

Juliet placed her hands on her hips and, finding no alternative, looked down at Seamus's footmen. "Come on then," she said. Seamus knew that her guilt over getting the footmen dismissed would keep her from doing anything else.

They arrived at her bedchamber door and the senior footman held up a hand, stopping her as two men swept into her room, frightening her lady's maid and causing the girl to drop Juliet's wash towels.

"It's all right, Anne, they're with me," she said as the men searched her room. "In a manner of speaking."

When the room had been deemed free of villains, the two junior footmen stepped out onto the balcony. And the senior footman drew the balcony curtains and then walked back to the bedchamber door.

"We'll be just outside if you need us," he said, closing it.

"Anne, get those poor men on the balcony some blankets, would you," Juliet ordered and then stepped into the washroom.

She disrobed, thankful to be alone, and in the isolation of the washroom and away from concerned eyes, Juliet cried, the terrifying ordeal she had just suffered not very far from behind her.

Enigma stared at the Welshman, her blood boiling. "You knew I wanted to speak with her."

"I didn't think a little thing like that would be strong enough to lift the bed off the floor."

Men constantly underestimated women and Enigma rolled her eyes at their stupidity.

"Well, now you know better," she smirked, looking at the white bandages around his thick head. "So, if Lady Juliet is working for Whitehall and knows of the code and Seamus McCurren is her lover and also working for Whitehall, then we can conclude . . . ?"

"Seamus McCurren knows about the code," Mister Collin said, and Enigma smiled, pleased with his conclusion.

"However," she said, pacing up and down her office, "if Lady Juliet was interviewing the clerk at the *Herald*, then they have not gotten very far in their investigation and will have no way of linking the code to Dante's."

"Then why does McCurren come here so often?"

"He comes for me." Enigma smiled. "He comes for the challenge of matching wits with me."

Mister Collin's eyes narrowed, as he no doubt realized the truth of her words. After all, Seamus McCurren played only at the proprietor's table. "So what do we do now that we know the Foreign Office has found our code?" he asked.

"They haven't found the code," she mused, "merely the markers."

Enigma stared at the walls as she considered her plan of attack. The gentlemen of the Foreign Office could look all they liked, but they would never find her code. Even the brilliant Seamus McCurren had only detected her coded markers.

Still.

"Keep following McCurren," she said to the Welshman.

"Right." The Welshman left and Enigma turned to Mister Collin. "Send for Lord Harrington. Have him come back to town as quickly as possible and then have Mister Matthews settle up the books and call in any debts owed us."

"That could take several days," Mister Collin reminded her.

Enigma nodded. "We need to meet with the French to arrange for new markers before we leave London and that will also take time to arrange. However, we should be prepared." She thought about the alluring Seamus McCurren and what he was capable of discerning. "We might have to leave quickly."

But she wasn't finished playing their game just yet.

Twenty-seven

❧

Juliet looked out at the beautifully attired guests at the ball, just happy to be out of the house.

She plastered a smile to her face as she chatted with people she disliked, knowing that in part the DunDonell Ball was being given on her behalf. But Juliet was tired of being polite and begging forgiveness from the matrons of the *ton* for something that she hadn't even done.

Bloody Harrington!

Still, she supposed that she should try to regain her reputation. Choosing to decline an invitation was one thing, but not being invited anywhere was an entirely different matter. And now that Seamus McCurren had well and truly barred her from the Foreign Office, Juliet would need to occupy herself in some fashion.

Perhaps she should contact Oxford? But as she thought of the eager professor who hung on her every word, Juliet's skin crawled. No, if she were to work on any mathematical suppositions, they would be researched entirely on her own.

She sighed, picturing her life sitting before a desk with a pile of papers and a worn wooden pencil. Juliet was so lost in her dismal daydream that she did not hear Robert Barksdale approach her from behind.

"Enjoying yourself?"

Juliet turned and stared. "Yes, thank you," she said, smiling uncertainly, unsure of Robert's motives.

It was the first time since the scandal that he had approached her in public and heads were discreetly turning in their direction.

"Would you care to dance, Lady Juliet?" Robert's heart was on his sleeve as he held out his arm for all the guests to see.

"I'll dance with you once," Juliet agreed, thankful that her long gloves would hide her wounds from him.

"One dance is more than I had hoped for." Robert smiled, then took her in his arms for the first dance of the evening.

"How have you been, Robert?" Juliet stared at his chest.

"Miserable."

She let her eyes touch his and then moved on, saying, "Good."

"I deserved that."

"And quite a bit more."

"But as you can see, this time I am asking you in full view of the *ton* to be my bride."

Her eyes flew to his and she all but stopped on the ballroom floor.

"And your father?" she could not help asking.

"I told the earl to give the estate to one of his many by-blows."

Juliet laughed. "Oh, yes, bringing up the man's illegitimate children was the course I would have chosen."

"No, it is not." Robert shook his head, certain. "You would have told the earl to go hang himself the first time he threatened to cut you off." Juliet blushed, remembering the distasteful meeting with her own father. "That's why I'm absolutely besotted with you. Marry me, Juliet?"

Juliet stared at the possibility of a normal life, a husband, children. It was so very tempting. As they reached the end of the dance floor, she stepped off with Lord Barksdale following after her.

Seamus leaned to his right and stretched his neck so that he might watch Juliet dancing with that bastard Barksdale. But they had just left the ballroom floor and for a moment Seamus lost sight of her.

"Excuse me," Seamus said to several gentlemen with whom he had been conversing, but he never took his eyes off Barksdale's back.

He could see the edge of Juliet's pink gown, but the rest of her was obscured by Robert Barksdale as the man led her to the far wall for a bit of privacy.

"Bastard," he mumbled, his lips curling with distaste.

Lord Barksdale's brown curls covered his eyes as he bent his head to speak with Juliet. The lass was shaking her head and the closer Seamus came to her, he saw that she was upset.

"Are you all right, Lady Juliet?" Seamus met her eyes, worried that she had not yet recovered from her ordeal. "You looked distressed."

Lord Barksdale glanced over his shoulder, his jaw tense. "The lady is none of your concern."

"Perhaps the lady would like to answer for herself?" Seamus held the younger man's gaze along with his threat. "Lady Juliet?"

"I shall speak with you later, Lord Barksdale," Juliet said.

Barksdale looked at her and, after a long pause, reluctantly bowed, saying, "I look forward to hearing your answer."

The lass blushed, no doubt a result of Robert having posed a highly inappropriate question. Seamus was itching to flatten the English prick, but as he was at his brother's own ball, he stood his ground and forced the bastard to knock shoulders with him as he walked away.

"Are you sure you're all right, lass?"

"No," Juliet admitted and the corner of his mouth lifted at her unerring honesty.

Seamus turned toward the ballroom, staring at the retreating figure of Lord Barksdale. "Has Robert Barksdale asked you to . . . to become his mistress?" Seamus mumbled, his fists clenched.

"How dare you." Seamus glanced at Juliet, confused by the rage shaking in her voice. "Are you seriously standing here, concerned with my future, when you are solely responsible for having me dismissed and for holding me prisoner in my own home?"

Seamus felt a stab of guilt, but the knife failed to withdraw from his chest.

"The guards are for your own protection, Juliet, and you are perfectly welcome to pursue your own interests," he reasoned.

"Which interests might those be, Mister McCurren? Needlepoint and the arrangement of flowers? I'd rather slit my own throat. Besides"—Juliet met his gaze, whispering—"if I agree to Lord Barksdale's proposal, I shall be under his protection . . . not yours."

"You're not . . ." Seamus paled, "You're not seriously considering Barksdale's proposal," he whispered, glancing about the room. "To become his mistress?"

Juliet's eyes sparkled a brilliant blue and she smiled maliciously. "Why not? I can enjoy all of the pleasures marriage has to offer a woman without any of the constraints."

"You can pursue your work without . . ." Seamus couldn't push the words passed the sinking feeling in his chest.

"Can I?" she asked, her eyes ablaze. "It was not my life's goal to become a cryptographer, but it did give me something with which to occupy my mind."

Seamus stilled, realizing for the first time the devastating consequences of an idle mind, particularly a mind as powerful as Juliet's. *This is all I have*. Her words bounced about his brain as he tried to imagine not having his books, his work, to challenge himself.

"I'm sorry, Juliet," Seamus said and she turned crimson.

"Don't you dare pity me, Seamus," she whispered with tears glistening in her eyes. "I do, after all, have motherhood to look forward to."

Stunned, he looked down at Juliet, his stomach seizing. "The bastard asked you to marry him?"

"He has the special license in his pocket."

"When?" Seamus felt his throat closing.

"Tomorrow, if I am of a mind." Juliet curtsied. "Now, if you will excuse me. I think Felicity should be the first to know of my impending nuptials."

Seamus scanned the room for Felicity Appleton, and unable to find her, he grasped Juliet's arm. "She's gone home, I'm afraid."

"Felicity did not inform me that she was leaving," Juliet said, truly concerned.

"It seems Lord Appleton was fatigued and she was accompanying him back to their home. She asked me to inform you of her departure, which is why I sought you out." Seamus smiled at how well his lie was falling into place as he continued to move them toward the front door. "I'll drive you home, if you like."

"Yes, all right." Juliet nodded, clearly relieved at being able to leave so early. "Thank you, Mister McCurren."

"Not at all." Seamus assisted her into his conveyance and then gave the driver directions before climbing in after her.

Juliet sat, staring at the window. Their eyes met in the reflection of the glass. She reached out and yanked the velvet curtain closed then settled back against the squabs.

The noise on the street faded in favor of the rhythmic

clomping of hooves and Seamus knew that time was running short. "Will you live in the country with Barksdale?"

"The country?" It took her a moment to understand what he was asking. "I . . . we have not discussed the matter of our primary residence."

Seamus stared at her profile, envisioning her gone. "What have you discussed?"

Her eyes narrowed and her head swung round as the carriage came to a stop. "That is none of your concern!"

She pushed past him before he could assist her down, only to stop on the walkway in front of his home. Juliet was shaking her head, saying, on an incredulous exhalation, "You've kidnapped me!"

"No." Seamus held up both hands, trying to think what the hell he had done. "I merely think you should consider Barksdale's proposal carefully."

"You take me home right now, Seamus McCurren." She climbed in his carriage, her arm crossed over her chest.

He took a deep breath and said, "No."

"No? No!"

"Juliet, just come inside and speak with me for ten minutes and then I'll drive you to your cousin's."

"Why? What good is ten minutes—"

"I just think you are not thinking clearly. You had a terrible shock with your kidnapping—"

"My *first* kidnapping," she spat.

"Ten minutes." His voice was soft, his eyes concerned.

Juliet stepped out of the carriage, lifting her skirts as she ascended his front steps mumbling, "Don't have much choice, do I?"

Seamus followed her up with no idea what the hell he was going to say. "My study, perhaps?"

A roll of her eyes was his only response and they walked into the book-lined room at odds.

"Would you like a drink?"

"If it will pass the ten minutes more quickly . . ." She shrugged and Seamus sighed. "Scotch, please."

He turned to the decanter and asked the wall, "Why are you marrying Lord Barksdale?"

"God, you are such a man."

"What the hell is that supposed to mean?" Seamus spun round as if he had been accused of murder.

"It means, Mister McCurren, that women have very little choice in these matters. I am a ruined woman who must sit round and pray for an offer and I've just received one."

"From a man that asked you first to be his mistress!" He thrust the crystal glass toward her.

"Robert apologized." She yanked the glass from his hand. "And besides, marrying Lord Barksdale is the only sensible thing to do."

It was and he knew it, which irritated him further. "And since when have you done anything sensible?"

"And when have you done anything not perfectly sensible?" It was an insult; they both knew it. Juliet smiled. "Has it been ten minutes?"

"No." Seamus took the glass from her hands and threw it against the wall.

"Oh, you're absolutely mad," she said sarcastically as she walked toward the scotch-covered wall. "Your scullery maid will be all a fluster, poor thing. Perhaps, I should hire her when Robert and I marr—"

Seamus had Juliet pressed against the wall before she knew what had hit her. He was kissing her deep and long and with more passion than he had ever known, but it wasn't enough.

His hands slid round her back and splayed the expanse, pulling her flush to his body. She moaned into his mouth as he surged deeper, drinking in everything she had to offer while offering her everything he had.

"You're not marrying Robert bloody Barksdale," Seamus

commanded against her lips and then picked her up and carried her to the carpet in front of the fire.

Her backside had scarcely touched the ground before he was kissing her. Seamus stripped her of her ball gown. He tossed it toward his feet and sighed with satisfaction when he felt her arms curl round his neck.

He was untying his cravat with one hand when she whispered, "Seamus?"

He kissed her deeply, not wanting to hear her deny him.

"Don't think, Juliet," he breathed, kissing her again. "For once in your life, please, just stop thinking."

Seamus could see her doing just that so he caressed her breast and kissed her senseless. He sighed with satisfaction when he felt her hands pushing his jacket from his shoulders.

Juliet watched him eagerly as he shrugged out of his jacket and she could scarcely breathe. He stared with equal anticipation at her remaining garments, trying to discern the fastest method of discarding them.

But he had hesitated too long.

He smiled his encouragement as Juliet fought with her chemise and then it was his turn. He placed both hands on her waist and slid her drawers from her slender hips.

Seamus lifted his head, and in the candlelight that warmed them both, he stared down at the most breathtaking woman he had ever seen.

She was so damn beautiful.

He met her eye, unable to speak, and Juliet stared back, whispering, "Teach me, Seamus."

His stomach flipped, knowing she would learn.

God, how this woman would learn.

Seamus placed his hand on her waist and watched as his fingers glided over the spectacular curve of her right hip. He splayed his hand across her belly, the tip of his last finger getting lost in the thatch of alluring curls between her thighs. He stared at his hands on Juliet's body with such a deep sense of possession that it startled him.

Troubled, he turned Juliet to face him and bent his head to kiss her. He parted her lips, sliding his tongue into her mouth as his hands slid over her bare backside while his mind claimed her as his.

It was the dead of winter and she should have been cold. Instead, she was anything but. The heat in his eyes and the warmth of his touch was setting her alight.

"I want you to teach me, Seamus," she whispered into his mouth, knowing no other man from whom she could learn. His golden eyes met hers and for one terrifying moment she thought he would deny her. "Teach me."

He would. She could see his decision etched in his features, and she let out the breath she had been holding, only to suck it in again when he kissed the hollow of her throat. Juliet reveled in the feel of his lips pressed against so vulnerable a place.

Seamus was taking an eternity unbuttoning his waistcoat and Juliet found herself rising to her knees to help him out of it. It fell to the floor and her breath was becoming labored as each stud on his shirt gave way, revealing that magnificent chest.

The hard plains of his stomach contracted as Juliet unfastened the remaining studs. Not bothering with the cuffs, he turned the sleeves of the linen shirt inside out. When he was free, they reached for each other, his hands on her lower back and hers on his shoulders.

Seamus kissed her again, crushing her breasts to his bare chest. Her nipples tingled as if they had just been awoken to a new purpose and she wanted to feel more. His head lowered and he took her left breast in his mouth. She moaned. Impatient, she pushed on his shoulders and Seamus stood up, ripping his trousers from his body.

My lord, he was stunning.

Juliet was shaking with desire, but Seamus must have thought it was from the chill of the study because he lay her beneath a blanket and joined her. He did not say a word as his mouth returned to her breast. He lightly raked his teeth across her nipple and Juliet jumped, her nails digging into his muscular back.

"Do that again," she begged and Juliet saw him grin before shifting his dark head to her right breast.

She closed her eyes, bracing herself to be overwhelmed, but after a moment her brows furrowed and she opened her eyes.

He was watching her and she hit him in the shoulder, demanding, "Seam—" But his name died on her lips, converting to "Oh" as he took her nipple into his mouth.

His lips moved between her breasts and he softly kissed his way down her stomach. But when his mouth continued to descend, Juliet slowly closed her thighs.

"I'm going to bring you to climax, Juliet." She heard his baritone brogue in the air.

Her thighs were eased apart by gentle caresses of masculine hands, and she could feel his ragged breath before she felt the heat of his mouth. Her mind leapt at new sensations while her body melted into the carpet.

He laved deeper and Juliet could feel the moisture of his mouth mingling with the heat between her thighs.

Seamus moaned as he tasted her desire and Juliet grew hotter still. She stole a peek at her spectacular tutor; his broad shoulders and bare back were so beautiful. He probed again and her eyes drifted closed, focusing on the lesson he was teaching her.

The pleasure he was giving her turned to urgency, but she didn't know for what.

"Seamus?" Juliet asked, wanting more, and he gave it to her. Caressing and laving, focusing his attention on a particular protrusion as if he knew her body better than she did herself.

She attempted to move away from him but his strong hands held the tops of her thighs, keeping her where he wanted her to be. Seamus continued his ministrations until her nipples began to harden and she arched her back, opening herself to him before fracturing into incalculable pieces.

Juliet did not breathe, did not think, did not even move until she was sure that she had felt every spectacular rush of sensation.

"No wonder men think of nothing else."

"It is better with some than with others." Seamus smiled, pleased with himself.

"Well, you're not going to disappoint me, are you?"

Seamus was busy crawling over Juliet, the taste of her pleasure still fresh in his mind.

"Disappoint you?" was all he could manage, his life's goal to be buried inside her.

"Your drawers, remember?" She was looking up at him, smiling. "I want to see you, Seamus."

The appeal was flattering, but it would involve getting off her and his body was downright rebelling.

"All right, lass," Seamus said, knowing he would have to shed his garments either way.

He stood, fussing with the drawstring to his drawers, and Juliet came to her knees. The blanket fell away from her spectacular breasts, turning her nipples a pebbled pink. Seamus looked at the lust in her eyes and he grew harder still.

"I would never want to disappoint you, Juliet." He grinned, watching her eyes carefully as he dropped his drawers.

She took a sharp breath and stared at his erection. He was afraid that she would change her mind when she ordered on an airy breath, "Turn around."

"Why?" Seamus asked, curious as to how her mind worked.

"You have the most magnificent backside in your buckskins and I want to see if . . . Oh, yes . . ." She was speaking to herself. "I much prefer your bare backside to your buckskins."

Seamus laughed and then crawled over her, pushing her onto her back.

Juliet looked up at him and Seamus could not help kissing her. He never seemed to be able to stop himself from kissing her.

He lowered himself on top of her naked body and closed his eyes, shaking with need. She spread her legs, a quick study, and Seamus began rocking his hips, teaching her the rhythm of lovemaking and reigniting her desire.

"Oh, Seamus," she lifted her hips to meet his. "You feel so . . . right."

"Wait until I'm inside you, Juliet," he whispered, unsure if he could.

Seamus placed himself at her entrance and stared down at the brilliant women he would make love to. He closed his eyes with anticipation, but he hesitated. She was an innocent unjustly accused, and if he were to take her virtue, so, too, would he take the proof of her innocence.

"Juliet, once I've . . ." He shook his head, his arms shaking with want of her. "There's no turning back."

"I do realize that, Seamus," Juliet said, annoyed. "Now stop thinking, because at the moment I am more interested in your exquisite body than your exquisite mind."

Seamus grinned to himself, gathering Juliet in his arms. "I'm sorry," he whispered, easing forward. Juliet closed her eyes and bit her lip and he bit his, but eventually she withdrew her nails from digging into the flesh on his back. "Are you all right, Juliet?"

"Yes, but I must confess I liked climaxing better."

"This gets better, I promise you." Seamus surged forward gently, teaching her with each languid stroke. He kissed her to ease his path, but the clever Juliet caught on quickly and emulated his movements.

God above, she felt . . . "right."

"Oh," she moaned in surprise as he buried himself to the hilt.

Seamus balled his hands into fists as he concentrated on her needs, not his. But with each feminine gasp of discovery, he could feel himself losing control. His steady strokes were becoming increasingly urgent and he was not sure how much longer he could restrain himself as she cried out with each of his thrusts.

"Open yourself to me, Juliet," he whispered in her ear.

Her hands slid down his back and her cries became more frequent until finally they were one long moan broken only by the need for her to breathe.

"Seamus?" she managed.

"Yes?" He could not think as he buried himself in her warmth.

"Can a woman peak more than once?"

A flash of lust stole the breath from his lungs so it took a moment for him to answer.

"Oh, God, yes," he said, speaking more of the pleasure she was giving him than to answering her question.

"Good, because . . ." And then he felt her feminine muscles tightening around him and for the first time in his life Seamus lost control.

Twenty-eight

In the foggy corners of his mind, Seamus heard the bed-chamber door open. He took a deep breath of contentment and mumbled against the silk sheets as he lay on his stom-ach, "Come back to bed, Juliet," with the hope of making love to her in the morning light.

Last night he had made love to her in the study, in his chair, and in his bed, but he had yet to make love to Juliet in the morning light.

Soft footsteps drew nearer the bed and he smiled with anticipation.

"I'd rather you get the fuck up."

Seamus was so startled by his older brother's voice that he flipped over, wrapping himself in his sheets as tightly as his newfound predicament.

"Daniel!" He stated the obvious, lifting the sheet to cover his naked hips. "What are you—"

His heart stopped and he went still, faced with the wrath of the three other gentlemen littered about his bedchamber.

Seamus glanced to his right and saw the eerie silence of the Earl of Wessex staring back at him from a corner chair, his countenance as cold and as hard as ice.

A flash of bright color drew his eye to Christian St. John, who paced back and forth like the wind bouncing off the sides of a highland canyon. The man was mumbling to himself as he stared at the floor and Seamus followed his movements, straining to hear what curses were being cast upon him.

"I knew it," Christian was saying. He stopped and looked at Daniel, who was still standing over him. "I knew it."

"What the hell are you talking about, Christian?" Daniel erupted, his turquoise eyes burning into Seamus. "None of us knew what a bloody idiot my brother was until this morning. Give me a drink, Gilbert, before I flatten the stupid git." Daniel ran his hands through his auburn hair and then remembered to close the bedchamber door.

The Duke of Glenbroke rose like an ancient oak and tried to steady the disturbance of the others.

"Perhaps," the duke began, lifting a drink to Daniel as he closed the ground between them in two strides, "we should hear what Seamus has to say for himself."

"Yes, I am most anxious to hear what explanation Mister McCurren has to offer for bedding Lady Juliet," the Earl of Wessex said, the chill in his voice reaching across the room and plunging deep into his chest.

Christian stopped pacing and joined the other men as they all stared at Seamus, demanding an answer.

"I don't have one." Seamus stared back.

"You don't have one." Daniel exploded. "You don't bloody have one!" His brother came around the side of the bed so that they were face to face, eye to eye. "You just ruined the lass that we"—his arm swept over the room— "were trying very hard to salvage, and all you can say for yourself is 'I don't have one'!"

Seamus opened his mouth and shook his head, but all that escaped was air.

"I knew it," Christian said again, prompting Daniel to spin round.

"You knew what, Christian?" he asked, annoyed.

"I knew he was in love with Juliet Pervill."

Seamus went rigid, his mind protesting Christian's claim. "I'm not in love with Lady Juliet."

"Aye, you are, Seamus." Daniel nodded, betraying him. "You told me you wanted to kiss the lass the first time you met her."

He groaned at the implication that he had set about to seduce Juliet, then he waited a few moments for the anger in the room to subside before looking up at the other men.

"Aye, I did want to kiss her but that was—"

"So." The duke took a step forward, trying to understand. "You are *not* in love with Juliet Pervill?"

"No," Seamus answered, looking to his left.

"Then you are merely a libertine?" the earl asked from the right.

"No!" Seamus cringed.

"Well, if you are not a libertine . . ." Christian stepped around the winged-back chair, his Nordic blue eyes clear. "That would leave only one answer to this little problem."

A large hand clasped Seamus's shoulder and then squeezed so hard that it all but broke his collarbone. "You'll ask Lady Juliet Pervill to marry you," his brother ordered.

Seamus couldn't breathe and his head snapped round so that he might read the level of sincerity in his brother's turquoise eyes.

"This afternoon," the duke added as the other gentlemen stared at Seamus, nodding their agreement.

"Aye," he agreed, knowing that asking for Juliet's hand was the honorable thing to do and that he would have done so himself.

But not quite so soon.

* * *

"How are you feeling?"

Juliet sighed, wishing she had never told Felicity what had happened last night. She should have realized her virtuous cousin would not understand. But she had to explain to Felicity why she had been out until four in the morning. And truth be told, Juliet had been bursting to share the momentous event with her dearest friend.

She was a woman now, well and true, and Juliet couldn't be happier.

Her cousin had thought it a great tragedy, of course, but Juliet forgave Felicity her ignorance.

"I feel wonderful." If a bit sore.

"You could be carrying his child, Juliet." Her cousin's eyes were soft and void of reproach. "So, you had better eat something."

"Oh, I shall. I am absolutely famished." Juliet pushed herself upright.

"Well, I'm pleased you've slept for so long as I think we can now discuss what happened with clear heads."

"I was perfectly clearheaded last night," she said, annoyed.

Felicity rose, pouring them both coffee, saying, "I beg to differ."

"You just don't understand, Felicity." Juliet sighed, dismissing her cousin's uninformed advice.

"Don't be so condescending, Juliet. You could have created a child last night and you have no husband. What else is there to understand?"

"Passion."

Felicity's eyes went cold and Juliet stilled. "You think I know nothing of passion?"

"I didn't say that."

"Just because I do not wear my heart on my sleeve does not mean I have never desired to be with a man."

"Really?"

"Yes, really!"

"Sorry, I just . . . Well, I had no idea."

"Neither does he, which is rather the point, Juliet. A lady does not take to bed any gentleman she fancies."

"A respectable lady does not, I agree. But if you will remember, I am no longer a respectable lady."

"That is not true. The *ton* was coming round."

"Were they?" Juliet raised a doubtful brow.

"Yes, the scandal was all but forgotten but now . . ." Felicity sipped her coffee, agitated. "Thank the lord no one will ever know of this misstep."

"What do you mean?"

"Christian dropped by this morning," her cousin said and Juliet stilled. "He knew how upset I had been when I could not find you at the ball."

"But I was told you left early because your father was . . . ill." Of course Lord Appleton had not been ill.

"Who on earth told you that?"

That lying Scot!

"Never mind." Juliet shook her head, her heart racing with the urgency of her question. "What did you tell Christian?"

"That you had made your way home."

"And?" She couldn't breathe.

Felicity looked at the counterpane. "Christian could see that I was distraught and he asked if you were well. I began to cry . . . and—"

"You told him!"

Juliet sucked in a breath but no air was left in the room. Her hand flew to her throat in a vain effort to ease her breathing.

"Juliet!" Felicity reached for a newspaper and began fanning her furiously. The light began to dim and Juliet made another futile attempt at breathing. "Mister Barnes!" her cousin shouted to the senior footman. "Send for Countess Per—"

"If . . ." Juliet held up a hand to still the footman's

progress. "You bring my mother into this situation . . ." She had to breathe. "I will *never* forgive you."

Frustrated tears filled Juliet's eyes and she could see the shock on Felicity's face when her cousin realized that she meant it.

"You may leave, Mister Barnes." Felicity turned away from her, the hurt thick in her soft voice. "I'll not tell your mother."

"Thank you." Juliet took a shaky breath and her clammy forehead began to cool.

She forced herself to the edge of the bed, taking another breath, and actually felt the air slipping down her lungs rather than being stuck between her shoulders.

"Here you are." Her cousin handed Juliet a cup of coffee with such grace that no one would ever suspect that she was angry. "It doesn't matter. Your mother will know soon enough," Felicity said as if she was sure.

Juliet stared at her cousin in no mood for the perpetual sunshine that spouted from Felicity's perfect mouth. Yet something in the manner in which she was looking at her made Juliet ask, "What do you mean, my 'mother will know soon enough'?"

"Don't you see?" Felicity smiled. "He'll have to marry you now."

"Who? Robert?" Juliet shook her head, confused. "He's only just proposed!"

"Robert Barksdale proposed to you?" Felicity asked, shocked.

"Yes, last night. I was so tired when I arrived home that I forgot to tell you."

"You forgot to tell me that a man offered to make you his wife?" Felicity just stared at her, dumbfounded.

"My mind was . . . occupied."

"Yes, I am sure that it was, but how did you go from a marriage proposal to another man's bed?" Felicity was angry and then swept it away with a wave of her hand. "I'm sorry, Juliet. It doesn't matter any longer. I woke you to give you time to ready yourself."

"Ready myself for what?"

"Seamus McCurren will arrive this afternoon to make you an offer."

"What!" Juliet jumped to her feet. "How could you possibly know his intentions?"

"Christian . . ." Felicity hesitated. "Christian went to Daniel and Daniel—"

"Did what? What did Daniel do?"

"He enlisted the aid of Wessex and Glenbroke to have a chat with Seamus."

Juliet was going to be ill.

"Mister McCurren should have asked for your hand last night and our four friends merely pointed out his oversight."

"Four?"

"Christian accompanied them, of course."

Juliet's mind drained of everything but the image of a disgruntled Seamus McCurren as he took his obligatory vows to the plain Lady Juliet Pervill.

It was a nightmare and Felicity kept adding to the ugly scene.

"He'll marry you and then you can live in his town home, which is not really all that far from ours." Juliet just turned and stared at her cousin, unable to form any words. "And if you are not already increasing, you soon will be. And if ever I marry, we can raise the cousins together, as we were raised."

Juliet dropped to her knees as Felicity planned the details of her life, which prompted her cousin to look down, asking, "What are you doing?"

"Praying." Juliet kept her eyes closed and curled her fingers over her hands. "Praying that God will strike me dead."

"Don't say such horrible things," Felicity gasped.

But at the moment Juliet did not care, wanting only for this afternoon never to arrive.

Freshly bathed, Seamus was pulling his shirt over his head when he heard his bedchamber door open.

"You're still here?" Seamus asked, glancing at Christian before violently jabbing at his shirttail as it disappeared beneath his buckskins.

"Still here," Christian said, walking to a chair. "Do you mind if I join you?"

"Yes," Seamus said, but he didn't really. He was glad for the company but not willing to talk about last night. Not willing to talk about Juliet. "I didn't see Ian with your merry little band."

"He's gone for the weekend." Christian poured them both long drinks. "I think it had something to do with your sister-in-law's plea for eligible gentlemen to attend her ball."

"Eligible?" Seamus swung his cravat around his neck. "Yes, the lady is not yet aware of the fear that word strikes in the gentlemen of the *ton*."

Christian took a sip of brandy as Seamus focused his attention on tying the silk noose around his neck. "And how does marriage strike you?"

Seamus's hands jerked at the silk.

"Damnation!" He stared at the misshapen cravat in the mirror, stared at anything but his insightful friend.

"I'll summon your valet, if you answer the question."

Seamus stared into the mirror, knowing there was no getting away from the man.

"I don't know." Seamus turned away from his reflection and sat in a chair opposite St. John's. "I suppose it strikes me about as well as it strikes any man."

"Well, my friend," Christian said, crossing his legs, "I believe I can help you."

"Really?" Seamus asked, knowing there was no getting out of this truss. "How's that?" he asked, grinning.

"Marry her."

"Marry Juliet Pervill?" Seamus laughed, leaning forward and snatching Christian's drink from his hand. "Right. If you had not been imbibing at such an early hour, you would recall that you, along with three very large and powerful gentlemen, determined not a half hour ago that offering for the girl was my only course of action."

"Oh, I remember." Christian nodded, snatching his brandy snifter back. "But I mean *really* marry her. Not out of a sense of obligation or because you are being forced to do so, but because you want to marry her."

"What difference does it make?" Seamus bent down and pulled on one boot. "We will be man and wife either way."

"Come on, Seamus." Christian sounded irritated, which was so rare that Seamus looked up to hear him out. "It makes a huge difference to a woman whether her husband marries her out of love or obligation."

"I'm sorry to disappoint you, Christian, but I don't want to marry Lady Juliet."

"Why not?"

Why not? A simple question, which should have been easy to answer. But it wasn't.

"Juliet is from good stock, if you disregard her father." Christian waved the man away. "And the lady has the added bonus of being a great deal of fun."

"It's not that simple, Christian."

"Why not?"

"Have you ever thought about your place in life, Christian?" Seamus tried to explain. "I mean who you are in this world, who others perceive you to be?"

"That's easy." Christian lifted his brandy. "I'm the spare."

"Right, precisely so, and I'm—"

"The clever one." Christian nodded, understanding.

"Yes," Seamus sighed, knowing Christian would not take that declaration as arrogance. "I'm the clever one, always have been."

"Oh, I think I take your meaning." Christian stared at the carved wooden ceiling, trying to put his thoughts into words. "You don't want to marry a woman more clever than yourself?"

Seamus froze, ashamed at the implication when put in those unflattering terms. "That was not precisely my mean—"

"Challenges your place in the world, so to speak?"

"Yes, I suppose so," Seamus muttered and Christian laughed at him like the good friend that he was.

"Good God, Seamus." Christian was shaking his head. "I pray to God that I marry a woman a good deal more kind, more clever, and bloody well more handsome than me." Christian grinned. "Although if my wife were a better layabout than I, I might myself feel the sting of competition."

"You're making me feel rather petty, St. John."

"You are being rather petty, and arrogant, and at the moment . . . bloody stupid. The girl is your perfect match, Seamus." Christian hit his temple twice with his forefinger to illustrate his point.

"You are in love with Juliet Pervill and you have fallen so hard that you cannot even see it. If the girl is more clever than you, then you will bloody well just have to swallow your pride and find a new place in life beside your bloody brilliant wife."

Seamus was speechless, struck dumb by the truth behind Christian's unexpected wisdom.

He was in love with Juliet Pervill, knew in his heart of hearts that was the reason why he had made love to her last night; to claim her as his, his match, his lover, and his future wife.

Not bloody Barksdale's.

"Thank you, Christian," he said, the weight of an unexpected proposal lifting from his shoulders.

"You're welcome, you stupid bastard."

Twenty-nine

Juliet sat with her cousin in the library, waiting like a condemned woman for the inevitable call of the gentleman being forced to ask for her hand.

She paced the musty rows of books that lined the walls of the site of her ruination and looked down at a Latin copy of *The Odyssey*, which seem wholly appropriate to this situation.

She glanced at Felicity, who was laboring over an intricate drawing, trying to avoid making awkward conversation.

They had fought again about whether to inform the countess of Mister McCurren's eminent proposal. Juliet could not look her mother in the eye and confess that she was as wanton as the *ton* believed her to be.

She curled her feet beneath her backside and stared at the Latin words blurring before her eyes. She was so filled with the dread, embarrassment, and anticipation of seeing Seamus again that she could not think clearly.

"Are you all right?" Felicity asked, watching her.

"No."

"I know you, Juliet."

"Meaning?" Juliet asked, offended.

"Meaning, I can see you struggling with your decision. Don't forget I have seen you with Mister McCurren."

"So."

"You're in love with him."

"I am not!"

"You took the man to bed, Juliet. You're not *that* reckless unless your heart is involved."

Was she in love with Seamus?

She had wanted him and in all honesty wanted him still, but she was not so naive as to confuse lust with love.

"You will not understand this, Felicity, being the paragon of virtue that you are." Felicity glared at her. "But I wanted the man. It is as simple as that."

"Juliet!"

"What? Are you telling me you've never wanted a man, never dreamt of being in a man's bed?" she asked, more of an accusation than she had intended.

"Of course I have."

"You have?" Juliet looked up, shocked.

"On more than one occasion, but I realize that if we were all to give in to our baser instincts, the social structure of Britain would collapse."

"And I would wager half the *ton*'s marriages are a result of ladies giving in to their baser instincts."

"Half?" Felicity looked at her with skepticism. They were interrupted by a knock at the library door.

"A gentleman requests an audience." The dignified butler bowed, handing Felicity a calling card.

Her cousin set down her sketch and, without reading the name on the white card, nodded. "Very well, send Mister McCurren in."

Juliet rose to her feet and straightened her jade morning gown while her stomach performed somersaults of apprehension.

"Juliet?"

"What?"

"Just because you are being forced to make this decision does not mean that it is not the correct decision to make." She stared at Felicity, unable to believe the extent of her betrayal.

"Nor does it mean that it is."

"It is the only decision you have, Juliet." Felicity did not even blink.

"Is it?" Anger overcame her trepidation, and by the time the handsome Scot had entered the parlor, Juliet was feigning a welcoming smile.

Seamus bowed toward Felicity, who had resumed her drawing, and then turned to Juliet.

"Good afternoon, Mister McCurren," she said as if they had never met. "I must say I am surprised to see you here. I would have thought we had seen quite enough of one another last night." Juliet ignored Felicity's gasp, noting with a great deal of satisfaction that Seamus's confident stance faltered just a bit.

Seamus held her eyes with that steady golden stare and she could see the muscles in his jaw pulsing below neatly trimmed sideburns.

"I was hoping to speak with you in private, Lady Juliet."

"What on earth for, Mister McCurren?"

Seamus stared at her, clearly not knowing what to say when Felicity came to his aid, suggesting, "Perhaps a stroll in the garden will provide you the privacy you require, Mister McCurren."

Seamus offered Juliet his arm and she hesitated, fearful of touching him, afraid it would further muddle her mind.

"Do you think it advisable for us to be alone, Felicity?" Juliet asked with exaggerated sincerity.

Seamus's face colored in what she would ordinarily label embarrassment.

"We could always call on the countess to chaperone," Felicity threatened, forcing Juliet to concede.

"The garden is just this way." Juliet took his arm and the ensuing jolt bore a hole straight through her stomach.

They walked to the back of the house in silence. Seamus escorted her through the French doors, placing his hand on the small of her back. Juliet stiffened, recalling the feel of those hands on her bare flesh.

"Why are you here, Seamus?" she demanded ungraciously as he ushered her outside.

"You know why," he said to the trees. "I have spoken with . . ." He glanced at her, revising. "I wanted to speak with you about what occurred . . . last night."

"What about it?" Juliet asked as if they had shared nothing more than a fine glass of wine.

Frustration crossed over his face. "Juliet."

"Why *are* you here, Mister McCurren?" Juliet said with utmost formality.

"You may not be aware, Lady Juliet, that in addition to my work with the Foreign Office," Seamus began as if swallowing an unpleasant tonic, "I am also the second son of the Earl of DunDonell and have acquired several estates of my own."

"How nice for you." She smiled brightly.

Annoyed, Seamus raised his voice. "Stop making this so damn difficult, Juliet." They walked on and he made a second attempt. "The point is, I am well landed with a rather substantial inheritance."

"So?"

"I have come to ask for your hand in marriage," he all but growled.

"You mean you were ordered to ask for my hand." She held his eye and watched guilt contort his handsome features. "I know all about your little . . . meeting this morning." Juliet walked farther down the narrow path.

"I do hope our friends did not injure your arm when they twisted it."

"It was not like that, Juliet."

She ignored him. "So the question before me is whether or not to marry the man that had me dismissed from the Foreign Office before taking me to bed?" Juliet studied Seamus as if he were one of her mathematical equations.

"I don't recall being the only one bent on seduction last night, *Lady* Juliet."

She felt as though he had slapped her. "No." She composed herself, hiding her wounded pride. "I suppose you were not."

"I'm sorry." He shook his head. "That was . . ." *Cruel?* "Uncalled for."

Juliet lifted her chin and stepped into the gazebo at the far end of the garden. "If I were to agree to marry you, Mister McCurren, what duties would I be expected to perform?"

"Duties?" His brows furrowed. He followed her into the wooden structure. "I'm not sure I understand."

"Yes, that is a problem, but I suppose if I were to speak slowly, we might manage to communicate." Seamus rocked back on his heels as insulted as she had hoped he would be. "What will I be required to do as your wife?" she rephrased, speaking as if the man were a simpleton.

Seamus chose to overlook her slight.

"The usual, I suppose." He shrugged. "Manage the domestic affairs at the town house, the manor house, the cottage at the seaside. Raise any children we may produce."

"And how large a crop do you anticipate?"

"I hadn't really thought about it." He completely missed her sarcasm. "My mother produced seven children."

Produced! *Seven!*

"Any other duties?"

"Nothing more than you've already performed." He grinned and bent his head to kiss her but Juliet took a step backward.

"Yes, last night was rather nice," she agreed. "However, as you are the first gentleman I have made love to, I really have nothing with which to compare."

Seamus's mouth fell open at the possibility of being refused. "I'm afraid I am more interested in pursuing my research than tending your domestic garden."

"You could be carrying my child, Juliet!"

"The *ton* is littered with the bastards of its libertines."

Furious, Seamus looked Juliet in the eye. "I am no libertine, and you know it."

"Nor do you wish to be a husband. After living through my parent's blessed union, you will understand if I am not too keen on the idea of marriage."

"You're refusing me?" Seamus asked, incredulous, his gold eyes molten.

"Yes."

"I'll not beg you, Juliet." They stared at one another. Juliet bit her lip, praying that, in a moment of weakness, she would not change her mind. He bowed, adding curtly, "Good afternoon."

Seamus entered Angelo's fencing club the following morning and quickly found himself looking down his cork-tipped foil at his fencing instructor, ready to begin a match.

"En garde," his opponent said, taking a defensive stance.

Seamus watched the dexterous swordsman carefully, seeking any advantage as they circled one another. Eager for a fight, Seamus attacked in a series of three short thrusts that put the instructor on his heels.

He was just going in for the kill when from the side of the room he heard someone yell, "McCurren."

He lost his concentration long enough for his instructor to parry, striking him in the chest.

The instructor laughed, saying, "You did very well, Mister McCurren, up until the moment when I killed you."

Annoyed, Seamus turned his head to see who had so

rudely interrupted his match. His eyes widened when he saw the dangerous look in Christian St. John's focused eyes.

"Has something happened?" Seamus asked, wiping off the sweat that trickled down his chest.

"No." He was caught off guard when his friend hauled back and belted him in the jaw.

The room dimmed and Seamus lost his balance, falling to the floor. He looked up in shock and stared as Christian stripped from the waist up.

"Get up, McCurren!" Christian unsheathed a foil with a metallic hiss.

"What the hell are you doing, Christian?" Seamus asked, pushing himself upright.

"I'm challenging you to a duel, you blackguard," his friend growled through clenched teeth.

"What?"

"You heard me."

"Why?"

Christian glanced round at Angelo's busy fencing room and took a step forward so that they would not be overheard. "I spoke to Lady Felicity this morning and she informed me that there would be no wedding."

Seamus stiffened, not taking kindly to his private affairs being discussed in public. "That is none of your concern, St. John."

"Like hell." Christian took a step back and uncorked his foil, raising it as he warned, "En garde."

"Are you mad?"

St. John took a step forward and swiped at Seamus's chest. A hint of blood seeped from the shallow wound.

"En garde," Christian repeated with a raised brow and a deadly tone.

A crowd began to gather. "Very well, Christian." He uncorked his own foil.

Christian's anger betrayed him and he lunged before he

was in position and Seamus countered easily, scratching his friend's arm to bring the man to his senses.

Unfortunately, it seemed to have the reverse effect.

"You bastard." Christian lunged a second time, and if Seamus had not jumped wildly to his right, the foil would have run him through.

Stunned, Seamus parried each vicious blow until his lungs were burning.

"St. John," someone called out from the crowd, but Seamus dared not take his attention off Christian's deadly foil.

"Christian!" he heard a familiar voice shout. Seamus stole a glance to his left and watched as Juliet grabbed an onlooker's foil and stabbed Christian in the backside.

"Oww!" Christian turned around abruptly, his large eyes going wide when he saw Juliet standing there. "Juliet! What on earth are you doing here?"

Christian glanced around at the half-dressed members of the exclusively male club, rightfully appalled.

"Felicity told me you were coming here." Juliet took Christian's arm and pulled him to one side. "And why you were coming," she said meaningfully, as Christian rubbed his backside.

The show ended, and the other gentlemen in the room dispersed, allowing them to speak freely.

"Felicity should never have told you. This is a matter of honor between gentlemen and—"

"I refused him, Christian."

Seamus closed his eyes and locked his hands behind his head.

"What?"

"I refused Seamus's offer."

"I could have killed him." Christian looked horrified, and they both stared at the blood trickling down Seamus's bare chest. "Why did you not tell me?"

"Because it is none of your bloody business." Seamus

slipped on his shirt, more miserable than he had been when he arrived.

"Why on earth would you refuse him?" Christian whispered, staring down at Juliet. Seamus tried to appear disinterested in her answer.

"Oh, I don't know, Christian," she growled and the man took a step back. "Perhaps the fact that you threatened to kill the man if he did not make the offer."

Furious, Juliet threw the foil in her hand to the wooden floor and stormed out.

"I was defending her honor." Christian shrugged, confused by Juliet's anger.

"Believe me, St. John." Seamus stared longingly at Juliet's retreating back. "The lady does not need defending."

Thirty

Seamus waited two days for Juliet to come to him, to come to her senses. But she did not and the thought that she might have accepted Lord Barksdale's offer out of anger was driving him mad.

At ten o'clock that evening, he gave up all pretense of indifference and called for his horse, determined to speak with her.

Seamus leapt atop his mount, reassessing his unenviable position. He was in love with Juliet Pervill and the longer he went without having her in his bed, the more he realized just how much he wanted her for his wife. However, thanks to the interference of his blasted friends, the woman would never believe the sincerity of his desire to marry her.

He knew how stubborn Juliet was, knew that nothing he could say would persuade her, not now.

But he had to try.

Seamus arrived at her house at half past ten and waited

impatiently for the butler to answer Lord Appleton's door. "Is Countess Pervill available?" The countess might be able to persuade her daughter of his sincerity.

"I'm afraid Countess Pervill and Lady Felicity have left for the evening."

"Lord Appleton, perhaps?" Seamus asked, desperate.

"His club, I'm afraid."

"Lady Juliet?" Seamus inquired, bowing to the inevitability of confrontation.

"Yes." The man smiled, nodding.

"Are my footmen guarding her properly?"

"They never leave her side," the butler said with obvious approval of the precaution.

"I'll just verify that they are on duty as ordered, if you don't mind."

"Not at all, Mister McCurren."

Seamus handed the man his greatcoat and hat and then bounded up the staircase. Two footmen stood guard at Juliet's door. "Wait for me in the parlor," he ordered.

The footmen glanced at one another, confused, and then started down the corridor while Seamus opened Juliet's sitting room door.

He headed straight for her balcony and asked the two freezing footmen, "Where is Lady Juliet?"

"The lady has retired to her bedchamber."

Seamus nodded. "Wait for me downstairs in the parlor."

"Thank you, Mister McCurren," the footman said, pleased to be relieved of a winter's night duty.

Seamus knocked on Juliet's bedchamber door, more nervous than he could have thought possible. "Come in."

He found her in bed and all the eloquent words he had rehearsed flew from his head. "Why did you refuse my offer?"

"You know why." Juliet snapped her book shut, rolling her eyes as she stood up from her bed.

Trying not to stare through her thin dressing gown,

Seamus concentrated on what she was saying. "I'm sorry you found out about the meeting."

"I'm not." She was shrugging her shoulders. "I mean, it is only fair that we both know you were forced to make the offer."

He could not deny the truth and Juliet walked to her dressing table then sat down to brush her hair before he had thought how to respond.

He tried to sound convincing. "I wasn't forc—"

"So Christian was merely offering you his congratulations when he sliced open your chest?" She raised her eyebrows to punctuate the question. "And I suppose you had invited four gentlemen around for tea the morning after . . ."

"You can't marry Barksdale."

Juliet spun around in her chair, asking, "Why not?"

Her eyes held his with such intensity that Seamus was having a difficult time thinking. "Because he's an idiot."

"And you're an ass."

Juliet turned away from him and tilted her head to the side as she continued to brush her long hair. He watched her in the mirror and was stunned to see a tear fall from the corner of her beautiful eyes. He watched it roll down her cheek, and his heart ripped in two.

"Juliet," he whispered, walking to her and reaching out to rub her shoulder with his right hand. "I'm so sorry. Marry Barksdale if that will make you happy."

Even if it would kill him.

But he hadn't said the right thing. Seamus could see that he had only upset her more when she put both elbows on the vanity and covered her face.

He swept her luscious hair to one side and bent down to kiss the back of her neck.

"Don't cry, Juliet," Seamus begged, turning her head so that he could kiss her on the cheek.

His lips were moistened by her delicate tears and he followed their path, kissing them away. She tilted her head to the side, abandoning her sorrow to his comfort. Her head fell back against his shoulder as her right hand drifted up to caress the back of his head.

The air was pushed from his lungs and his heart leapt with the need to hold her. His left hand slid around Juliet's waist; his right hand drifted to her breast. He squeezed softly, eliciting an encouraging moan.

Seamus eased Juliet to her feet, kicking the chair from between them. He drew her to him and smiled when he saw Juliet close her eyes in the reflection of the mirror.

The thought that the touch of his body had given her pleasure made him want to give her so much more. He dipped his hand between her breasts and untied her silky robe, letting it fall to the floor.

Seamus stared at the mirror, looking at Juliet in nothing more than a thin nightdress that made visible every curve of her beautiful body. He kissed the other side of her neck, remembering how she had felt beneath him, how he had felt when he made love to her.

He wanted to feel like that again, to confirm that what he had experienced in her arms was real, that his mind had not embellished his memory during the long nights without her.

His left hand swept down her neck, taking the left sleeve of her nightdress with him. He kissed her bare shoulder, her skin so flawless, so soft. Seamus was breathing hard and his eyes skimmed over the curves that hinted at the full breasts he knew were hiding beneath the nightdress.

His right hand was on her other shoulder and he took a step back, pulling down her right sleeve. He stared in the mirror, his eyes following the nightdress as it fluttered to the floor. His breath caught and he stared in the mirror at a nude Juliet, his memory flawless.

Seamus kissed her and avoided looking her in the eye as he carried her to bed, afraid that she would stop him, stop this from happening if he did.

He stripped quickly and climbed over her, only then

looking her in the eye. Neither of them spoke as he set about comforting her. He touched her gently, reverently, as they drew nearer to becoming one.

She began kissing him back, consoling him as much as he was comforting her. He rolled on his back, needing to know that she wanted him.

He leaned against the pillows and Juliet straddled him, placing her hands on his shoulders and leaving them eye to eye. She didn't kiss him or caress him; they merely stared at one another as she sank down his length.

Neither of them breathed, until she lifted herself, only to have their breath stolen when she sank down again. Seamus grasped her backside to aid in the rhythm of their breathing, their lovemaking.

Her breathing became more rapid as did her movements. Seamus moaned, but he dare not look away from the eyes that saw him so clearly.

Tears began forming in her eyes, but he did not know why. His hands slid to her hips and he penetrated more fully. Her eyes remained fixed on his. She was close to her peak and Seamus raced to catch her.

He reached up and caressed her cheek and Juliet sank down, causing them to climax as one.

His entire body was trembling and nothing else existed.

He stared into her beautiful eyes, shaken.

"Marry me?" Seamus asked before he knew what he was saying.

He had asked for her hand before, but this time he felt no sense of obligation, no guilt, only a terrifying desire for her to say yes.

"You bastard," she whispered, the sound of devastation in her voice. "Is that why you came here, to coerce me into marrying you?"

"I . . ." Seamus wanted to deny it, to tell her that he was there because he wanted her and nothing more, but it wasn't true.

He had come because he didn't want anyone else to have her. She was his.

Juliet pushed away from him, scrabbling off the bed. "You thought if you made love to me again, that I would consent to be your wife? Get out," she whispered. He could not move and anger contorted her features as she shoved him in the chest. "Get out!"

He just stared at her, not understanding what the hell had just happened, not understanding how their incredible lovemaking had resulted in her screaming at him.

"Very well, then, I shall leave." Juliet was out of bed and covering her beautiful body with a silk sheet before Seamus could stop her.

"Juliet." What could he say?

She stopped at her bedchamber door and turned to him.

"So kind of you to ask, but I'm afraid I must refuse your offer, Mister McCurren. You see, I have a bit of a scandalous reputation that I have yet to earn and now that I have crossed *you* off the list"—she smiled—"I can move on to Lord Barksdale."

His jaw clamped shut and he climbed out of bed. "Don't, Juliet."

Juliet cupped her hand to her ear. "I'm sorry, I must not have heard correctly, for a moment you sounded like a jealous husband. But then again you're not my husband." She cocked her head to the side. "Are you, Seamus?"

Before she left him for Barksdale, Seamus took careful aim and then let his words fly.

"Well, you've one thing to recommend you to the rakes of the *ton*." Juliet turned to meet his eye, her lovely long hair cascading down the cobalt sheet she held to her chest. "You're bright if not beautiful."

Her mouth fell open and Seamus could see that he had struck dead center. Tears welled in her bright blue eyes, and as he witnessed the depth of her wound, Seamus was unsettled to find that his verbal blow had made him bleed far more than Juliet.

He stood, naked before her, unable to move through his shame and guilt to comfort her. Seamus blinked and she was gone. He staggered backward, his shaky legs barely able to hold him until he sank to the mattress. He placed his head in his hands and stared at the floor in shock.

For twenty-six years he had been alone, had felt out of place in the world. Not until he had met Juliet Pervill had Seamus realized that there were others like him and the relief, the elation of that discovery, had been beyond measure.

Yet only when he had made love to Juliet, when he held her in his arms, had Seamus truly understood that Juliet was his. Slated by God, his match in both mind and spirit, and what had he done, but driven her straight into the arms of another man.

He wondered what Juliet would calculate to be the odds of his meeting another woman with a mind equal to his own. She would know, of course. He laughed painfully then sucked in the bitterness that burned the back of his throat, mingling with the familiar cold of desolation and his perpetual loneliness.

Thirty-one

※

It had been two days since they had left town, and Juliet sat with her mother in their drawing room, staring out the window at the waning moon.

She sighed for the hundredth time, prompting her mother to breach the two-day silence. "Did you tell him?"

"What?" Juliet flipped a page of a newspaper.

"That you love him?"

"I don't love him." She flipped another page, having read nothing.

"Of course you do. You didn't even ask to whom I was referring."

"I'm not in love with Seamus McCurren."

"Then why did you go to him?"

"What are you talking about, Mother?" Juliet looked up from her paper, confused.

"When you escaped from your kidnappers, you went to him." Her mother raised an accusing brow. "Not me, not Felicity—"

"He works for the Foreign Office. It was only logical—"

"Bullocks." Her mother looked down at her cross-stitch and Juliet's jaw dropped at her mother's crudeness. "We both know why you went to him that day and why you have run off to the country. You're scared."

"I'm not scared of Seamus McCurren."

"Of your feelings for him, you stupid girl," her mother lectured affectionately. "You are so afraid that he will not love you in return that you have fled to the country."

She was in love with him, had been for quite some time, but men like Seamus McCurren did not love women like her. "I don't want to talk about it, Mother."

It was far too painful.

Juliet looked down at an advertisement of fashion plates for the spring season and tried not to think. Ball gowns, riding gowns, day gowns . . . mourning gowns. She read on.

"When is Felicity coming to visit?"

"Next week." Her mother pulled a stitch.

"Perhaps we should have a ball while she is here."

"If that would take your mind off Seamus McCurren." Her mother met her eye and she rolled hers.

She flipped a page and her nose wrinkled. "Mother, listen to this."

Juliet lifted the newspaper and read aloud the description of the pictured gown.

Madame Maria's Modiste

Welcome spring in this stunning muslin gown where fashion meets function. The many layers of quality muslin are trimmed by the finest of colorful silk ribbon. Stroll across the Serpentine wearing this gown and you are sure to turn heads. This design can be fashioned with varieties of fabrics for spring. Please,

*call on Madame Maria's to be the first to wear
London's latest fashions.*

"Doesn't that sound odd to you?" Juliet continued to stare at the page as she spoke.

"Madame Maria, was it?" Her mother pulled another stitch of the pale silk thread. "Poor woman is assuredly foreign, which is no doubt why she butchers our language while peddling her wares to poor, unsuspecting country girls eager to purchase town fashions."

"What do you mean 'butchers our language'?"

The countess looked up from her embroidery as if she had failed as a mother.

"Well, darling, one would never say 'with varieties of fabrics,' would one. Any lady with a minimum of breeding would have written 'with a variety of fabrics.' 'Variety' is, of course, already plural in this instance, so why on earth would one say 'varieties of fabrics' unless the woman was a foreigner and unfamiliar with the subtlety of the English language."

Juliet froze. "Pardon?"

Her mother looked down at her intricate creation, losing interest. "I said Madame Maria was undoubtedly a foreigner, Italian most likely, unfamiliar with the subtleties of the English language."

With varieties of fabrics. Juliet stared at the paragraph and thought, *With varieties of fabrics.*

"Mother, throw me your pencil," Juliet said, agitated.

"I do not 'throw' things, Juliet." Her mother was busy stabbing the linen on one of the many marks she had made with the pencil she kept in her embroidery basket. "If you wish to—"

"Throw me the pencil, Mother!" Juliet shouted and her mother's head snapped up, hearing Juliet's uncommon distress.

Their eyes meet and her mother picked up the pencil

and threw it across the small sitting area. Juliet caught it, her hands shaking as she began to work with her feet still curled under her.

She ignored her mother's gaze as her eyes darted from letter to letter and word to word. And then she thought of Seamus and his description of the cryptographer as "orderly."

The person who had written the E code had an organized mind, creating a simple system of cryptography that was virtually impossible to detect.

Juliet looked again and then whispered to herself, "No wonder Seamus only found the markers," before glancing up. "Mother, I must return to London. Would you be so kind as to send my things to Felicity's?"

"You're not leaving now?" her mother asked, appalled. "It is the middle of the night."

"It is ten o'clock in the evening, Mother, and if I leave tonight, I can be in London tomorrow evening." She kissed the countess on the cheek. "Don't worry. I shall take a battalion of footmen with me."

"It is the footmen I worry for," her mother quipped over raised brows.

Enigma sat at her table and smiled to herself when Seamus McCurren entered her establishment.

"Ah, Mister McCurren," Youngblood said. "Do join the table, we were just getting started."

The cards went flying about the table and Enigma glanced at Youngblood's cards and then watched the expressions of the men around her. The old man had nothing, the young gentleman thought he did, the fat man wasn't sure, and Mister McCurren . . .

She had no idea.

A surge of excitement went through her and she placed two fingers on Youngblood's thigh, knowing it was not the card he would have played. He tossed the card that she had ordered and Mister McCurren raised a brow ever so slightly, surprised.

McCurren won the trick and laid a second card down and Enigma tried not to envision his beautiful hands on her body. Her attraction to the man who had broken her code was becoming distracting at a time in which she needed none.

But she could not help herself.

She placed four fingers against Youngblood's thigh and watched the intelligence burning in the golden eyes of the man across from her. She watched his full lips, the precision of his sideburns. He was a man who liked control and she was more than willing to give him the reins.

Stimulated, her hand drifted to Youngblood's cock and she caressed his length. His green eyes darted to hers, but when he saw her looking at Seamus McCurren, his jaw pulsed with anger.

She touched three fingers against Youngblood's elegant thigh and grinned as she stroked him, knowing how much he liked to be handled. His pretty eyes were having a difficult time staying open and it took him a moment to throw out the card.

Her attention returned to Seamus McCurren, whose gaze had wandered elsewhere.

"Are we in need of redecorating, Mister McCurren?"

"Not at all," Seamus said to Dante's beautiful bawd, while keeping his eyes on the short man with a bandage wrapped around his head. A thought crawled up the back of his mind and took root, spreading an uneasiness that left him cold. He tried to shake it off but the sensation of apprehension grew until he finally asked the stocky little man, "Do you work here?"

"Yes sir," the man said and the instant he heard the Welsh tones he knew why he was so uneasy. This Welshman was the man Juliet had described as having rescued her.

Seamus took a steadying breath, inhaling the implications of this man standing here, in Dante's employ. But the longer he sat, the more intensely he could feel Young-blood's eyes on him. He could feel the eyes of the man that had kidnapped Juliet, had intended to kill her.

"Might I have a brandy then." Seamus smiled, using all of his control to keep from shooting the proprietor of Dante's where he sat.

But avenging Juliet's kidnapping would do him no good, and as he played his hand of cards, he contemplated the deeper game.

"Nicely done, Mister Youngblood." Seamus nodded to his adversary, who had concealed a pit of French vipers in his den of iniquity.

"I've never been complimented for taking a man's money, Mister McCurren."

"I'm not complimenting your taking my blunt, Mister Youngblood," he said to the creator of the E code. "I am complimenting your outplaying me."

The proprietor's lover grinned and Seamus's eyes narrowed. He glanced about the room, glanced at the influential men seated around him and the half-dozen upstairs.

Dante's was the perfect venue for the cryptographer's needs.

Ply the gentleman of the *ton*, of Parliament, with drink and women then relay the information gathered in their weakened state to France.

However, as Seamus stared at Mister Youngblood and his superiority of play, he realized that Lord Harrington had not been the only gentleman coerced into service by France. There would be others being blackmailed for a myriad of unseemly reasons, the least of which was a gaming debt.

"I'm afraid I am finished for the evening."

Seamus rose and Youngblood's lover asked, "Is she expecting you so early?"

Irritated and overcome by his own guilt, Seamus met the woman's cold, indigo eyes. "Unfortunately, I have no lady expecting me at all."

"No lady?" The bawd raised an eyebrow. "We've no ladies here, Mister McCurren, but surely you see something you like."

The woman sat back in her chair seductively and Youngblood's head snapped round as she continued to smile at Seamus in carnal speculation.

"While Dante's is indeed entertaining, I'm afraid it does not offer the quality of companionship to which I am accustomed."

Youngblood's glare shot daggers at the woman as he said, "You see, Mister McCurren prefers ladies, my dear, not secondhand whores."

"If you will excuse me?" Madame Richard met Youngblood's gaze as she stood. "I'm off to earn you a bit of blunt."

Three gentlemen at the table jumped on the rare opportunity, rising, but the bawd called to the ever-present head of security.

"Mister Collin," she said, and Seamus stared at the fury in Mister Youngblood's eyes, confused. "Have we an available room upstairs?"

"Yes, Madame Richard."

"Show me," she said and they disappeared from sight.

Thirty-two

❧❧❧

$Falcon$ glanced at the Duke of Glenbroke when a knock sounded at their private room of White's, interrupting their chess match.

The young duke shrugged his enormous shoulders and then looked toward the door, saying, "Enter."

But rather than a footman delivering a message as Falcon had expected, the fair figure of the Marquess Shelton stood in the door.

"Sorry to disturb you," the marquess said, closing the door, fully aware as were the other members of the *ton* that they were never to be disturbed while enjoying their weekly match.

"I assume it is important?" Falcon asked, turning in his chair.

Ian Shelton was a powerful man, not only physically but mentally, and Falcon silently approved of the close friendship between these two young men.

"Yes." The marquess sat in one of the vacant chairs and looked at him. "I believe that it is."

"Well," the duke demanded.

"I came to tell you about my fascinating weekend."

Ian St. John smiled at the duke, who rolled his eyes, saying, "A bachelor should never tell a married man of his exploits, particularly 'fascinating' exploits."

"Ah, but this one, I think, will be of interest to our lordship as much as to you, Your Grace."

Falcon raised a brow, intrigued, "Do tell us of your weekend, Shelton."

"It began with a journey to the estate of Lord Harrington."

"The bastard who ruined Juliet Pervill?" the duke growled as Ian leaned forward and handed Falcon his invitation.

" 'A meeting of the minds'?" Falcon asked, both of them ignoring the duke entirely. "What on earth does that mean?"

"Exactly what I wanted to know."

"And did you find out?" Falcon asked.

The marquess raised both blond brows. "I'm not sure. We were shown into the drawing room before dinner and told by Harrington that the purpose of his coordinating the 'first of many' gatherings"—it was Falcon's turn to raise a brow—"was for influential members of society to come together to discuss in a comfortable environment the issues facing our great nation."

"What did you discuss?" the duke asked, curious.

"Everything from Napoleon to surplus corn crops."

Falcon thought for a moment and then asked, "And how did Harrington appear?"

"Very interested"—the marquess met his eye—"which was rather odd since he has not attended a single session of Parliament for as long as I have been a member."

"I've never seen him either," the duke confirmed.

"But that is not all," Shelton said, "When I went to my room, I found a pretty little chambermaid waiting to warm my bed." Falcon waited. "Talkative little thing, Mira, wanted to know all about me and the House of Lords as she removed my trousers."

"Sacrificed yourself for your country, did you, Ian?" The duke smiled, stealing a glance in Falcon's direction.

"Good God, no." The marquess laughed. "I could hear the girl's sex clapping the moment I entered the room."

"A professional woman?" Falcon elicited an opinion.

"From the way she moved, I've no doubt of it," Ian said. "But why so talkative?"

"Good question," the duke asked.

"I'll have Lord Harrington investigated, this chambermaid, too. Mira, you said the girl's name was."

"Mira," Shelton confirmed. "Brown hair, midnight blue eyes, and a birthmark on her right breast."

The duke raised a brow, adding a sardonic grin. "Laboring hard for the cause of freedom?"

"You know me, Your Grace," the marquess said. "Anything for the crown."

"It is not your crown falling off that I'm worried about." The duke laughed and Falcon chuckled. "More in the vicinity of the family jewels, I should think."

As the marquess glared at his powerful friend, his lips remaining firmly closed, Falcon's mind returned to the reason Ian St. John had called.

" 'A meeting of the minds'?" Falcon mused as if their conversation had never strayed.

The only question was, whose was the mind behind Lord Harrington's meeting? And what did that mind want to know?

Thirty-three

❧

Enigma stood with arms outstretched when the door to Madame Maria's was flung open with a violent ringing of the bell above the modiste shop door.

She turned to look at the offensive interruption as the woman ordered her footmen to remain outside. Madame Maria jotted down the last measurement she had taken of Enigma's trim waist before bobbing her head.

"Excuse me, Madame Richard." Maria's words were forced by a vulgar Italian intonation as if the sounds were fermented deep within her belly.

Enigma gave a nod of consent for the modiste's departure and then she turned to look at the woman who had disturbed them.

The girl was certainly small to be so loud and her English lineage could clearly be seen in her fair skin and clear blue eyes. She might even at some point be called pretty, given a few more years on the vine.

"Buongiorno, Madame Maria," the girl said and Enigma lowered her arms, sensing a lengthy and meaningless conversation.

"Good afternoon, Lady Juliet."

Enigma's head snapped round, giving the girl a second look. This was the woman the brilliant Seamus McCurren had been bedding?

Unbelievable!

"Yes, good afternoon, Madame Maria," Lady Juliet said and then turned to her and apologized. "I'm so sorry to interrupt your fitting."

Enigma smoothed down the tight silk on what she knew to be an exceptional figure. "Take all the time you need, my dear," Enigma replied, meaning every word. "I'm in no hurry."

The girl turned back to the modiste to hasten their exchange. "I was wondering if I might see your last month's advertisements?" Maria's brows asked the question for her and Lady Juliet explained, "There was a beautiful gown that I was considering purchasing in one of your advertisements but I cannot seem to remember which paper—"

"Ah, *si*." Madame Maria handed Lady Juliet a stack of newspapers and then walked over to Enigma to finish taking her measurements.

"Madame Maria, who writes the adverts for your gowns?"

"I hire a skinny man at the paper." The modiste continued taking measurements while Enigma stood watching Lady Juliet from the corner of her eye.

The girl nodded and she looked down, her mouth moving as she read. But it was not until Lady Juliet's finger began to stab at the pages of newsprint that Enigma realized what the woman was doing.

She was counting.

Enigma stared more closely, reading the girl's lips as

Lady Juliet counted to ten, over and over again. The lady turned the page and continued to count, her eyes getting closer to the words as she concentrated on them.

And then the girl smiled, and deep within the woman's intelligent eyes, Enigma saw her allure to Seamus McCurren.

Her heart was beating with excitement at being this close to being detected, this close to a woman capable of doing so.

"Madame Maria makes lovely gowns, does she not?" Enigma could not help speaking with a woman as gifted as she.

Lady Juliet looked up as though unsure if the question was addressed to her. "Yes, they are very beautiful." The girl smiled, adding, "Might I keep these?" to the busy modiste.

Madame Maria shrugged, delighted by the compliment. "Certainly, take as many adverts as you wish."

"Thank you so very much, Madame Maria." Juliet grinned triumphantly and, being a well-bred English lady, turned to Enigma and said, "Good day."

"Good day." She smiled, adding, "Lady Juliet Pervill, was it not?"

"Yes." The girl stopped on the threshold of the door, stunned. "I'm sorry but have we been introduced?" she asked and Enigma respected her even more.

"No, my name is Madame Richard," Enigma said pleasantly. "And perhaps now that we have been introduced, we shall meet again?"

"Yes, perhaps we shall." Lady Juliet met her eye before turning to leave and saying, "Thank you again, Madame Maria."

The door closed and Enigma grinned, contemplating what use she would make of this information and more importantly . . . what use she would make of Juliet Pervill.

"Mister Habernathy, you've no idea how happy I am to see you."

"Good afternoon, Lady Juliet." James Habernathy smiled, pleased to see her again. "Where is your guard?" he asked, confused.

"I left them on the front steps, but I don't have time to explain." She walked to Seamus's desk and riffled through his papers. "I think I may have identified our French cryptographer."

"Really?" Mister Habernathy looked stunned.

"Yes." Juliet tried not to be annoyed at his surprise of her intellectual ability. "And the last thing I need at the moment is two footmen following me about. I need to verify a few things before I present my findings to Falcon or I shall never be reinstated with the Foreign Office."

"Oh, yes, I see." Mister Habernathy nodded. "It wouldn't do to make an error, and if you will forgive me for saying so, Lady Juliet, I thought it rather unfair that you had been dismissed at all."

Juliet's hands stilled and she stopped herself from crying. "Why no, Mister Habernathy, I don't mind your saying so at all." Her loyal secretary blushed and Juliet eased his embarrassment. "Now, we have two hours to prepare."

"Prepare for what?"

"For our meeting with the architect of the E code."

"I think I've identified our cryptographer." Seamus stared at the Duke of Glenbroke and then Falcon, having located them in a private room at White's.

"Thank you, Mister McCurren, but I am afraid that we already know who the man is." Falcon moved a pawn and, without looking up, said, "Lord Harrington was found dead in his town home from an overdose of laudanum not three hours ago. While the blackguard's death is not surprising to anyone who knew him, it was the unfortunate mauling of his solicitor by two dogs that rather convinced me."

"His solicitor is dead?" Seamus asked, horrified.

"Oh, yes torn to pieces on the steps of his front door."

Falcon sighed. "Unnecessary that, although the solicitor's death does suggest his complicity in the matter of Lord Harrington's collaboration."

"We also have information pertaining to several week-end gatherings where prominent gentlemen were asked to discuss their views on the political direction in which Britain is heading."

Seamus shook his head. "I'm sorry but you have made a mistake about Lord Harrington."

"What makes you think so?" The duke's eyes had sharpened to steel.

"A little more than a month ago, Lord Harrington lost his town home during a card game to Lord Pervill."

"Yes, Mister McCurren, we know all that," the old man said impatiently.

Seamus continued, undeterred. "What you may not know is the name of the establishment where the transfer took place. A well-respected gaming hell by the name of Dante's Inferno."

"I know of it." The duke nodded.

Seamus cleared his throat, having difficulty admitting the remainder of the details. "I, myself, am a frequent visitor of that particular hell as the hell's proprietor, a one Mister Lucas Youngblood, provides the only gaming challenge for me in town."

"Go on," Falcon said, understanding Seamus's need for intellectual stimulation.

"Several weeks ago, I was a patron at Dante's alongside Lord Harrington." Seamus snorted. "If Mister Youngblood was an equal match for me, then Lord Harrington would have been a sitting duck."

"Meaning?" The duke wanted clarification.

"Meaning . . ." Falcon took over his enlightenment. "Mister Youngblood fleeced the fool and made off with Harrington's estate."

"No doubt solicitors were involved in the transfer of

property, which would explain why both Harrington and his solicitor have been made conveniently dead."

"Yes, I sent round a representative of the Foreign Office to interview Lord Harrington's solicitor just yesterday."

"Imagine the amount of information flowing through Dante's." Seamus glanced from one man to the other. "From blackmail, to drunkenness, to the secrets whispered to attentive whores."

The duke stared at Falcon, uncomfortable with the infinite and disastrous possibilities.

"I'll send my men to seize Dante's Inferno straight away." Falcon said.

Seamus nodded. "I'll be in my office looking over my files to see if I can prove my supposition."

The duke rose, ending the conversation. "And I will speak with the prime minister."

Thirty-four

‿❧❧‿

It was two o'clock in the afternoon and Dante's Inferno was empty.

Enigma finished writing a missive to the emperor and then sealed the letter with her symbol of black wax arrows. She tucked the priceless piece of information in her reticule and moved on to other matters.

"Have you transferred the money as I've specified, Mister Matthews?"

"Yes, Madame Richard." Her accountant bobbed his head like a frightened turtle. "Everything was transferred precisely as you instructed."

"Excellent, Mister Matthews, because it is a great deal of money and if I for one moment believed that you were embezzling—"

"Oh, no, Madame Richard! I would never do such a thing," her accountant protested, and as she looked into his dull little eyes, she believed him.

"You shall accompany us to Hyde Park, where you will

move your luggage to a coach that is traveling to Scotland as previously arranged." And then she turned to Mister Matthews as if she had just remembered. "You've taken care of the other matter, I am sure?"

"Yes." The man bobbed again, "The profitability of Dante's Inferno made the business of insuring the establishment rather straightforward. We had several gentlemen, regular patrons of Dante's, who were more than pleased to provide the protection requested."

"Excellent work, Mister Matthews." Enigma smiled brilliantly and the accountant blushed at her attention. "Oh, and tell Mister Collin that I wish to speak with him before we depart."

Her accountant left and within minutes the satisfying Mister Collin was opening her office door. Smiling, she walked toward him, her hand sliding over his taut buttocks the moment she touched him.

"Are you ready to set up shop elsewhere, darling, or are you still angry with me about Youngblood?" Mister Collin smiled and she allowed him to kiss her, caress her, before she dislodged herself from his arms, saying, "I shall be waiting for you in the carriage when you have finished in here."

Enigma walked out the front door of Dante's Inferno for the last time with absolutely no regrets. She had made an enormous amount of money, and with this last exchange of British secrets with the French, she would be able to retire a very rich woman.

But Enigma knew that she would not.

She was addicted to the game of making money off men who underestimated her and of making love to men who did not. It was a perfect life for a woman such as she, but inevitably every game came to an end so that another might begin.

Enigma settled onto the squabs in her landau next to her accountant and opposite her front man, Mister Youngblood.

The three of them waited in silence, staring at Dante's façade as they waited for Mister Collin. Yet, while the men stared at the front door, Enigma stared at her office window.

The vermillion curtains fluttered, licked by orange flames that Mister Collin had unleashed. She smiled and the front door of the most successful hell in London opened and her obedient bodyguard walked out to join her.

Jack Collin settled into the crowded carriage next to the pretty Mister Youngblood and then banged on the roof, shouting, "Hyde Park."

They ambled forward, and as Enigma smiled across at Mister Youngblood, they could hear distant shouts of "Fire!" but it would not matter.

The fire would consume Dante's along with half the buildings on their street, and there was not a damn thing anyone could do to stop it.

"Well, now that we are all together, I suppose it would be best to review our plan." They made their way to Hyde Park and she continued to talk to her faithful servants. "Mister Matthews has made the financial arrangements for our relocation and will be traveling to Scotland, where he will wait three days before boarding our ship."

"Yes, Madame Richard," the accountant said, to indicate that he understood her instructions clearly.

The carriage turned into the park then stopped in a wooded area as they waited for Mister Matthews's conveyance to arrive.

"The only difficulty I see in the entire plan, Mister Matthews . . ." She turned to look at her gifted accountant. "Is the large amount of money that has been stolen from me." The little accountant went white when Mister Collin pulled out his knife and stared down at him.

"No!"

"I really don't like being robbed, Mister Matthews." Enigma nodded to Mister Collin. "And I won't tolerate embezzlement," she said as her bodyguard reached out and stabbed Mister Youngblood on the left side, smiling all the while.

Her accountant started to swoon as he stared at the dead man seated across from her.

"Listen to me, Mister Matthews," she cooed, keeping him conscious. "You are an important facet of my trade and I very much value your contribution." Enigma smiled. "So, from this moment forth, I would like for you to increase your wages by one pound per week."

Her accountant stared at Mister Youngblood's corpse and then at the man who had killed him. "That is very . . . generous of you, Madame Richard."

"Oh, you have earned every penny of the increase, Mister Matthews." She looked at her bodyguard for confirmation. "Hasn't he, Mister Collin."

"Yes," Jack Collin begrudgingly agreed as he stared out the window.

The second carriage arrived and Mister Matthews bolted for the door, but Enigma stopped him.

"Now don't forget to wait three days before meeting us on board our ship." Her accountant nodded, stepping to the ground. "And Mister Matthews, if you disappoint me . . ." Her indigo eyes were cold and then warmth returned to them. "Oh, but you won't, will you, Edgar."

"I would never think of disappointing you, Madame Richard." Her accountant bowed, terrified. "Three days?"

Enigma smiled. "Three days." Mister Collin closed the landau door.

"He'll be there," Mister Collin concluded, wiping the blood from his large knife.

"I know," she said and then moved on to her next task. "What time is it?"

"Half past three."

Enigma sighed, "What are we going to do for half a bloody hour?"

Her bodyguard smiled and she laughed. "You are not

sincerely proposing that we rut in the same conveyance as Mister Youngblood's corpse?"

His eyes were hot, making her burn. "I couldn't think of a better use of a half hour."

Enigma looked him up and down and began to unbutton her pelisse, saying, "You're a vindictive bastard aren't you, Jack?"

"Yes, but nowhere near as vindictive as you," he said with admiration clinging to every word and every touch.

Seamus hurried back to the Foreign Office in the hopes of catching his secretary James Habernathy before the man left for the evening.

"James?" Seamus called, opening the door, but the office was empty.

Seamus gave a groan of disappointment as he moved quickly toward his desk. He pulled out all of the E code files and was beginning to sort them out, to see if he could prove the arrogant Mister Youngblood's involvement, when he found himself in need of a pencil.

He searched his desk drawer and, finding nothing, glanced at Juliet's smaller desk. The desk would be moved out tomorrow and he would not have to endure the pain of losing her every time he walked into the room.

But for now it was there and Seamus was sure she had a multitude of pencils tucked away in one of her tiny drawers. He rose then forced himself to walk to her side of the office, the signs of Juliet's unforgettable presence still lingering in the room, lingering in his heart.

He pushed away his pain as he continued to search and then something caught his eye. He lifted the newspaper and saw Juliet's hasty handwriting, and the hair on the back of his neck stood on end.

She had found something, had scribbled away at the letters of the description of the spring gown until Seamus had no notion what was left. He reread the description, trying to think as Juliet did, trying to match that brilliant mind of hers.

But as he workèd and failed to crack the code, he thought of the E cryptographer . . . order and control. He tried again and failed. Seamus was beginning to panic when he thought of the reason why Juliet would come to the Foreign Office. She was trying to catch the cryptographer on her own because he had given her no one to work with.

He tried again, putting himself in Juliet's mathematical mind. Numbers. He began to count. One, three . . . Order and control. Five—

Seamus rose alongside his fear as he counted to ten and found the words.

Meets . . . by . . . Serpentine . . . heads . . . for . . .
first . . .

Today was February first. He had to assume that the meeting was taking place today and that Juliet was going to attend. That she was going to place herself in harm's way. Panicked, he yanked his watch from his waistcoat, breaking the golden fob. Five minutes to four o'clock.

"God, no." Seamus dropped the advertisement and ran to the stables.

His horse was just being unsaddled when Seamus stopped the man and took the reins. He jumped atop his mount and sent him flying toward the park, toward Juliet.

Seamus tried to concentrate on the roads, the fastest method of getting to the Serpentine, but all he could think about was Juliet. If something were to happen to her . . . He could not envision life without her, could not bare the thought of returning to the loneliness and isolation of not being understood.

But it was not just her mind or her humor. It was her face, her delightful freckled nose, those beautiful blue eyes, her mouth. His chest tightened as he remembered kissing that mouth, remembered the experience of making love to Juliet, the experience of being in love with Juliet Pervill.

He was in love with her, and if anything were to happen to his Juliet—

A bell tower chimed, announcing the four o'clock hour. Seamus's chest was pounding as hard as his horse's hooves, but he knew it was not from his ride. He was becoming enveloped by dark thoughts of losing her.

For if Juliet died, Seamus knew that he would never again live.

Thirty-five

⤬⤬

As Juliet stood in Hyde Park with Mister Habernathy by her side, she tried to ignore her growing sense of anticipation. She had come to the park to catch her cryptographer, to prove to Seamus and his lordship that she very much deserved her place within the Foreign Office.

"Let us sit on this bench," Juliet whispered to her loyal friend. "It will give us a perfect view of the Serpentine."

"Yes," Mister Habernathy agreed and they sat down. "I've instructed your driver to be prepared to leave at a moment's notice."

"Thank you, Mister Habernathy," Juliet said, turning to meet the man's kind eyes. "Thank you for coming with me rather than going to his lordship."

"Lady Juliet." Mister Habernathy grinned. "I would not miss your besting Mister McCurren for all the world, and besides, his lordship ordered me to keep an eye on you."

"Did he really?" she asked, stunned.

"Weeks ago. But with Mister McCurren's footmen at your side there has been no need."

Juliet chuckled and then glanced at her pocket watch. "Four o'clock." She stared at the head of the Serpentine and then heard an insistent quack.

Juliet looked down at a pretty little duck that was looking back at her. The duck had quacked, thinking she was a source of food, and then other ducks began to gather at her skirts. The first duck quacked again, becoming less adorable by the minute, and Juliet thrust her hand out, saying, "Shoo," then gazed back at the bridge over the Serpentine, which remained blessedly deserted.

Then there arose a chorus of quacks and Juliet looked down at the seven ducks that had abandoned the water in favor of her provision. Several heads turned in her direction and Juliet cringed.

"I'll attend to them." Mister Habernathy stood, shooing the ducks away, but they parted for him like the Red Sea then ran back to their provider.

Juliet sighed. "There is nothing for it, Mister Habernathy. Animals have always thought me one of their kind."

She reached down to dig up a handful of dirt and then walked to the long water, a half-dozen ducks in tow. Juliet cast the cold clumps of earth out over the pond and the greedy little ducks went swimming after them.

Dusting off her soiled gloves, she glanced at the Serpentine when a pleasant voice asked from behind, "Feeding the water fowl, Lady Juliet, wasn't it?"

Juliet turned to look at a beautiful blond woman, and it took several moments for her to realize with whom she was speaking. "I met you at Madame Maria's?"

"That's it exactly." The woman smiled. "Did you find the gown you were hoping to purchase?"

"Uh." Juliet glanced over her shoulder at the Serpentine, distracted, and then turned back to the woman. *What was her name?* "No, I'm afraid not."

"Well," the stunning woman said, about to impart her wisdom when Juliet saw a large man walking toward them over the woman's right shoulder. "Perhaps you can describe the gown to Madame Maria and she can create something even more becoming."

"Yes," Juliet murmured, but her eyes grew wide when the large man passed them, a nasty scar marring the left side of his face. A face she had seen in the office of the *London Herald* just three days prior to the E code appearing in that very publication. "That is an excellent suggestion. Now, if you will excuse me, I'm afraid we are expected elsewhere."

Mister Habernathy bowed and the lady inclined her head, "I look forward to seeing you very soon, Lady Juliet."

"Me also," Juliet said, taking James's arm and slowly following their man.

Got you!

The man with the scar stopped by the Serpentine bridge and then greeted an older and much smaller man. The pair appeared, to anyone but herself, to be old friends having unexpectedly crossed paths in the park.

But she knew better.

"That's him, the one with the scar. I've seen him before at the *Herald*," she whispered to Mister Habernathy, who watched as the smaller man gave the taller a parcel before receiving a missive in return. "Follow the cryptographer. We must stop the supply of information. The Frenchman is of less importance."

"Right." Mister Habernathy deferred to her logic and they turned to the left, increasing their pace.

The man with the scar walked deeper into the park and Juliet began to fear that they would not be able to follow him without detection. She was just formulating a secondary plan when they rounded a bend in the trail and caught sight of the cryptographer's conveyance.

"Run back to the carriage and have my driver cut through the park just there," she ordered James while keeping a watchful eye on the cryptographer. "I'll observe which direction his landau is heading, and with any luck, we can catch sight of him before he exits the park."

"I don't think—"

"I can't run in this gown, James." Juliet met her secretary's eye. "Either you do it or we lose the cryptographer altogether."

James nodded and began running back toward Juliet's carriage. He was no more than fifty yards away when Juliet heard a pistol cock behind her back.

"Would you be so kind as to join me, Lady Juliet?"

Her brows furrowed as she turned toward the beautiful woman from Madame Maria's. Realization struck. Only a woman would have thought to use a lady's advertisement to send her code.

"You."

The woman smiled, watching as she put two and two together. "Yes."

Juliet's mouth opened to call for James, but he was already on his way back, fear in his eyes.

"Move," the lady said and Juliet had no choice but to walk toward the woman's conveyance.

However, as they neared the door of the landau, Juliet looked over her shoulder in confusion as the lady seemed totally unconcerned by James Habernathy's dogged pursuit. He was no more than twenty feet from her when the man with the scar stepped out from behind a tree.

Time stopped and Juliet ran toward James, but it was too late. The man stabbed James in the stomach, and all she could do was stand there and watch. James fell to his knees, his rapid puffs of breath visible in the cold winter air. Juliet continued to run toward him, but the man with the scar scooped her up on his way to the lady's conveyance.

He threw Juliet inside the landau. The woman from Madame Maria's was already seated as he closed the door. Juliet glanced out the window, tears streaming down her face as she watched James collapse, the puffs of breath that affirmed his life now gone.

The carriage lurched forward and Juliet stared across at the man with the empty eyes. He smirked as she cried and Juliet lost control. She kicked him and struck out at his face.

The brutal man caught her painfully by the wrist as the woman to her left began to laugh, "Careful with this one, Mister Collin. The lady is not as tame as she appears."

Juliet turned her head to the left, asking angrily, "How do you know me?"

"I had you followed, my dear."

Juliet paled, remembering the instance in front of Felicity's house. "For how long?"

"Since you began disrupting my code and for as long as you have been Seamus McCurren's lover."

Juliet felt ill.

"What do you want from me?" she asked, wondering why they had not already killed her.

"To meet you, speak with you." The lady stared at her. "It is not often that I come across a person, much less a woman, capable of understanding me."

Juliet looked at her lap, trying not to comprehend. "I understand nothing about you," she lied.

"Don't you?" The woman grinned, knowing that Juliet did. "Have you never sat in a parlor room, praying for God to strike you dead so that you would not have to suffer another word from some fool? Have you never wanted to stuff the condescension in a gentleman's voice down his arrogant throat? Have you never wanted to test the limits of your mind, Lady Juliet?"

The woman looked into her soul, seeing the true reason she had joined the Foreign Office.

Uncomfortable, Juliet asked, "So boredom has led you to betray your country?"

The lady laughed. "I have no country," she said, holding out her lovely hands. "I simply have myself."

"Then why sell secrets that will cause the death of nations?"

"Because I can?" Her eyes blazed darker, a deeper blue. "What do I care if men kill one another? I'm in trade. I trade the opportunity to beat me at the gaming table for gentlemen's money, and I trade English secrets for even more money."

"It is not the money you want." Juliet met the woman's cerulean eyes, her turn to see clearly. "You want to enjoy the game. You want to feel superior to the minds you meet . . . the minds you best."

The woman grinned, sitting back. "Seamus McCurren has quite good taste. Do you not think, Mister Collin?"

The enormous man looked Juliet up and down, his lip pulled back with distaste. "No."

"Never mind, my dear." The lady patted Juliet's left knee. "Mister Collin is more interested in beauty than brains." The traitor's eyes brightened, warmed. "Not like the absorbing Seamus McCurren."

The woman practically purred and Juliet bristled, as did, she noted with interest, Mister Collin.

"Comely and clever," the lady pronounced aloud. "What more could an intelligent girl want in a man?"

"Oh, I don't know." Juliet looked at the vicious man seated across from her. "However, I'm quite sure that a propensity to murder people would be low on *my* list."

"Really?" The cryptographer looked perplexed. "I've always found that proclivity rather useful."

"Yes, I've noticed." Juliet closed her eyes to dispel the image of James Habernathy with a knife sticking in his belly. "I'm finished speaking with you," she said, so the woman would not have the satisfaction of seeing her weep.

"Oh, but I have yet to tell you your choices, Lady Juliet." The large man grinned and Juliet held his eyes, trying not to show the depth of her fear. "As a mathematically minded madame, I have earned a great deal of blunt, but with you assisting me . . . We could make much, much more."

"Why on earth would I help you?"

"To test the limits of your mind." She must have seen that Juliet was unmoved so she added, "And because Mister Collin will take days to kill Mister McCurren if you do not." Juliet stilled, frozen by fear. "Or better yet"—the woman chuckled, amusing herself further—"I could make you one of my whores. According to Lord Harrington, you already have *that* proclivity."

The man scoffed. "I don't think she would earn you much."

"Perhaps not," the brilliant bawd agreed, feigning disappointment as she looked Juliet over. "There you are then. Run the numbers of my gaming book or I let Mister Collin kill Mister McCurren then you." The lady looked from Juliet to her servant, curious. "How do you lean, Mister Collin?"

"The knife."

"Oh, dear, but you have irritated Mister Collin." The lady sighed. "The knife is very painful, my dear. Are you sure you will not reconsider my off—"

"Pardon me." They heard from outside the carriage.

Their conveyance slowed and Enigma sat up, instantly alert. "See who it is," she ordered Mister Collin.

Her bodyguard nodded then pulled a pistol from his jacket. He carefully pulled the red velvet to one side, saying, "I can't see the man speaking," the bodyguard whispered. "His back is turned—"

Mister Collin's next sound was a grunt of surprise as Juliet kicked him in the chest with both feet, knocking his pistol out of his hand.

"Go," Enigma yelled at the driver just as the girl opened the carriage door.

The landau lunged forward as did Lady Juliet, but Mister Collin yanked her back by her hair before the girl made it out of the conveyance.

Lady Juliet cried out and it was then that Enigma saw him, Seamus McCurren. His golden eyes turned murderous. He raised a pistol as he rode, and the instant before he shot Mister Collin in the forehead, she envied Juliet Pervill.

But now was the time for self-preservation, not envy.

Mister Collin's corpse was dangling from the carriage, slowing them down, so Enigma kicked him loose. Both she and Lady Juliet were lifted by a jarring bump as the back wheel of the landau ran over Jack Collin's large frame.

Seamus McCurren had yet to slow and Enigma was beginning to seriously fear for her own life.

She pulled the smaller woman against her right side, her pistol to the back of the girl's head as Enigma shouted out the door, "If you want her so badly, Mister McCurren, by all means, take her."

Seamus McCurren's eyes grew large with fear and he steered his mount wide as she pushed Juliet Pervill out the carriage door. Enigma watched him leap from his horse before it stopped galloping. He rushed to her side and then bent to one knee over the unconscious woman.

Enigma reached out and closed the door as her carriage sped forward, vaguely wondering why she had not shot the girl before pushing her out.

Her heart constricted, already knowing the answer.

She had spent her entire life looking for a man of equal ability and in the end had resentfully settled for fleecing the men she inevitably found wanting. She had made an enormous amount of money doing it and no doubt would again. But in her heart of hearts, Enigma knew that she would give it all up to be understood . . . to find her counterpart.

She laughed aloud, surprised to find that after all of her financial success, she was still a woman, a woman looking for her mate, her intellectual match.

And then she heard it, a muffled click.

Her mouth dropped as she lifted her head. She met the

cold green eyes of Lucas Youngblood and he smiled weakly with Mister Collin's pistol pointing at her heart.

Mister Youngblood took a gargled breath and blood poured from the side of his pretty mouth as he whispered, "Bitch," just before pulling the trigger.

Thirty-six

❧❧

Seamus turned his head at the sound of gunfire, but quickly lost interest when soldiers surrounded the landau as it attempted to exit Hyde Park.

His attention, his world, was focused on the woman lying on the ground. He gathered Juliet in his arms and she winced, chilling him to the bone.

"Juliet, darling, are you all right?" Seamus whispered, but she did not respond. He closed his eyes and touched his forehead to hers to feel her warmth, her life. "Juliet," he breathed, kissing her lips.

But when she still did not respond, Seamus scooped her up in his arms and mounted his horse. *But where to go?* He could not think as panic was clouding his judgment.

Felicity's house was not far and a physician could be quickly summoned. Five minutes. It would take no more than five minutes to ride there.

"Juliet?" He needed to hear her voice, see her beautiful

eyes, to assure himself the she would survive his stupidity. "Juliet!"

Seamus looked down at her face, her freckles appearing lighter. *Was she getting pale?* God, please, not his Juliet.

They were at Felicity's home and he slid off his horse and climbed the stairs shouting, "Open the bloody door," as he banged the brass kick plate with the tip of his right boot.

"Juliet," he called again as he ran into the house. "Can you hear me, darling? Are you all right?"

Felicity was running into the entryway, fear in her eyes.

"Well, Seamus, I would feel a great deal better if you would stop banging me about." Seamus smiled, swallowing the lump in his throat. "I mean honestly, don't you think the fall I took from that damn carriage was jarring enough?"

The efficient Felicity was quietly ordering her butler to summon a physician as she herself ran up the stairs ahead of Seamus to ready Juliet's bedchamber.

"And why on earth would you bring me here?" Juliet was rubbing her head and squinting as if the light was painful. "It would have been much more sensible to take me directly to the physician. Now, poor old Doctor Barton will be forced to drag all of his apparatus—"

Seamus lifted the girl to his lips and kissed her hard, relieved that his love was alive and for the most part well. "Shut up, Juliet."

It must have been the besotted look in his eyes, because rather than argue, Juliet just smiled, saying, "Very well, Seamus."

Seamus watched as she closed her beautiful eyes and then nuzzled his neck, allowing him, for the first time since their meeting, to take care of her.

They reached Juliet's bedchamber and Seamus grinned, stepping past the settee where it all had began. He carried Juliet to the bed where they had made love and gently set her down, settling on one knee at the side of the cobalt counterpane.

"How do you feel?" He stared at her eyes so that she would not lie to him.

"A few cuts and bruises, but otherwise I'm perfectly fine." Juliet brushed his hair out of his eyes and smiled a little half smile that made him want to devour her.

He leaned forward and kissed the adorable freckles on her perfect nose, before kissing her beautiful mouth. He lifted his head and brushed a leaf from her hair.

"Seamus?"

"Yes," he said, the happiest man on earth.

"This never would have happened if you hadn't gotten me dismissed." She could not resist pointing this out, and his head dropped, a defeated man.

"Juliet." He rose.

She sat up, propping herself on the many silk pillows. "You know I'm right. You never should have gotten me dismissed from the Foreign Office just because I threatened your pride."

"Juliet," he shouted out of frustration. "I resigned from the Foreign Office because I had fallen in love with you!"

"You really are in love with me, aren't you?" Her bright blue eyes grew brighter with her tears.

"Yes," he said, feeling vulnerable. "Why else would I have resigned when we both bloody well know that I'm the better cryptographer?"

She laughed. "Do we?"

"Mmm." Seamus grinned, scooting her over so that he could lie beside her.

"We shall see about that."

"What do you mean, we shall see about that?"

"Nothing." She kissed him and his heart leapt.

"Marry me." he ordered.

"If you apologize for calling me homely," she countered.

"You called me dim-witted."

"It is not the same." He could see the hurt in her eyes.

"Juliet, do you remember the rogue in the corridor at the Foreign Office?"

"Yes."

"Do you remember what I said to you?"

"No."

"I said that beautiful women should not be allowed in a building full of unmarried men."

Juliet smiled. "You did say that, didn't you."

"I thought you beautiful then, Juliet. That night, I just . . ." He looked into her eyes, ashamed. "I just could not stand the thought of another man touching you, and I wanted you to feel the same amount of pain that I was feeling."

"I did."

"I know, Juliet, and I'm so very sorry for hurting you."

"It seems we both know how to cut with our tongues," she pointed out.

"The curse of being clever, I'm afraid."

"I never had this problem with Robert."

"Ouch, she draws first blood." Seamus kissed her on the neck. "But as I'm the one marrying you, Robert Barksdale can—"

"I don't recall accepting either one of your offers."

Seamus met her amused eyes. "Marry me, my darling Juliet?" he asked with all his heart.

And being a very clever woman, she saw his sincerity, whispering, "Yes."

Epilogue

❧❦❧

"*Seamus*, what are you doing!"

"Nothing," Seamus said, perplexed by Juliet's anger. "I'm just sitting at my desk!"

"You know James is injured and yet you ordered him to bring you a laden tray of coffee and biscuits?"

"I did no such thing," he protested, half listening to his wife and colleague.

"It's all right, Mrs. McCurren, I am feeling right as rain," Mister Habernathy said as he set the tray on Seamus's larger desk.

"See," Seamus said absently as he continued to read. "Not my fault at all."

"Are you quite sure, James?" his bride asked their devoted secretary. "Perhaps you should take another week off."

"No," the man said adamantly. "Thank you, madam, but if I am being entirely truthful, it is far more restful at the Foreign Office than at home with my five children."

Juliet laughed. "Very well, then, you can recuperate here

if you promise not to retrieve any more coffee, luncheon trays, or heavy documents."

"I swear it," Mister Habernathy said, his hand on his heart, as he backed out of the office door.

"What are you doing?"

"Nothing really," Seamus mumbled, continuing to read. "Don't you have anything to decrypt?"

"No." His wife sighed heavily. "Honestly, sometimes I wish the French were not so thick and provided me with a bit of a challenge."

"Uh-huh." Seamus was scarcely paying attention.

"Do you ever feel that way?" she mused, more to herself than to him.

"Why don't you work on one of your mathematic suppositions?" Seamus suggested so that she would leave him alone.

"I was working on a new theory." Juliet walked up behind him and began playing with the hair at the nape of his neck just as Seamus was getting to an interesting portion of the newspaper he was reading. "Are you familiar with the work of Pascal?"

"Not now, Juliet." He brushed her away, both of them aware of the amorous mood her discussions of mathematical theory put him in.

"He was a Greek mathematician who founded a school for both men and women—"

"Not now." Seamus dropped his chair to the floor, his heart racing as he continued to read.

"You've found something?" Juliet asked, hearing in his tone that he had.

"Get me a piece of paper and a pencil." He knew his wife would forgive his rudeness in the state of discovery.

"Here." Juliet handed him the things he had requested and then stood back to let him work, trusting his ability to decode and knowing that he would confer with her if he needed assistance.

Seamus read the article four times, seeing the pattern clearly. Yet as he wrote the words, his face turned as pale as the sheet of paper his wife had handed him.

"Darling?" he asked, hoping to God he was wrong. "Who is speaking in the House of Lords Friday next?"

"Don't be foolish, Seamus. You know very well that Ian St. John is scheduled to address the House. He has been working on his speech for weeks now." And then she glanced at him, holding her breath. "Why do you ask?"

"Because"—Seamus met her eye—"the French have just offered one thousand pounds for his assassination."